The Obstinate Land

Other Books by Harold Keith

The Bluejay Boarders

Brief Garland

Rifles for Watie
1958 Newbery Medal
Lewis Carroll Shelf Award, 1964
ALA Notable Children's Books, 1957

Komantcia
NEW YORK TIMES Best Book, 1965

Sports and Games

Susy's Scoundrel
Western Heritage Award, 1975
Western Writers Association Spur Award, 1975

THE
OBSTINATE LAND

By Harold Keith

Thomas Y. Crowell Company

New York

for my sister

DIANA POLING

LIBRARY OF CONGRESS CATALOGING IN PUBLICATION DATA

Keith, Harold, The obstinate land.
SUMMARY: During a hard winter the father of a
pioneering German family settling the Cherokee strip
in Oklahoma freezes to death and his fourteen-year-
old son must assume responsibility for the
struggling family.
[1. German Americans—Fiction. 2. Oklahoma—
History—Fiction. 3. Frontier and pioneer life—
Oklahoma—Fiction] I. Title. PZ7.K2550f
[Fic]   77-1826 ISBN 0-690-01319-1

2   3   4   5   6   7   8   9   10

CONTENTS

AUTHOR'S NOTE

————◆—●—◆————

Research for this novel was gleaned mainly from personal sources and from historical materials in the University of Oklahoma library.

Both my grandfathers, Jim Kee of Quinlan, Oklahoma, and Columbus B. Keith of Avard, Oklahoma, pioneered farms in the old Cherokee Strip and told me about it when I was a boy. Anecdotes of the era have been passed down through both sides of our family.

The personal source to whom I owe the most is my cousin Robert Kee, who is a farmer-rancher living near Quinlan, Oklahoma, in the old Strip. His wife, Kathryn, kindly typed his letters to me. They also read the story in manuscript.

From several homesteading accounts in *Chronicles of Oklahoma*, the state's historical quarterly, I particularly drew on interviews with two German pioneers, Mrs. Fannie L. Eisele, who lived on a farm near Covington, Oklahoma, and Otto Koeltzow, who developed a claim in Greer County, Oklahoma, and whose reminiscences were edited by Dr. A. M. Gibson, the university's George Lynn Cross Research Professor of History.

From the *Indian-Pioneer Papers* in the university's Western History Collection, Library Division, I found many interviews with Cherokee Strip pioneers, both men and women, accumulated in the 1930s; particularly helpful were those researched and written by Linnaeus B. Ranck, an auctioneer from Gage, Oklahoma.

A succession of personal interviews with German pioneer families of southwestern Texas appearing in *The Cattleman*, 1938-40, were useful, particularly the stories of such German ranchers as Orlanda Thallman, Heinrich Rothe, Casper Real, David Karbach, Friedrick Holekamp, Henry Hoerster, Jacob Linn, Martin Dittmar, Henry Keese, and Heinrich Conrad Kothmann. Miss Myrtle Murray, district agent for the Texas A&M Extension department, wrote the series.

The files of three Woodward, Oklahoma Territory, newspapers, the *News*, the *Advocate*, and the *Jeffersonian* (1893, 1894, and 1895) were also excellent sources. I'm grateful to the Oklahoma Historical Society of Oklahoma City for letting me see them and make notes. They give a fine flavor of the exact period of the book.

The dust storm described in Chapter 7 was influenced by an account of a similar storm related by Dr. George M. Sutton, the university's George Lynn Cross Research Professor of Zoology, during a lecture at Stovall Museum.

Mattie Cooper's Arkansas dialect was hard to pin down until I had the good fortune to discover old files of the magazine *Dialect Notes*, containing several studies by Dr. J. W. Carr, associate professor of English and Modern Languages at the University of Arkansas, 1901-06. Material for the series "A List of Words from Northwest Arkansas," which appeared just after the turn of the century, was obtained from his students at Fayetteville.

Sandra Jordan, the Thomas Y. Crowell Company editor with whom I worked on this book, made many invaluable suggestions.

Others who assisted were Mrs. Alice Timmons, former Western History specialist of the university, the late D. H. Cotten, the late Henry Bass, the late George Shirk, Dr. Don Robinson, Lillian Faulk, Leland Wolf, Walter Hansmeyer, George Woods, and the late Clarence Boyd. Suzanne Kee of Beaver, Oklahoma, typed the manuscript.

Mrs. Wilna Tipps, director of Children's Services at the Pioneer Multi-County Library of Norman, Oklahoma, kept urging me to do the story after I had researched much of it but then let it lie unwritten while turning to books in other fields.

I am grateful to Dr. James K. Zink, director of the University of Oklahoma Library, and to Mrs. Mary Esther Saxon, assistant professor of bibliography and fourth-floor librarian, for providing the faculty study in which I researched and wrote this book.

Harold Keith
University of Oklahoma
August 23, 1974

THE STONES
OF OWNERSHIP

Fritz Romberg relaxed his grip on the bridle reins and squinted into the sun. Beneath his blond hair that spiraled in tiny curls and ringlets, beads of sweat ran off his tan face and down inside his cotton shirt that smelled old and stale. A gentle, docile boy, he was small for his thirteen years, but strong, wiry, and not afraid of anyone.

His eyes scanned the terrain and found it fascinating. There was not a single house in sight, nor fence, nor road—just the covered wagon he rode beside and the straw-colored prairie grass rippling in the breeze. He could hear the soft chirping of prairie chickens calling to their young, and cattle—brown, black, and tawny, some streaked, some spotty—freckled the landscape and were feeding on it. The cattlemen who owned these herds and grazed them on free public land fiercely opposed the invasion by homesteaders.

"Look, Fritz," called out Frederic Romberg, the father, leaning out of the wagon to look up at his elder son. Frederic's thick

1

yellow hair was parted in the middle and his deeply studious eyes looked clear through you. With a long arm, he gestured widely. "No timber, no stumps, no rocks. It's land that's shouting to be farmed." His voice was musical and pleasantly baritone.

Fritz eased his weight in the saddle of his horse, Valentine, and thought about something that fat Peter Popplebaum had told him outside the church at Navasota, back in south Texas. "My father says your father's daft. It's madness to go to those prairies where such absolute necessities as fuel, building material, and fencing will be hard to find and probably cost ready money." Nettled, Fritz had replied, "Where else in the world can you get a whole farm for a fifteen-dollar filing fee?" But he couldn't help feeling vaguely uneasy. Had his father been unwise?

Removing his hat, he let the hot wind blow through his hair. He understood his father's enthusiasm. Developing his own farm, where they would have a home of their own and not be obligated to any man, was a dream that Frederic had long cherished.

It would be a difficult life, Fritz knew, but not as difficult as the one they had left behind in Texas where a baby sister had died in the sickly climate and they had fought the boll weevil, army worm, and the tyranny of the wealthy German landowner for whom they had worked as tenants and sharecroppers. On Sundays they sometimes had had to rise at three in the morning in order to walk to church on time. But now that was all behind them.

The boy felt happy and excited. He liked the sweet air and the delightful chill of it at night no matter what the daytime heat had been. He would never forget his feeling of enchantment the previous afternoon when, seated on the prairie with a plate of food, he kept seeing the sky in all directions beneath his horse's belly no matter where the animal grazed around him. He was exhilarated by the lonely magnificence of the country, and the sense of freedom it inspired. It was like being in a boat on the ocean with no land in sight.

He stole a concerned look across the front of the wagon toward

Freda, his mother, sitting stiff and straight in the rope-bottom chair next to his father. She was homesick and discouraged, he knew.

"What do you think of it, Mother?" he called to her.

"You can look a long way and see nothing," she replied sadly. Although her face was thin, she still retained the remnants of beauty—good bones, neat hair, a gentle mouth, and wise eyes that were usually warm and cheerful.

Fritz felt sorry for her. She had hated to leave, perhaps for all time, Fredericke, the small daughter who lay in the cemetery back at Navasota. She also disliked leaving her nieces and nephews of whom she was very fond.

At a recent campsite she had seen a large rock with the words "You are now leaving Texas" inscribed upon it. Realizing that she had torn up the roots binding her to relatives and friends, she had dropped her face into her hands and sobbed unrestrainedly. It was one of the few times Fritz had ever seen her cry.

It was the third day of the Cherokee Strip land run in northwest Oklahoma Territory. The U.S. government was giving 160 acres of public land to the first settlers to reach it and file a claim. In return, the settlers had to live on it five years and improve it. Then it became theirs. Driving hard from sunup to sundown, Frederic Romberg had ignored the racing settlers who had dropped off ponies or jumped out of buggies to pound down stakes in the eastern two-thirds of the new country.

His goal was a choice piece of land in the semiarid western uplands, a part of the Strip not yet settled. It lay along the fertile Hackberry Creek valley, not far from the newly built Santa Fe Railroad angling down from Kiowa, Kansas. In choosing it, Frederic had been mindful that the railroad would make markets more accessible.

"Towns will soon spring up along the railroad," he predicted.

Frederic had found this spot of special excellence while on a scouting trip the previous autumn. It was land enriched by the creek's deposit of alluvium in floodtime and by the washing down

3

of the surrounding topsoil. It would produce in abundance. There was also a spring and near it a grassy knoll that would protect a home from the wind. And now they were nearing it.

Fritz pushed back his hat and sleeved the sweat off his forehead. It was late September of 1893, and the nation was caught in the coils of drought and financial panic. Neither land nor livestock had much value. Horses were given away and calves killed when born to keep them from eating what grass the drought left. Many who had lost hope of getting ahead in the older settlements turned toward Oklahoma. It seemed to Fritz that each hummock of grass waved them onward.

Twisting in the saddle, the boy looked down into the wagon. Jacob, his younger brother, was asleep in the back. Sarah, his four-year-old sister, was walking behind the wagon for exercise. Unknown to her mother, the little girl was wearing a freshly starched apron and her church shoes. Sarah smiled shyly at him, knowing that her elder brother would not betray her.

Fritz smiled to himself. Sarah liked to wear freshly washed and ironed clothing. She would have changed her dress three and four times daily had Freda permitted it. Even in this flat wilderness he had seen her brush her hair before climbing out of the wagon to walk.

She looks as if she's making a social call, Fritz thought. He knew they probably would meet nobody. But he was mistaken.

In late afternoon they came upon a wagon that was mired in the mud of a small creek. It had a white top, three towheaded children, a brindle cow, a yellow dog, and a pervading air of restlessness. The driver was unloading his heaviest luggage. The family had climbed out to lessen the weight. One of the children was a girl Sarah's age.

"My old mules air plum wore out," whined the man in a singsong voice.

Frederic stopped his team. "Leave the rest of your belongings in the wagon," he counseled, "we'll pull you out."

Fritz was proud of how correctly his father spoke the English language. He had learned while attending an English language class taught by Anton Vonfeld, the Lutheran pastor back in south Texas, and had taught his whole family in turn. Painfully conscious of their limitations in a strange world, the German settlers were eager to learn the right way in everything.

Fritz slid off Valentine and tied him to the wagon's iron brake. Frederic stepped on a front wheel and jumped to the grass below.

"We're beholden to you," said the man. He unhooked the traces behind his team and drove them out of the mud, leaving his wagon in it.

Fritz helped his father take their big gray team out of the doubletrees and couple them to the stranger's vehicle.

"Giddap!" called Frederic, shaking out the lines. Flexing their muscles, the Romberg grays towed the wagon to dry land.

Fritz took off his shoes and wiped the wet sand off them onto the grass. He hoped someday he would grow and mature and have Frederic's ability to deal promptly and effectively with emergencies.

That night the two families camped together by the creek. Its water was so bitter that they couldn't drink it. Even the horses would have no more than a sniff.

"It's gyppy," muttered the stranger, disgust in his tones.

The Rombergs shared the drinking water from their barrel. Fritz saw that it was getting low.

Before dinner Fritz and Jacob brushed the grays and washed down their shoulders with water from the creek. Then they fed them oats from the small store in the bottom of the wagon. While the two mothers prepared supper, Sarah and the small daughter from the other family thrust their bare feet into the creek, watching the water bugs skate along its surface.

The two men talked, mostly about farming and finding homesteads. Fritz listened. Someday he too would own his own farm.

It was the tradition of tightly knit German families for sons to stay with their parents and work for them until marriage. Then the parents would set up that son in farming, furnishing as a stake a

5

team of mules, a wagon, farm tools, seed for planting, horse feed, and one hundred dollars in cash. That was another reason the Rombergs were going to Oklahoma. Frederic could never have earned that much cash in Texas.

"We come clear from Beaver City to make the run," said the man, "but we got lost in a big pasture. Then we seed a ranch house an' tried to settle on a quarter section close to it, but the owner of the ranch run us off. He said it was too dry there fer farmin' and that they had a 'free grass law' that lets his livestock range at will but makes us homesteaders fence our crops. But fencin' costs too much. I wish I'd stayed at Beaver City or gone to the Texas Panhandle. Lotsa farmin' over thar, we hears."

Frederic nodded. "You're right," he said, "but you have to buy the land. A lot of it is bringing five dollars an acre. That's eight hundred dollars for a quarter section. Maybe it's worth it, but I don't have that kind of money. At Bowie, Texas, I saw a copy of the *Tascosa Pioneer* in a wagonyard. It said that the railroads and large ranch owners are working together to develop the Texas Panhandle country. The more homesteaders they bring in, the higher the land values become."

The Arkansas man spat tobacco juice onto the grass and nodded vigorously. "No-man's-land, where we come from, is boomin' too. Beaver City, its capital, has got a thousand people. They got a church there an' they've had schools fer eight year. Houses, dugouts, and shacks is rizin' all over thet country. What's holdin' up homesteadin' here?"

Frederic looked at him soberly, as if surprised at the other's lack of information.

"The ranchmen," he said, "they're organized. And they're determined. They expect to pasture their herds here forever. But that's foolish. Everybody knows that you can't keep a big tract of land like this Strip idle with only one inhabitant of the township living on it when adjoining states have forty people to the square mile."

Frederic's eyes swept the prairie around them. "This country right here is just about the last free land there is anyplace," he said. "I'm going to put down my stakes right here in this Strip."

"Whereabouts in the Strip is you headed?"

Frederic told him as best he could. "Better join us," he invited. "We'd be glad to have you for neighbors."

The other man looked indecisive. "I'll think on it," he said. "With the cow, we hev to travel slow. We kin always foller yer wagon tracks."

He probably won't follow them, Fritz mused. He looks as if he wants to make his own wagon tracks. Many made the Strip run from mere curiosity or wanderlust.

That night, as Fritz lay wrapped in a blanket on the grass beneath the stars, he heard the baying of a coyote, a long, weird, blood-curdling laugh that died away in smothered yaps and gurgles. He thought it the wildest, most stirring music that he had ever listened to.

Sitting up, he looked at Valentine standing nearby, his dark form silhouetted against the sky. Ears cocked forward, the horse was listening too.

"What do you think of that, boy?" Fritz spoke to him softly. Arching his head around, the horse took a step toward him and pushed against Fritz with his nose. Fritz laughed silently. A perfect understanding existed between them. Sometimes Fritz talked to the animal as if he were a human being. Listening gravely, the horse always seemed to understand.

Next morning the two wagons parted. Little Sarah regretted the leave-taking from her newfound playmate.

"Good-bye," she called just before Fritz lifted her into the Romberg wagon. "Your dress is pretty. Your earrings are pretty. Your hair sure is pretty." As they drove off, she sat in the back of the wagon looking out so that she could wave to her friend until she passed from sight.

All day they drove through the September heat. They had no trouble bearing it because the air seemed thinner and drier. Sound carried well across the flatness. Once when a quail whistled

7

sharply nearby, Fritz's ears rang from the vibrations. The grass waved and the wagon jolted. The canvas top flapped in the breeze. Occasionally they saw prairie chicken, wild turkey, and antelope.

To Fritz it was a bewitching sight. He had been reared where hills and tall forest trees shut off the view, but this prairie land of great distance was more alluring. It seemed to be holding out its hands to settlers.

Frederic kept peering ahead, looking for a big cottonwood tree that he said would guide them to their homestead.

Fritz ducked his head and wiped his mouth on the sleeve of his homespun shirt. "How will we know that it's our land?" he asked.

"It isn't our land yet," said Frederic. "We have to beat everybody else to it. We have to put down our stakes in it first."

"How is it marked?" asked Freda.

"By the stones of ownership," Frederic replied. "Several years ago the whole Strip was surveyed and laid out in sections one mile square. There are four farm sites of 160 acres in each section. They are called quarter sections, or quarters. Stones bearing the numbers of each tract of land were set at the corners of each farm site. The first thing we'll do is find our corner stones so we can be sure we're the only persons on that particular claim. Then we've got ninety days to go to the Woodward land office and file on it. If nobody else has filed on it sooner, it's ours."

Little Jacob's face darkened. "What if we find somebody else on our land, Father?" he asked. "What will you do? Shoot them with your pistol?"

Frederic's mouth softened into a smile. "*Nau, nau.* There won't be anybody else on our land," he assured the boy. "Nobody knows about it but me. It's beginning to look like we're the only ones in the whole country anyhow." He was wrong.

Just before sundown, while they camped near a small creek, a cowboy rode up on a bay horse. He was big and burly with cool, quick eyes and a no-nonsense way about him. He smelled of sweat, leather, and cigarette tobacco.

Fritz had eyes only for the man's costume, especially his tan hat

with a chin strap, his holstered gun, and his leather chaps with
nickel conchas running down each leg. His spurs had steel rowels
shaped like the petals of a daisy.

The only touch of color on him was a purple scarf coiled neatly
around his neck and a pair of yellow sleeve-holders. He looked like
something of a dandy. The stranger just stared at them and their
outfit, as if he resented them and all their kind.

"Good evening," Frederic greeted him. He gestured toward the
food. "Won't you join us?"

For a moment, the other did not reply. He frowned belligerently
at them, especially at their wagon with the tubs, water jugs,
carpenter tools, and plows swinging from it.

He shifted his weight in the saddle. "If you plan to settle around
here, you'd better bring plenty of nerve along because yore gonna
need it," he said. "We don't want you plowin' up our range. It's
right side up already."

Frederic stood, brushing the crumbs from his lips. "My name's
Romberg," he said, "and this is my family. We're making the
Cherokee Strip land run. We're not in Texas, are we?"

The man moved his feet in the stirrups and the little pear-shaped
pendants on his spurs jingled like Christmas bells.

"No, yore not in Texas. But yore not welcome anyways. And if
you plan to stay round here you'd better sing small or have yore
harp in tune." Hard-jawed and hazel-eyed, he glared at Frederic.
There was pride in his eyes and a sadness so deep that it seemed to
reach back into old hurts and other times.

Frederic was patient with him. "You know, of course, that the
United States government has thrown the Strip open to settlement.
We've come farther west than most families, I know. But this is
still the Strip. We've acted strictly within the law. I see no reason
why we can't all get along together. There's lots of room out
here."

"Naw there ain't!" disputed the cowboy. "It's gittin' smaller
ever day. Yore not the first settlers here. Some wagons made the
run two days ago from Higgins, Texas, the southwestern entry

point. Other nesters came on the railroad from Higgins. The whole country's startin' to fill up.''

That surprised the Rombergs. They hadn't known that settlers were coming from the west.

Nine-year-old Jacob Romberg was looking at the stranger's revolver, sheathed low on one hip.

''Where'd you get that ratchety old gun?'' the boy blurted out suddenly. ''I'll bet it won't shoot across the creek yonder.'' He scowled fearlessly up at the cowboy.

''Jacob!'' Freda Romberg's low voice reprimanded. Her face coloring, she faced the stranger. ''I'm sorry he spoke to you like that, sir. It's been a long trip and I'm afraid he's become stubborn and crotchety.''

The cowboy touched his finger to his hat. ''That's all right, mam.''

Turning, he fixed little Jacob with a penetrating stare. ''Do you have fever with them fits?'' he asked the lad.

Freda laughed merrily. It was the first time Fritz had heard her laugh in days. Spreading a Turkey-red damask tablecloth on the prairie, she placed plates on all four corners to anchor it against the wind and set out bone-handled knives, forks, and spoons after wiping them carefully with a dishcloth.

Looking up at the stranger, she said, ''Are you sure you won't eat with us? We have plenty.''

The cowboy looked as if he were refusing, but apparently thought better of it.

''I might take a slug of that coffee,'' he said.

When he got off his horse, Fritz saw that his legs were bowed like a hoop. He had seen cowboys in south Texas, but never one with legs warped like these. The fire was crackling cheerfully. The grays were stamping about in search of green sprigs of grass.

''This seems a healthy country,'' said Frederic. ''We came from south Texas where it's low and wet.''

The cowboy let his eyes feast almost worshipfully over the prairie.

"It's so healthy here that if anybody wanted to start a graveyard they'd have to shoot somebody," he said. It was obvious that the grassy range was his religion.

Frederic showed him a map, indicating approximately the location of their claim.

The cowboy accepted the big porcelain cup from Freda, nodding his thanks. He pointed to some low hills lying in the west. He warned them that there was no trail, just signs. He pointed out other landmarks for them to follow. He advised them that their location was practically surrounded by the holdings of Sam Womble, the biggest rancher in the area, and that they could reach it by midmorning of the following day. Then he handed his empty cup to Freda, thanking her.

Mounting, he rode off, his long body draped over the cantle of his saddle as he balanced himself gracefully, the reins held lazily in one hand. The music of his tinkling spurs lingered on the wind.

He looks as if he owns the whole prairie, Fritz thought as he watched him go.

"Heavens," said Freda, "we don't even know his name."

"I doubt if he wanted us to know it," Fritz replied, and resumed eating.

Next morning they got started early. It was a big day in their lives. At last they would see their homesite. The country became a little rougher. Occasionally they would encounter red buttes salted with veins of white gypsum whose crystals shone brilliantly in the sun. Patches of salt grass, sumac, yucca, and wild plum grew alongside the shortgrass and the sage. Sand dunes glistened in the distance.

To their surprise, they saw fresh wagon tracks. Then the morning sun flashed on two parallel lines of steel, and passing beneath telegraph wires that hummed mysteriously, they crossed the Santa Fe railroad. Later they came to a white flag fastened on a stick. A covered wagon stood nearby, but its team and occupants were gone.

Fritz frowned, fanning himself with his hat. He hadn't expected

11

to find settlers this far west. Frederic's eyes scanned the landscape. He was looking for his cottonwood tree. Half an hour later Sarah saw it.

"There's the tree!" she cried. "It won't be long now."

When they reached the old sentinel, they saw that its waxy leaves were turning a buttery yellow. Frederic halted the wagon in its shade and they all got out. Fritz fitted his fingers into the grooves of its heavily furrowed trunk and listened to its whispering leaves that sounded like rain falling.

"The homesite is right over there," said Frederic, pointing with one arm, "right along Hackberry Creek." Hurrying them back into the wagon, he shook out the lines. The grays broke into a trot. When they veered alongside the stream, it was dry.

Frederic kept looking ahead as he drove. His chin was outthrust. The wind parted his black beard, blowing it back over each shoulder. The reins flowed from his hands down the backs of the grays. Freda sat stiff and quiet, her hands folded. The wagon kept on jolting and its canvas top kept snapping in the breeze. Fritz's mind was in a turmoil. He knew how much this meant to his father.

Then he saw his father's face transfixed with surprise and dismay at something ahead.

Fritz looked ahead, too. He saw a man plowing in a field. A partially erected house of planks stood near a grassy bluff. Smoke curled out of its stick and mud chimney. Near it, a woman was bent over, hanging wet garments on sage hummocks near what looked like a spring. A girl was helping her. A smaller girl played in the yard with a red dog. The dog was barking at their approach.

Bitterness surged through Fritz. Somebody else was entrenched on what they had all believed would be the Romberg corner of the promised land.

NEIGHBORS

Frederic drove the wagon into the yard. The woman went on scrubbing clothes across a washboard, although she did not take her eyes off them. To Fritz, she looked sullen and tired. Frederic handed the lines to Freda and got out.

"I'm Frederic Romberg," he said, his face working strangely. "I've had this quarter section picked out for a homestead ever since I found it on a scouting trip last year. The Strip run started only three days ago. How have you made all these improvements in three days? How did you get here so soon?"

"We're here, ain't we?" she replied wearily and went on washing. It was obvious to Fritz that they were Sooners, people who had slipped past the soldiers guarding the border several days before the run.

Fritz let his eyes play over them. They looked poor and shiftless. The two girls were both barefoot, and they both had drifts of freckles across their noses. The older girl, who looked about twelve, had a long neck and black hair scraggly as a bird's nest. Her dress was little more than worn blue fabric over a red petticoat. The younger girl, about Sarah's age, stood with her finger in her mouth and kept wrinkling and sniffling her nose.

In the field, the woman's husband quickly unhooked his mule team. Driving the mules ahead of him, he approached, his nervous eyes darting from face to face, as if trying to ascertain the intentions of the Rombergs.

He tied his mules to the wheel of his wagon, lifted out a rifle, and slouched up to them. He was bald and his head was round as an orange.

Again Frederic introduced himself, and in a voice that was tight with emotion explained about previously having scouted the land.

"I don't mind being beaten," he concluded, "provided we both started at noon on September sixteenth, the legal starting hour."

The bald man did not speak. He just stood there, looking shifty and defiant.

"May I ask your name?" Frederic inquired.

"You may," replied the other coolly. "It's Cooper. Orvus Cooper." Reaching into a pocket of his ragged jeans, he drew out a plug of tobacco and, without taking his eyes off Frederic, turned his mouth sideways to bite off a fragment with his yellow teeth.

Fritz sat his horse stiffly, clenching and unclenching his fists. Little Jacob's lips were thrust out angrily. Sarah sank lower and lower into her chair. Freda seemed the calmest of them all. She just sat quietly, holding the reins in her small hands.

Frederic planted his feet resolutely. The rifle did not frighten him, Fritz knew. He said, "We made the run fair and square, driving hard from the legal starting point after coming clear from southeast Texas. Now I find you on the place with a house half built and you breaking your fourth acre of prairie sod. How do you explain this extraordinary speed? Do you claim that you've made all these improvements in the last day and one half?"

The man reached into his pocket and pulled out a folded bit of paper.

"This here's my registration certificate," Cooper said, "an' I got two witnesses that'll swear my claim is legitimate and my certificate legal." He held it out for Frederic to inspect. Fritz on the horse sat frozen and silent.

Frederic made no move to take it. "You got here so long ago that you apparently don't know that the government stopped issuing registration certificates several days before the run started," he said. "The certificates were being sold openly at some places and honest people were having to stand too long in line waiting to get them. Even if you had a hundred registration certificates, they wouldn't explain all this plowing"—he waved one arm at the field—"and all this building."

Cooper thrust the certificate back into his pocket. A surly look came into his face.

"It's jest like you an' me is playin' a game of checkers fer this place," he said smoothly and testily. "I've jumped. Now it's yore move." With his right hand, he patted the stock of his Winchester.

Hands trembling, Fritz chafed at the injustice of the matter. This was unlawful possession, bold and presumptuous, backed by a gun. A feeling of helplessness and despair washed over him. They had no place else to go. Orvus Cooper watched them like a cat.

When Fritz saw his father draw a long breath and turn back to the wagon, he knew that they had lost that farm forever. For a moment Fritz thought that his father had been foolish to come so far for a farm whose acquisition depended purely upon chance. Then, feeling guilty, he rejected the idea and a warm feeling of loyalty washed over him.

Frederic drove silently, his face set in hard lines of defeat. The blow was difficult to bear. Sensing his pain, Fritz rode Valentine closely alongside the wagon, wishing that he could somehow comfort his father. He began to feel uneasy. Now that they had lost their favored place, they were really on their own. What could they do?

Finally Frederic spoke. "There's no court, no witnesses out here," he said. "I have no way in the world of proving that he settled early. And we couldn't afford a lawyer if we found one.''

He drove a little farther. "It was the only decent farm site in the area," he added. "I saw most of the others when I was here last year."

Fritz saw a happy look steal into his mother's face. "I'm sorry for you, Frederic," she said. "Now we can go back to Texas."

Frederic turned and looked at her. "No, Freda," he said, "we're not going back to Texas. We're going to find another homestead here."

Tears clouded Freda's eyes. She raised her chin, saying nothing. German wives usually obeyed their husbands. Fritz ran his fingers through his hair and looked at her. The shadowing despair in her face worried him.

It was Jacob who saw the light spring wagon standing in a hollow between two small knolls. A shred of tent was staked beside it. Horses were hobbled. A spring flowed nearby. Frederic got out and went up to speak to the owner.

A bright-eyed, kind-faced young woman peered out at him from beneath the canvas top. She wore a sunbonnet.

"I'm housecleaning," she said. "My man's gone to Woodward to file a title on our claim. I just thought I'd put things in shape."

At the sound of the cheerful voice, Freda got down, too. Frederic introduced his whole family. He told her about losing the favored farm to the Sooner, Orvus Cooper.

Fritz was impressed with the woman's cleanliness. The floor of the wagon and the board siding had been scrubbed. The improvised cupboards were clean and neat. On the sage nearby blankets and comforters were hung to air and in the sunshine outside the tent the cooking utensils gleamed. Everything was as neat as Freda's own wagon.

It was all meager, scanty, and somehow lacking and yet there was happiness in the woman's face.

"I'm patched," she said, "but I'm not dirty." She was right, Fritz saw. Her blue calico dress was mended and her efforts to beautify it were wistful and pathetic. But it was neither ragged nor

16

unclean. Her sunbonnet was starched and beneath it beamed a face as brown as that of a gypsy.

Her name was Daisy Patterson. She told them that for the past three years her husband had been a government surveyor. Liking the country, he had homesteaded the quarter section on which the wagon stood.

"He says there's another quarter next to the place you lost that hasn't been filed on. It would make a pretty fair farm," she said, pointing westward. "It's rolling and has a small canyon, but the land is hard and the soil goes down four or five feet. This is all ranch land in here. Sam Womble, the biggest rancher in this part of the Strip, lives close by. He'll fight you every way he can. He hates nesters, as he calls us."

Frederic decided to inspect it. On the way, they passed a ranch house with barns and corrals sprawled all about it. Frederic stopped the wagon at the gate.

A man came out and the Rombergs got their first look at Sam Womble, a little man wearing a black hat and calfskin boots with green mule-ear tugs hanging down on both sides to pull them on with. In one small, plump hand he held a glowing cigarette.

Frederic introduced himself, explained that he was about to file nearby and asked directions to the claim. The man acknowledged that he was Sam Womble, but he did not tell them where to go. He drew deeply on his cigarette and was seized with a sudden fit of coughing that lasted half a minute. When he got his breath, his watery eyes blazed with anger.

In a voice that was gruff and gravelly, he attacked all nesters, wanting to know why they were coming in, trying to farm land totally unsuited for crops. "All you do is scratch the land," he charged.

Frederic answered, "God did not create this country just for the cattleman. You've had the free use of it for years. But you can't have it all. The government says we can stake out claims for agriculture. I intend to turn mine into a fine farm."

Womble dropped his cigarette and ground it into the grass with

17

his boot heel. "I know you muleheaded Dutch," he said scornfully. "You live cheap and work for low pay. If a whole settlement of you was stood on its head, I doubt if anybody could shake one hundred dollars out of all your pockets. You'll starve to death out here. This land's treacherous to farm. It won't raise nothin' but grass."

Frederic looked him squarely in the eye. "We'll show you," he said. "What are you going to do with your cattle when homesteaders come in and settle on the range you've been using but do not own?"

"This is free grass country," retorted Womble. "You nesters are going to have a tough time protecting your crops from our herds."

Frederic reached out toward one of the grays and extricated a part of its tail that was tangled in the doubletree. "Since we are going to be neighbors," he said, "I hope we can live together in peace and help each other as neighbors should."

Womble eyed him slowly and insolently from head to foot. Then another coughing spell shook him. Turning his back on them, he walked to the house. The Romberg wagon moved on.

His face dull and set, Fritz touched Valentine's flanks with his heels, following the wagon. They would have two hostile neighbors, Cooper and Womble. It wasn't an encouraging way to begin life in a new land.

After a short trip, they arrived at approximately the spot Daisy Patterson had told them about. Near the lip of a small canyon stood a big hackberry tree. Near it, half a dozen young cottonwoods rustled in the wind, their leaves sounding to Fritz like the low murmur of voices.

Stay, the voices seemed to urge. It's beautiful here. Trust us. You'll learn to like it.

Fritz stretched his neck to see better. He liked it already. It was far better than south Texas. It was flat and dry and the soil was red, but it would belong to them. There would be no rent to pay, no landlord clamping a yoke on their necks.

After looking it over, Frederic decided to take it. The minute his feet touched the ground, he seemed to forget about losing the farm he wanted to Orvus Cooper, whose home they could see half a mile distant.

He helped Freda out of the wagon. Jacob and Sarah leaped out. They all walked around. The shortgrass felt springy to Fritz's feet.

With the toe of one shoe, Frederic pressed down and flattened a segment of red soil protruding from a gopher hill. He stooped and picked up a handful of it, spreading it over one palm. Fritz understood his father's excitement. He knew that few German farmers owned an acre of land. Their pride in possessing even a prairie farm was almost pathetic. It would be their home and they would guard it with desperate passion.

From the brink of the canyon, Frederic pointed to the knee-deep grass below.

"Look, Freda," he said, "cows could live down there all winter and come out fat in the spring."

Freda took a long, slow glance all around. "It all looks so big and strange," she said, "so far away and lonely."

They decided to camp on the spot. The sun swung low. The land was softening with shadows. The air was surprisingly cool. After dinner Fritz laid his bedroll, pulled off his boots, and stretched out with a sigh.

At daybreak, Freda's startled cry from the back of the wagon awakened him. "Look," she breathed, pointing. Fritz saw them. Two deer were staring at her in big-eyed wonder from the canyon below.

Frederic and Fritz searched in vain for the corner stones. As they rested at the wagon, a rider came up from the canyon's edge. A young man, he wore a leather cap and homespun clothing. The abnormal alignment of his brown eyes, which were crossed toward each other, was noticeable. He had thick, protruding lips and an

19

expression so pensive and boyish that you wanted to put your arm around him and draw him to you. He was Ray Patterson, the husband of the young woman in the covered wagon. He didn't seem at all sensitive about his crossed eyes.

"No wonder you can't find your stones," he said, "Sam Womble probably stole 'em. He stole mine but I'm a surveyor and it didn't take me long to locate others nearby. I don't have my instruments here, but I'll show you how to mark your land and we'll figure out your numbers from those on the nearest stones you can find."

He soon found a stone on an adjoining quarter section. With a spring tape, which he kept in a pocket, he measured the circumference of a hind wheel on the Romberg wagon, tied a red handkerchief around its rim, and with Frederic driving in as straight a line as possible, they counted the rounds of the wheel until the quarter section was measured.

"I'll bring my instruments over later and run your lines again, just to be sure," Patterson said as he untied his red kerchief and thrust it into his pocket.

"Womble's got his own system of holding his range," he explained. "I've got a friend in the Woodward land office who told me all about him. At first he didn't own any of the land. To protect his water rights, he homesteaded the quarter section where his house and barns are. Then he had each of his cowboys file on quarter sections along the stream. He paid all the filing fees, put up a shack dwelling for each cowboy, and paid the government the cash amount per acre necessary to get title to the land.

"Thus he not only owns the land on both sides of the stream, but also gained control of the grass back of these water claims because no other ranchman would want it without having access to water. Whenever a homesteader comes in on that back part, Womble runs them out. He's shrewd and ruthless."

There was much to be done. Living quarters had to be built and furnished, a barn and chicken house constructed. A well must be dug, fences built. A water trough for the horses must be provided.

First, the wagon was unloaded. Most of the items Frederic had fetched with him from Germany in strong chests, in order to protect them from the sea air on the boat to Texas: a plow, all instruments necessary for garden and vineyard cultivation, complete harness outfits, tools for building a house and furniture, locks, belts, hinges, nails of all kinds, and iron chains of different strengths and sizes. Now he was transplanting all of it to the Strip. There was even a lump of putty and a small diamond with which to cut glass panes to fit windows. Soon it was all neatly stacked on the prairie.

The next thing to do, Frederic decided, was to go to Woodward, a new town on the Panhandle line of the Santa Fe railroad, and file on his claim at the government land office. Woodward lay twenty-seven miles east, but with the wagon lightened by the unloading, the grays could reach it easily in a day. The whole family went.

Frederic also wanted to procure a quantity of winter seed wheat, if possible. He had heard that in Kansas the Santa Fe railroad had distributed it gratis to the Russian and German settlers. He was convinced that it was superior to corn or spring wheat in this northwest Strip climate.

Soon they encountered the Woodward road, just two ruts blown deep by the prevailing southwest wind. After traveling so long across uncharted grasslands, it seemed like a hard-surfaced highway to Fritz. The prairie on both sides was green and rolling.

In midmorning they met a bearded settler in a wagon hauling water in a barrel. He said that it was for his wife to cook with and his livestock to drink.

"Why don't you dig your own well?" Frederic asked.

"Because I live in the Panhandle, eighteen miles away, and we have to dig down two hundred feet to reach water," the man explained. "It's jest as near to water one way as the other and I'd druther get mine along horizontal rather than perpendicular lines." Fritz wondered how deep the Rombergs would have to dig when it came time to sink their well.

21

Although Woodward was only a few years old, Fritz was surprised at its rapid growth. As the Romberg wagon rolled up the crooked main street with Fritz flanking it on Valentine, he got his first sight of a spick-and-span frontier cattle town. New frame buildings had been erected along both sides of the street, and the beat of hammers, the rasping of saws, and the smell of the fresh-cut lumber foretold the coming of others.

The town's hitching posts were lined with saddle horses and occasionally a buggy or wagon could be seen. The board sidewalks were crowded, the saloons and restaurants filled, and the mercantile stores were busy equipping ranchmen and homesteaders.

Frederic found a lawyer who prepared their filing papers for application to homestead. Fritz saw the excitement come into his father's face as he signed the application with his full name, Frederic Ernst Romberg. After a trip to the government land office, they were the proud possessors of 160 acres that cost Frederic only $16.50, the filing fee. But the depot agent had no winter seed wheat.

However, he did have something else piled on the floor that Fritz wanted very much, a stack of old newspapers. Apparently they were destined for the trash can.

"Please, *mynheer*, may I have these?" he asked so beseechingly that he was promptly also given several aged magazines. In Texas, Fritz had read hungrily everything he could borrow on any subject from the school library or from Anton Vonfeld, the Lutheran pastor. Sometimes he would go to sleep while reading and his mother would have to take the book from his hands.

As Frederic moved with his dignified stride in and out of the buildings or about the streets, he politely lifted his high-crowned German hat to every man he met. Back in Navasota, it was the German custom for men to take off their hats to one another in the street. Fritz had always admired the graceful ease with which his father did this while uttering his *"Guter Tag"* or *"Adieu."*

However, in Woodward men apparently had not heard of the custom. None of them tipped their wide low-crowned hats to anybody. And when they began to smile, and laugh, and look back with amusement at Frederic, Fritz felt his face reddening. He wished that his father would abandon the custom, and better yet, abandon the hat.

They bought a supply of groceries, a water barrel, corn for the horses, some lumber, a sod plow on the advice of Patterson, and a glass panel door for Freda. That left Frederic with only forty-eight dollars.

"Let's deposit all but five dollars in the bank," he proposed. Fritz, who had never seen a bank, went with his father while Freda took Jacob and Sarah on a tour of the stores.

The bank consisted of a small frame building, the front half of which was the lobby and the rear half the depository. Behind the counter that separated the two rooms stood an old iron safe, a desk, two chairs, and Jake Pryor, the banker, a small wizened man with sharp dancing eyes and a beard that covered his face almost to his eyes.

Near him on the table lay a Colt .45 revolver, a pad of bank notes, and several stacks of silver coins. They left forty-three dollars with him, accepted his receipt, and went out on the crowded street.

Everywhere they heard exciting talk of the Cherokee Strip land run and of the changes it had wrought.

"The run durn near depopulated Bluff City, Kansas, located jest above the border," chuckled an old fellow who wore his white hair and beard long and overflowing. "Its population dropped from 650 to 375 in half an hour. Now Bluff City's talkin' about issuin' a proclamation openin' up its own deserted country to settlement."

"Didja hear 'bout the holdup over on the Rock Island?" asked a lanky man in blue overalls. "The train was crossin' the Strip durin' the run. People was hangin' off the cars inside and outside. They looked like a million blackbirds that had swooped down and perched. A bunch of men stopped it and robbed the Pullman cars of all their ice and water. Things must be awful dry to do a thing like that."

"The drought is so bad in the northeastern part of the Strip that when Charley Whitman jumped out of his buggy to pound down his shingle, the ground was so hard he couldn't drive it down. So he went back to his home in Caldwell without a claim," related a third man. Fritz listened eagerly, storing it all up to tell his mother.

"What do we do next, Father?" he asked.

"Find mama, then head for the claim and begin building our dugout," replied Frederic. He acted as if he couldn't wait to get started.

THE DUGOUT

The task of building a home on the prairie,　where no wood or timber was available, began at once.

Because he had so little money with which to buy lumber, Frederic had to find a substitute that was cheap and plentiful. Like most homesteaders, he chose the buffalo grass. Its sinewy root-veined topsoil could be plowed into sod strips out of which a home might be built.

"Settlers couldn't make it here without the blessed buffalo grass," declared Frederic as he set the stakes for their dugout. "It provides food for the animals all year round and building material for homes and, with the help of the animals, fuel for the home. It's the most useful grass on God's footstool."

Selecting a well-drained spot in the canyon slope facing south, they dug a rectangular hole sixteen feet square. Frederic, using the grays and the sod plow, ripped up the tough soil in layers. With an axe, Fritz hewed these into rectangular blocks.

Then they switched to shovels and began shaping the interior of

25

the room, removing the earth and digging deeply enough for a man to stand upright without bumping his head on what was to be the ceiling.

That ceiling challenged the builder's art. After searching for three days, they found six miles distant some big cedars growing in the sand hills on land unoccupied by settlers. While Ray Patterson had told them that it was unlawful to cut wood for any purpose on government land, Frederic figured they had little choice. Fortunately they were not caught.

They cut and trimmed several logs. Fritz enjoyed the labor. The chips falling in feathery shavings from his light axe were redolent with the pungent cedar smell.

After transporting these logs back to the claim in their wagon, they laid the longest log, called the ridgepole, across the top of the dugout, through the center, from one side wall to the other, to support the roof. Pole rafters extending from the ridgepole rested on the tops of the walls on both sides. The long boards obtained at Woodward were placed across the rafters and nailed to them. Tar paper was fitted over the boards and sod spread thickly over that. Two stout poles were embedded in the front for the door facing, and Freda's glass-paned door was installed.

Meanwhile, Freda and the children planted turnips, which would defy the frost and grow all winter during the warm spells. Out of its young leaves they could, in a month after planting, have turnip greens.

Fritz wanted them to buy a young heifer that would grow and soon give milk.

"*Nein,*" said Frederic, "we have no fences yet. It would stray and get lost."

One day while Fritz was working outside he heard his mother, who was standing with him at roof level, cry out with fear, "Look quickly, Fritz! Crawling up the wall!"

Fritz looked. Below him in the dugout room a large rattlesnake had climbed halfway up the rough ends of one sod wall. Fritz walked around from the outside, entered the dugout, and with one thrust of his shovel cut off the snake's head. On the end of its tail the reptile had fifteen rattles and a button.

Freda's face was white. All her life she had feared snakes. Jacob and Sarah stood nearby, big-eyed, hands clutched.

"Every time I look at that wall I'll see that snake," Freda shuddered. Fritz carried it outside on his shovel and buried it. Then he shredded another full inch of dirt off the wall, cleaning it.

"Don't ever fight a rattlesnake," Frederic warned Jacob and Sarah later. "The bite of a rattler is poisonous. There's no medical help out here."

Meanwhile, the sod blocks were laid up in a wall, full-sized in front and filled in at the sides in the same manner that brick is laid but without any mortar. When they nailed apple boxes to the walls for cupboards, the sod was so hard that the nails held as if driven into wood.

Fritz never forgot the look on his mother's face when she entered that dark house of dirt for the first time. Cleanliness is a German housewifely virtue. Back in Texas, Freda had lived in a home of framed wood whose floors she scrubbed regularly and whose outside walls she kept washed down. No wonder she found this hard to bear.

"Let's sleep in it tonight," proposed Sarah. Frederic consented. But first they had supper in their new home.

Fritz set up the little topsy stove, which had two eyes, each covered with a stove lid. A small oven was contained in the first joint of the black stovepipe that extended through the ceiling. Since there was no wood, they had their first trial in burning dry cowchips, the standard fuel of the prairie.

"What's a cowchip, Fritz?" asked Jacob. He had never heard the term."

"A cowchip is what the cow leaves after she has walked on," Fritz replied.

Cow roses, Daisy Patterson had called them. These were first

27

kindled by a few handfuls of dry grass. They made a good bed of coals once the Rombergs learned how to bank them.

The whole family helped carry inside from the wagon the beds, quilts, comforters, and the trundle cot, which could be pushed under a larger bed during the day. Oil paper with a square of cheesecloth serving as a screen covered the lone window, admitting some light.

It was cool in the dugout. Everybody slept soundly until midnight. Then thunder began to grumble and lightning illuminated the oil-paper window. Fritz, sleeping on a straw tick by the door, was awakened by the rain outside swelling into a deluge. A wet earthy odor filled the air.

Fritz felt a drop of water strike his head. Another drop struck him, and then another. He got up and moved his bed back against the wall. Water was leaking into the dugout through the unfinished roof.

Freda got up, lit a lamp, and placed a tin kettle beneath the drip. For a moment, Fritz lay listening to the raindrops falling into the kettle.

The first pings were tenor ones. Then, as the kettle began to fill, each droplet struck a lower note until it sounded as if a piano tuner were running the musical scale as he evaluated the pitch of each descending key.

A second leak developed and Freda put a pan under it. A third drip started by the window and Freda placed a bucket beneath that. *Ping, pang, pong!* sang the raindrops joyously striking the cooking utensils.

"Ow!" said Jacob, sitting up in bed. "I'm getting soaked."

Frederic and Freda brought Jacob and Sarah into bed with them, but the leaks found them there, too. Faster and faster they came. Frederic and Freda sat up, putting on their coats. When Frederic donned his felt hat with the high crown Fritz had to laugh at the comic figure his father cut.

The oilcloth was placed over the bed to keep the children dry. The lamp was extinguished. Soon nearly everything was wet except the treasures in Freda's metal trunk and the bed protected by the oilcloth.

The situation was hardest of all on Freda, Fritz knew. First, the rattlesnake. And now, this.

"Please, Frederic," he could hear his mother softly imploring, "take us back to Texas."

It was then that Frederic, who had been the leader of the German singing society *Liedertafel* at Navasota, began singing German songs to cheer them. Soon they all joined in. Then Frederic lit the lamp and began reading aloud from a bound copy of Mark Twain's *Roughing It* that had been given to him by Pastor Vonfeld back in Texas.

Fritz laughed over Twain's description of the western "jackass rabbit" that "dropped his ears, set up his tail and left for San Francisco at a speed which can only be described as a flash and a vanish." Little Jacob began to chuckle, then Sarah. Finally, in spite of herself, Freda tittered too. They seemed to be laughing at their own plight, as well as at Twain's humor, Fritz thought.

Sitting against the wall with his coat on, he began to nod and drowse, and almost before he knew it, he was lulled to sleep by the mingling of their laughter with the noisy pelting of the raindrops into the kettles and pans.

When he awakened, the son shone brightly outside and the meadowlarks were splitting their throats. But it was still raining inside; the wet sod on the roof would drain for hours. However, his parents had been resourceful.

Despite the interior dripping, Fritz could hear a fire drawing in the stove and smell the smoke. He sat up, blinking, and a diverting sight met his eyes. Freda was frying pancakes while Frederic, still wearing his droll hat, held the family umbrella over her to protect her from the drips.

After that, they moved back to the covered wagon for several days until more tar paper could be laid on the dugout roof.

They had enough to eat because, in addition to the supplies they purchased in Woodward, they had brought food with them from south Texas. Freda had put up dried fruit and preserved meats. She had also baked a large quantity of bread and dried it out, so that it would not mold. On the long trip, they had often stopped in the evening to purchase milk from farmers. Then they would heat the milk and soak the dried-out bread in it. But no longer were there farmers to buy from.

Water became their chief problem. In West Creek, a mile away, where Freda had to do her washing, the water was heavy with gypsum. When they tried to lather it with soap it curdled like buttermilk. The grays would not drink it. The drinking water in the barrel was almost gone.

Freda asked Fritz to go to a buffalo wallow half a mile away and scoop up muddy water in a bucket. Then she strained it through a cloth and boiled it to make coffee. After it cooled, everybody drank it.

But Sarah and Jacob did not like coffee. Soon Sarah wanted a drink so badly that she cried. And Fritz, longing for a swallow of cold sweet water, thought often of the old well in south Texas. It then became Fritz's duty to harness the grays and haul the water barrel they had purchased at Woodward two miles to the Pattersons' to fill it with water from their spring. The spring at the Coopers' was much closer, but Frederic had forbidden any contact with them.

However, even this method wasn't satisfactory, since there were three horses to water besides five people. And additional quantities were needed to cook with.

"We must dig our own well," decided Frederic.

With a pick and shovel, Frederic and Fritz took turns with the digging, choosing a spot adjacent to the dugout door. Freda, Jacob, and Sarah carried away the dirt, placing much of it around the dugout to make it tighter and divert the rainwater away from the walls.

From morning to night, they stayed with their new labor. Jacob and Sarah were young, but they already knew all about hard work. They had learned from their parents. Until she was eight years old,

Freda had lived in Germany where she had learned to feed the cattle, clean their stalls, pick up the heads of grain that fell during harvest, and carry wood on her back. Wearing a willow basket strapped to her shoulders, she had also taken a paring knife and gathered dandelions for the geese. When Frederic, as a boy of fourteen, had finished school, his parents had hired him out to a German farmer to help with the rough farm work.

The first soil they dug for the well was black buffalo-grass dirt. Then came several feet of a hardpan subsoil, followed by a mixture of sand, clay, and rocks. As they descended, they walled it with native rock.

At thirty-one feet, water began to seep out of the sand. Would it, too, be gyppy? Freda lowered the dipper on a string to Frederic in the bottom of the well. They all listened breathlessly while Frederic raised his lantern and took an exploratory sip.

"Ach!" he muttered, his face puckering. Straightening, he spat it out.

"No good," he said.

"Father, let's see if the stock will drink it," Fritz proposed. He lowered a bucket, which Frederic partly filled. Then Fritz offered Valentine a drink.

The horse sniffed it, wrinkled his nose, and looked reproachfully at Fritz. Then he drank, cautiously but plentifully.

On another trip to Woodward to purchase a pump, well pulley, rope, and bucket, they had to withdraw more of their savings from Jake Pryor's bank. But now they had less water to haul from the Patterson spring. Frederic carved a watering trough from an old tree trunk they picked up on the way home, so they did not have to buy a new trough for the horses.

From Ray Patterson, they had learned that the Free Grass Law, favored by the ranchmen, permitted livestock to range at will but required homesteaders to fence their lands or assign their children the task of driving range cattle off their crops. This could be dangerous. Range cattle were often wild and ferocious. Although the matter had never come to a vote in the Strip, ranchmen like

Womble would enforce it as long as they had the upper hand.

Realizing that Womble's herds, or someone else's, might trespass on the kafir corn crop he planned for spring, Frederic decided to build a barbed-wire fence around his field while he had a little money.

Only a strong fence would do, he knew. "In this country anybody who can afford a fence with two strands of barbed wire and the posts closer than four rods apart will probably be looked upon as a plutocrat, but that's what we're going to have," he said. They bought the barbed wire at Woodward and their account in Jake Pryor's bank shrank a little more. It seemed there was no end to their needs.

"What are we going to use for posts, Father?" asked Fritz. Fence posts were priced at fifteen cents each at Woodward, an expense that they obviously could not bear.

"We'll have to go back to the sand hills, I guess," said Frederic.

It was hard, fatiguing work and required five days. There was also an element of risk. Patterson had warned them that if the ranchers, or their cowboys, saw them cutting trees on government land, they would report them to the marshals and it would cost them a stiff fine.

"But, like you, I hate to see all that good timber go to waste, so I believe I'll take my wagon and go with you," he concluded.

Again they were fortunate. Nobody saw them. The fences went up fast. Frederic was careful to erect his inside his boundary, allowing space for what someday would be a public road. Barbed wire was unfamiliar, so streamers were tied to it so that horses and cattle would see it and not blunder into it and cut themselves.

Many of Freda's turnips grew as large as milk crocks. They ate them all winter. They gave some to the Pattersons. Freda had brought from Texas such vegetables as kohlrabi, mustard, parsley, and leek for the spring sowing. She also brought flower plants and cuttings of vines and fruit trees.

After breaking and cultivating the sod within the fenced area, preparing it for the spring planting, they built a sod barn, leaving the east end open for coolness. Now the washing was done outdoors near the well. The clothes were soaked, then soaped, and the dirt was beaten out with a battling board rounded at the edges in order not to tear them.

For Fritz, the most enjoyable hours came at night when they sat around the cowchip fire in the dugout, each curled in his favorite position, while Frederic read to them or told them stories. They sang songs and read the Bible.

From the capital letters at the beginning of each chapter in the Bible, Freda taught the children their ABCs. Later they were promoted to the blue-back speller.

After the study hour the children put on their long nighties. Kneeling before their parents, they said their prayers, then threw their arms around each parent's neck and with a ''good night and pleasant dreams'' went to bed.

One day in late October, Sarah was missing. ''I saw her looking up the creek,'' said Freda. ''She's lonesome, I expect. There's nobody here for her to play with.''

Fritz went after her on Valentine. He found her two hundred yards from the Cooper house playing with the small Cooper girl who cast one startled look at his frowning face and scuttled for home like a flushed cottontail. When Fritz shot a look at the shack, he saw the older Cooper girl standing in the yard staring at him, her head protruding comically from her long skinny neck. She also looked nervous, as if remaining in the same township with him was taking an intolerable risk.

''What are you doing here, Sister?'' Fritz said sternly. ''You know Father doesn't want you associating with the Coopers.''

Sarah looked up at him, smiling trustfully. Her warm affection for him outweighed everything else.

''Look, Fritz,'' she said. Grasping him by a finger, she led him to their improvised playhouse. Rooms were outlined by walls of sand. Sofas were rocks upholstered with moss. The front door was marked by two small heaps of grass and there was absolutely no other way to enter.

"Tomorrow we're going to eat dinner in our new playhouse," she told him happily as he swung her into the saddle.

"No you're not," he said. "Father wouldn't like it. We're not having anything to do with the Coopers, don't you remember? They're Sooners."

The look on Sarah's face changed from puzzlement to hurt. It was difficult for her to regard a playmate as a foe.

In November the cold came upon them quietly and suddenly. The climate in northwest Oklahoma Territory was different from that of south Texas, they found.

Twists of prairie grass, which Fritz wound into long ropes, burned nicely but far too quickly. The same was true of sunflower stalks. Coal could be purchased in Woodward but it was expensive. Cowchips seemed to be the only alternative.

Freda, carrying a burlap sack, took Jacob and Sarah into Womble's pasture and they began to pick up cowchips. They had just got started when Mrs. Womble came out and drove them off. Behind her at the ranch house they saw smoke issuing from a fireplace chimney. A gigantic stack of cordwood lay in the yard. It had probably been taken from a government canyon, Freda decided.

"Why do you think you can steal from us?" the ranchman's wife asked as, hands on hips, she glared at them.

"We're not stealing them from you," protested little Jacob, his lower lip stuck out. "We're just borrowing them from your cows." But that logic failed to impress her.

"Get out and stay out," the woman stormed. "This is ranch country. You have no business in it. You can't take care of yourselves out here so you expect us to do it for you. If our cowhands catch you stealing timber from government land, they'll turn you in to the Federal marshals.''

Taking the wagon, Frederic and Fritz ranged widely looking for cowchips, but the prairie coal was hard to find except on the Womble range.

When it became dark, they usually went to bed to save fuel. Fritz, shivering in bed, couldn't help but remember Peter Popplebaum's warning back in Navasota.

''I wonder how the Coopers are keeping warm?'' said Freda, casting a glance at the Sooner cabin. ''I haven't seen any smoke coming out of their chimney.''

Sarah said, ''Zella told me that her father has gone to Kansas to find work, so they'll have money to buy food.''

Frederic frowned and turned away. He had also sought work so that he might increase their dwindling bank account. He had landed a hauling job at Fort Supply, only twenty-two miles distant. The job would start the following week.

On Frederic's last Sunday he read sermons to them from old issues of the *Christian Herald*. He led them in singing hymns. In the afternoon they took a long walk. They missed the Lutheran services they had attended in south Texas.

Three days later the northern sky darkened and a winter storm threatened. A careful search for cowchips yielding nothing. Frederic and Fritz drove the grays to Ray Patterson's dugout and found that his fuel supply also was exhausted.

Relaxing the reins, Frederic put one foot on the brake and looked at Patterson. ''Like everybody else, we'll be breaking the government law, but I feel it's a law that soon will be repealed,'' he said. ''A law is worthless unless behind it stands a warm living public opinion.''

Patterson came out drawing on his gloves. ''As long as there's vacant government land nearby with wood on it, I intend to have my share,'' he said, ''even if it is close to Womble's headquarters. We aren't cutting the wood to sell. We just want to keep our families warm.''

Frederic told him of Mrs. Womble's threat to have their cowboys turn them in to the Federal marshal if they caught them cutting wood on government land. Patterson fell silent.

Fritz's forehead puckered with thinking. "Father," he said, "why don't we cut it at night while their cowboys are sleeping? The moon's up. We can see."

Why not indeed, they reasoned. They decided to take the Romberg wagon and Patterson's mules.

CHRISTMAS
AT WOODWARD

Carrying guns and lanterns as well as axes, they went into the deepest canyon that Fritz had ever seen. The going was so rough that they took turns walking ahead and leading the mules. But once their axes began to bite, the wagon started to fill with sticks of cottonwood, chinaberry, and cedar.

"It's so still down here," panted Ray Patterson during a rest period. "Do you think Womble or his hands can hear the ringing of our axes?"

"I doubt if anybody will be outdoors listening this late at night," said Frederic. "If Womble hasn't coughed himself to death, he's probably sound asleep. Besides, we're in the bottom of a canyon. Sound won't carry well out of here."

At one thirty in the morning they were safely back at Patterson's and had divided the wood. The next night they returned with both teams and both wagons and took out two more loads. That solved the fuel problem at the Romberg and Patterson claims for some time.

But it didn't solve it at another claim.

The next day it turned bitterly cold. The gray sky spat sleet and the creek was frozen over. Frederic had gone to Fort Supply to start his hauling job, taking the grays and the wagon.

At about midmorning there came a knock on the Rombergs' dugout door. Fritz opened it.

Mattie, the older Cooper girl, stood outside, huddled in a ragged coat. As usual, she looked poised to run if he even wrinkled an eyebrow or drew a quick breath. She wore cheap cotton gloves and a man's hat tied down over her ears with a red bandanna. She looked cold, wretched, afraid.

"Mama wants to know if you-uns will give us some of yore wood," she said. "It's cold as blixum. My dad's off in Kansas workin'. We been lookin' but we cain't find ary more cowchips." Her words seemed to come from the back of her throat and she spoke with a slight lisp. She had walked the half mile against the freezing wind.

For the first time, Fritz saw her up close. Black tangled hair. Face white and thin. Lips blue with cold.

Surprised by her request, Fritz forgot to ask her in. He just stood there with the doorknob in his hand.

Scanning the faces inside the dugout, the girl seemed to read reluctance and hesitation on their countenances and to impute it to the dispute over the Cooper claim. Suddenly she lost her fear.

Her eyes blazed and Fritz saw that under the brim of the old hat they were as blue as the berries growing on the cedars in the badlands.

"We'll pay you-uns back when my dad gits home," she said, her low voice choked with emotion. "You-uns will be paid in full." Fritz was surprised to discover that a creature so young and shy had so much spunk and independence.

He stepped back. "I'll get my hat and coat," he said. Eyes brimming with mortification and hurt, she stared at their topsy stove glowing redly and at their woodbox filled with cottonwood and cedar.

Freda came forward. "Won't you come in and warm your-self?" she invited.

Mattie Cooper shrank back, shaking her head firmly. Apparent-ly she wanted no part of their slow hospitality. Then she turned and ran with an awkward lope back in the direction of her home.

Freda shook her head and made a clucking sound with her lips. "Poor thing," she said, "she was embarrassed to death. And she looked half frozen, too."

Fritz pulled on his coat. He had to give her credit. Despite her queer speech and her scrawniness, she was spirited. She'd put up a fight. He liked that.

He saddled Valentine. With a rope tied to his saddlehorn, he dragged a quantity of their stove wood to the Cooper cabin. He also took his axe. He knocked on their door.

Mattie Cooper opened it with Zella at her elbow. She didn't look quite so nettled this time. When she saw what he had brought she looked at him with surprise. She had taken off the hat and her tangled hair tumbled about the shoulders of the old coat like the ravelings of a rope. Zella had a quilt wrapped around her.

"What kind of a stove do you have?" Fritz asked.

"Same as yores," she said, "a monkey stove."

Fritz blew on his knuckles to warm them. He had never heard it called that. He said, "Do you want me to come in and start a fire for you? I brought some dry kindling to put under the green. I have matches, too."

The girl shot a look at him, a straight surprised look with the wonder not yet gone from it. She shook her head.

"We got lucifers an' bufferlo grass," she said. "We kin start it." He supposed she meant sulfur matches. He had never heard them called lucifers. She went back in.

Fritz dragged the wood to their back door and took his rope off it. As he coiled the rope he looked about the yard and saw that Orvus Cooper had made a few improvements. There was a sand-stone walk leading to the spring, but the plowed field wasn't fenced.

With his axe, he chopped the limbs to a length that would fit their stove.

As he mounted, their back door opened again.

Mattie came out and, crouching with her legs folded under her, began to pick up an armful of the fuel, watching him, still half afraid.

"Mama says thank you fer bustin' up the cook wood," she said.

Reaching for another stick, she glanced up again and this time her look was almost cordial. "Mama says yore welcome to take water from our spring anytime you want," she added.

When Fritz, back home, told them that, little Jacob scowled.

"It should have been our spring in the first place," he said. He turned to Fritz. "Brother, why did you give those Sooners part of our wood?"

Fritz hung his coat on a nail in the dirt wall. "Out here, the law of hospitality is very strict," he explained. "Father says that you have to feed and shelter your worst enemy if he comes to your house in need. If you refuse to help him, you'd better leave this country."

"When are the Wombles leaving the country, Brother?" asked Jacob, squinting shrewdly. "They sure didn't help us when we went over on their land for those cowchips."

Freda began to put plates around the small table they had brought from south Texas. "The Wombles are peculiar people," she said, and they let it go at that.

Later, when Fritz went outside to give Valentine several ears of corn, he saw gray smoke coiling from the flue of the Cooper shack.

That night, he thought about it. The small quantity of wood he had taken to them wouldn't last long. Despite their shortcomings, he hated to put that scarecrow of a girl to the embarrassment of having to call again to beg for more wood. He doubted that she'd do it. She'd probably prefer freezing to death.

All day he fought it out in his mind. After supper, he galloped to the Pattersons' and tied Valentine to a fence post. Borrowing

Ray's wagon and mules, he again drove to the canyon. This time he knew the way in the dark.

"I'll go with you," Patterson had offered generously, reaching for his gloves. "You'll need help. Heavenly scissors! It's cold enough out there to freeze the ears off a brass monkey."

Fritz shook his head. "Thank you," he said, "but I'd rather lone wolf it so I can keep all the glory to myself. Besides, you've already done your part, lending me your wagon and mules."

By midnight he had stilled his thudding axe and piled the wagon full. At one o'clock he had the wood neatly stacked in a rick in the Coopers' yard. At two he was back at the Pattersons' and had the mules unharnessed and turned into the feedlot. At three he was asleep in his own bed. Again he had encountered no marshals or ranchers.

That's the last time I'll do anything as silly as that, he told himself just before he dozed off. That sneaky Orvus Cooper can hustle his own firewood after this.

As the holidays drew near, Fritz lamented that this would be the first Yule they had celebrated without a Christmas Eve children's program at the church and a Yuletide sermon by a Lutheran pastor. There was no tree, no decorations, no relatives with whom to share the German custom of observing two days of worship and merrymaking.

But Frederic, who had returned from his hauling job, had a plan. Gradually it unfolded. Two hours before dawn on the morning of December twenty-fourth they dressed in their best and, working in the dark, loaded the wagon with quilts, blankets, utensils, food, and straw to thrust their feet into. After breakfast, Fritz harnessed the grays, backed them on each side of the wagon tongue and hooked them into the doubletrees.

With Fritz riding Valentine and Frederic shaking out the reins of the grays, they set out for Woodward. The cold shut down so hard that although Freda had wrapped the children in quilts and their feet were deep in the straw, they still became chilled. Wearing the quilts around them, they got out in the darkness and walked part of the distance behind the wagon to keep their toes warm. Frederic and Fritz took turns driving the grays and riding ahead on Valentine.

When the sun's great red eye came winking up through the buffalo grass, illuminating every square rod of the level prairie, the frost sparkled and Valentine threw a shadow ten times as long as himself. Fritz gasped at the new land's stark beauty.

What few farms there were could be identified by smoke rising from the ground, for nearly all the homesteaders lived in dugouts. There were few fences and no well-traveled roads, just trails. Creeks had to be forded, but that was easy because they were all dry.

In late afternoon, shivering, they pulled into Woodward, bits jingling and the town curs yapping at the horses' heels. They went at once to Hennessey's wagonyard, where the camp house was cozy in the glow of a big heating stove whose firebox was red as brick. Frederic bought a quart of whiskey at a saloon and a round of hot toddies warmed them all.

The main function of the wagonyard was to provide refuge for a traveler's horses, a place for his rig, and shelter for himself and his family. Alongside two walls in the camp house were built-in bunks two tiers high into some of which they unloaded their bedding. In the rear of the big room stood a small cookstove, a scuttle of coal, and a table and chairs.

Fritz was concerned about the expense until he saw what his father paid—fifty cents for the overnight stabling of the horses and twenty cents for the three flakes of prairie hay that with the corn they had brought from the dugout comprised the horses' food. No charge was levied for people staying in the camp house as long as they kept their horses in the yard.

This is almost like that first Bethlehem Christmas, Fritz thought as he warmed his hands and his backside. We're almost staying in a stable. It's only a few feet away.

For their first Christmas Eve meal in Oklahoma Territory,

Freda, using the kitchen range, heated a big pot of German bean soup and served with it an immense loaf of home-baked bread, which they spread with honey purchased that evening from a grocery store. As Frederic had suspected, few men were on the roads at Christmastime and they had the camp house all to themselves.

The town was agog with the excitement of the holidays. As the Rombergs walked about the crowded street they saw that the meat markets were filled with carcasses of wild turkey, deer, and antelope. There were even steaks from a fat young bear. Toys, candy, nuts, and sweetmeats were offered at the Post Office store. Bear and venison were served at a free luncheon at the Do Drop saloon where five musicians performed.

On the boardwalks there was hardly room to pass. Sometimes they had to go out into the street to get past the people. Fritz could have looked forever into the decorated store windows.

He stared with awe at a drugstore exhibit that showed a Christmas tree resplendent with many small candles held on by tin cup clamps and the first glass ball decorations and tinsel strings that he had ever seen. In a furniture store window stood half a dozen nickel-plated Daisy air rifles and a sled with steel runners and steering handles.

Most thrilling of all was the display in Wagner's dry goods store. The main window was a room. A little girl, a real live one, with curly hair, slept in a bed. She kept raising up on one elbow— and no wonder. Santa Claus was coming down the fireplace chimney. He had one foot on the floor and a new overshoe on it with the price tag still visible. Jacob and Sarah didn't want to leave that window.

That night they attended the Christmas Eve program of the Union Sunday school at the town school. There a jovial audience jammed the place. Gifts had been provided by the churches for every child. Presents for Jacob and Sarah were placed beneath the large cedar tree that was adorned with popcorn strings and colored paper chains.

A new chapel organ, only four feet high, sat in one corner of the room. Fritz caught his breath when he saw it. It had celluloid stops and nickel-plated pedal frames inlaid with Brussels carpeting. Its back was finished with shining panels and open fretwork. It seemed crying to be played but therein lay a problem.

"The ranchmen got together and purchased it for the church, but we haven't found anybody who can play it," the minister informed the congregation.

Fritz's hand shot up. "Sir," he said, "my mother can play it." He turned, smiling, to Freda.

What he said was true. In the Lutheran church at Navasota Freda had played the small organ and Frederic had led the choir. And Frederic had sung baritone and Fritz tenor in the male quartet of the community's German singing society.

"Hush, Fritz," stammered Freda, looking at her hands. "I haven't played for months."

But Frederic rose and escorted her to the organ. "You must excuse my wife for being *schei*," he said, "but it is true that she has not played since we came from Texas. However, I think that it will soon come back to her."

It did, too. A natural musician, Freda began to thumb the hymn book on the music rack and to explore the keyboard. At first her fingers were stiff, Fritz knew, and the touch of the keys seemed strange. Smiling and shaking her head when she flawed a note, she kept on.

Gradually the notes cleared. Using only two stops at first, she began the melody of *"Die Lorelei"* in tones so high and sweet that they suggested ethereal voices. Then she began pulling more stops and adding melodious harmonies.

"We need someone to lead the singing, too," added the minister. "My throat's so raspy from a cold that I can't do it. That's fortunate for the congregation. Any volunteers?"

This time Fritz waited, looking around the room. Nobody stepped forward. Again Fritz's hand jutted toward the ceiling.

44

"My father can," he said. A whisper of laughter arose and a polite patter of handclaps.

Frederic walked to the front. "Before my son volunteers our whole family, I'd better get the singing started," he said. "My name is Frederic Romberg. That's my wife, Freda, at the organ." He introduced Fritz, Jacob, and Sarah. Each of them stood in turn, smiling and bowing bashfully.

In the community singing that followed, all five Rombergs participated joyfully; they liked to sing and knew most of the old tunes by heart. Then, with Frederic singing the melody and Fritz adding his boyish tenor, they sang as a duet *"Stille Nacht,"* "Silent Night," once in English and then repeated it so softly in German that the audience sat hushed on the edge of its chairs as it strove to hear each note. After the sermon the Rombergs mingled with the congregation.

A girl came up to Fritz in the crowd. Tanned by the sun, even in winter, she had a long blonde braid that dropped over one shoulder. She kept twisting it with her left hand.

"My name is Dobie Quinlan," she said in an agreeable low-pitched voice. "My father helped buy that organ, but none of us can play a lick on it. Your mother plays beautifully. You sing good, too."

Fritz laughed. "Not good, just loud." He kept looking at her, and smiling. There was always something exciting about meeting new people, especially girls.

She wore a white muslin dress that held her tightly at the waist and breast. There was a pleasant fragrance on her, and her skirts rustled as she looked at him. It was the open look of a very pretty girl.

Behind her, Fritz saw her parents. The father, who was obviously one of the ranchmen of whom the minister had spoken, was a little man with sandy hair and a moustache. He wore a western hat and short black boots imprinted with a green butterfly with red and blue wing dots. Fritz wished that he could afford such a pair. The

45

man stayed close behind his daughter, Fritz observed, as if to shield her from any intrusion by strangers.

"What spread do you work for?" the girl asked.

"No spread at all," said Fritz. "We live in a dugout west of here."

Blinking in surprise, she backed up a step. "Then you're nesters," she said.

"We've farmed all our lives," Fritz went on. "We made the Strip run clear from south Texas. That's seven hundred miles." He laughed merrily. "Then yesterday we drove in a wagon twenty-seven miles from our claim to attend this program. We like long trips."

Her eyes, gray as thimbles, widened. "Then you won't mind visiting our *hacienda* sometime," she replied. "It's the Bob Quinlan ranch. We're located about fifteen miles west of here. Stop by sometime. I won't let our cowpunchers shoot you."

"Thank you," said Fritz. Then he added, gallantly, "If I have to be shot, I'd much rather be shot by you than by your cowboys." She's nice, he told himself. Wonder when I'll see her again?

At the camp house later, the stove's firebox had grayed but the big room was still warm. Sarah looked pleadingly at Frederic.

"Please, Father," she said, "tell us of Christmas when you were a boy back in Germany."

Lifting her into his lap, Frederic told the story as he had so often in other Yule seasons.

"We celebrated it German fashion, on Christmas Eve," he began. "We did not believe in Santa Claus. We were taught instead that the Christ child came down from heaven to trim the tree and leave the presents for us. On the eve of the Saviour's birth, the tinkling of a little bell would be heard outside German homes, then a knock on the door.

"A lady would appear as the herald of *Christ Kindlein*, the Christ child. She was dressed in white with a girdle of blue. Her face was veiled. Asking for the youngest child, she would ask the boy or girl to say a prayer as evidence of diligence in praying. Then she would give the child presents.''

Sarah listened with a sparkling face. Jacob grew uncommonly quiet, his eyes as big as buttons.

After Frederic finished the story and Sarah and Jacob were asleep, Fritz put fresh coal on the fire, Frederic brought out the whiskey, and they drank Christmas eggnog after which the three of them played cards until late in the night.

Next day, after Frederic said grace, Freda served her Christmas dinner, most of which she had brought precooked from the dugout but heated again in the camp house. It was mainly *bot boi* (hot pie), a dish that was not a pie at all but a rich stew of chicken, potatoes, and carrots with squares of egg noodles swimming in the broth. Since they had no chicken, Freda had substituted two wild rabbits, which Fritz had shot with Frederic's Colt revolver.

"Only wild rabbits must be used," said Freda. "The domestic ones do not have the proper flavor."

In early afternoon, they started the long trek back to the dugout. As they rode westward, Fritz thought that, because of his father's originality, it had not been a bad Christmas after all. They had spent it together, as a close family should.

The remainder of the winter was mild and uneventful. To their surprise, they discovered that buffalo grass, ripening on the ground, afforded good food for the horses all winter. Even when it snowed, Valentine and the grays learned to paw the snow off to reach it.

On Frederic's next return from his hauling job at Fort Supply, he brought exciting news. Bill Doolin, the territory's most notable outlaw, with a companion had robbed the Woodward depot of $6,540 in cash consigned to the army paymaster at Fort Supply. About dawn, the outlaws went to the railroad hotel in Woodward and woke up George Rourke, the Santa Fe station agent. They forced him to go to the depot and open the safe. The outlaws then rode southwest of Woodward, eluding a posse of cavalrymen led by Jonas Ritter, the veteran Indian scout.

"I won't get paid until next month," Frederic said. "Doolin got the payroll."

"I've heard about that Doolin," said Ray Patterson. "He's a bad one."

Fritz thought, I wish Doolin had ridden northeast of Woodward instead of southwest of it. I don't want him turning up out here.

March went by and spring came to the Strip. No two days were alike, Fritz thought. One would dawn clear and mild with the prairie lying in green splendor and the meadowlarks whistling their high sweet notes in the sunshine. But the next would be cold and wild with wind that blew the clouds so forcefully that their edges seemed raveled like the fringe of a surrey.

The level land was inviting to the plow and a joy to stump farmers from Texas. Leather lines tied over his left shoulder and under his right arm, Fritz trudged behind the grays and watched his father's new sod plow rip up the shortgrass soil, laying the root-veined ribbons bottom side up in the furrow.

April came and they sodded twenty acres more, planting it to kafir and sorghum cane. Fritz liked to watch the damp soil cascade off the blade and hear its soft crunching sound. He liked to smell the fresh-turned earth.

Ray Patterson helped them, and they helped him. There were no mechanical seed-planters in the country that first year. For the planting, they improvised, using a gallon syrup bucket into the side of which they punched a hole. Filling the bucket with seed, they replaced the lid tightly and ran an axle through it from end to end.

On every third round of the plow, they stopped and attached the bucket to it. As it rolled along on the shoulder of the furrow, a seed would drop with each revolution of the bucket and the next round of the plow would cover it shallowly. Afterward, Patterson and his team went back over the furrows with a brush harrow to cover any seed that had not been overlaid.

48

Each had their work to do. Although it was not as heavy as in Texas, Fritz knew that there would be more of it as they developed the farm. Back at Navasota, the whole Romberg family had arisen at four o'clock in the morning. There was milking to do by lantern light, livestock to feed, and the cleaning of the barn's stanchions and stalls. Then would come breakfast, after which the dishes were washed and the kitchen scrubbed. After Freda blew out the kerosene lamp just before sunrise, they went to the field to shuck corn.

Here in the Strip, Frederic decided to try fruit growing on a larger scale with seedlings obtained from Fort Supply. An orchard of peaches, apricots, and apples was planted, along with several rows of Irish potatoes. Frederic just turned the sod over the potatoes and forgot about them. Once the prairie soil had been plowed, it absorbed rainwater like a sponge. Everything seemed to grow well, including the grass along the creek on the disputed Cooper claim. Soon it became luxurious enough to cut for hay. One day they saw Orvus Cooper's drooping figure leveling it with a scythe and stacking it. A week later it wasn't there.

"I know where it went," Ray Patterson told them. "He sold it to Sam Womble. Womble wanted it to winter-feed his horses. Cooper got a good price for it, too."

Frederic's jaw set firmly. He never spoke, but Fritz knew what he was thinking. Hay was a good cash crop. If Cooper hadn't slipped in and preempted the place before the legal starting time, that profit could have belonged to the Rombergs.

Frederic was a close observer of nature. The intricate design of a butterfly's wing, the mother cottontail's custom of lining her nest with fur pulled from her breast, the delicately edged black wings of the scaled quail—none of this escaped him and he enjoyed pointing it out to his children. It was his theory that the mourning dove was misnamed, that its low cooing was more tender than sad.

Sarah was always trailing along at Frederic's heels. Once when she brought a drink of water in a small bucket to her father,

Frederic showed them a dove's nest. It was poorly constructed, since doves show little judgment in locating their homes. This one lay squarely in the road that ran from their dugout to the field. The nest was undisturbed because Frederic had gone to great pains to skirt it with his team and plow.

One day Sarah brought an old school reader to the field where Frederic was plowing. Stopping him, she would spell out the hard words and then ask him to pronounce them. Finally he became unwilling to delay his work by stopping, whereupon she walked in front of the team and he had to halt.

"Hold your horses, Daughter," he said, "I'm busy. We'll do it tonight."

Piqued, she threw the book onto the ground. Frederic draped his lines over the plow handle and without a word paddled her with the flat of his hand. It was one of the few times Fritz had ever seen his father administer physical punishment. Although Sarah cried, she knew that she deserved it, he could tell.

Fritz liked the smell of the Strip in the mornings when the Rombergs arose before dawn to do the chores. It was a fresh and invigorating smell, filled with the spicy whiff of the dewy range. He felt a yeasting within him to own his own farm. Someday, he would conquer this beautiful, stubborn land, compelling it to yield a profit to him as well as to his father.

He grew to like their dugout home; it had been easy to heat in winter and would be cool in summer, other settlers had told them. The roof no longer leaked. It was now grown over with grass, wild flowers, and weeds. The floor was as smooth and hard as oak. It could be swept and even mopped.

The new country had slowly begun to attract settlers. More dugout chimneys and small black spots of cultivated ground began to show every time they went to Woodward for supplies. Fritz had plowed a garden spot and Freda and the children had long since planted it. One morning, they found deer tracks in it.

May drew on, bringing with it warm winds, red sand daisies, and a visit from Daisy Patterson.

"I'm having a baby," Daisy announced breathlessly. Ray hung back, grinning. "Ray bought us a cow, too," she added.

"Frederic wants to find one for us," said Freda.

"You can have some of our milk," said Ray, "our cow gives four gallons a day."

Daisy brought a gift for Freda, a Rhode Island hen and a setting of eggs. "You'll have to watch her closely," warned Daisy. "The varmints are bad around a canyon.

"I'm going to ask the older Cooper girl to help me when the baby comes," Daisy added. "She volunteered. She knows quite a bit about doctoring and she's clean as a pin. She brought old Granny Phelps out of a bad case of asthma just before Christmas. She stayed three nights with Granny. Slept on a deerskin on the floor without a pillow. Next morning the lady of the house poured water over the girl's hands and told her to dry her face on her bonnet. They can't have much over there."

Fritz was surprised that any of the Coopers could do anything useful.

That afternoon he built a chicken house for the hen. He built it out of sod and added a perch. Over it he put a sod ceiling, roofed with tar paper, just like that atop their own dugout. He also contrived a nest out of prairie grass, which the hen promptly rearranged to suit her fancy. The children called her Flossie.

When the chickens hatched, the hen refused to take them into the hen house at night.

"Look where Flossie is," said Jacob in surprise the next morning. The hen had moved her brood outside near the dugout door, as close as she could get without coming in. Jacob had almost stepped on them as he went to water the horses.

Freda came to look, tying her apron behind her. "That's odd," she said, "I wonder if she stayed all night out here? That hen house looks lots warmer and safer."

"Maybe a snake got after them," said Frederic. "Martin Faust of Navasota once told me that a bull snake ate a dozen of their chicks, one after another."

51

*   *   *

A week later Fritz was riding Valentine along the creek when he saw the flash of a green dress and came upon Sarah and Zella Cooper playing with a small cottontail rabbit they had caught. Fritz dismounted.

As usual, Sarah seemed glad to see him. Taking him by the hand, she showed him how they were using black walnut hulls for cups and oak leaves for saucers in their playhouse.

"Look, Brother," she said, "Zella tied her ribbon around the rabbit's neck so that we can lariat him out." Although Zella was poised to run, she held her ground this time, eyeing Fritz distrustfully.

Fritz brushed a fly off his cheek and looked about. In spite of its yellow leash, the rabbit seemed quite tame as it nibbled at the handful of grass Zella held out to it. Although the girls seemed to be having fun together, learning to be neighbors, Fritz's duty was plain. His father had forbidden any social contact with the Sooners.

Placing Sarah in the saddle before him, Fritz started home with her.

With tears in her eyes, Sarah looked back over her shoulder at Zella standing in the path with her finger in her mouth. "Goodbye," called Sarah. "Your dress is pretty. Your bracelet is pretty. Your hair sure is pretty."

At home, Frederic approved of Fritz's action.

"I'd rather you didn't play with her," he told Sarah. "Play with Jacob."

COW-FRESH
ICE CREAM

———————◆—◆—◆———————

Frederic and the grays had gone to Fort Supply to haul freight,
Fritz was splitting wood in the backyard when he heard Jacob's
voice from the stable. "Brother! Brother! Here comes somebody.
And he's coming fast."

Hoofbeats drumming, a rider careened down the trail, his bay
horse in a dead run. The man had lost his hat. His brown hair was
blowing in the breeze.

Turning in at the Romberg dugout, he jerked the animal to a stop
and flung an iron picket pin in the dust at Fritz's feet. He was pale
and distraught. The bay was panting in noisy heaves.

"Rattler bit me on the leg," the man said. "You gotta fire goin'
in your dugout?"

Surprised and bewildered, Fritz nodded. The man slid out of the
saddle, grimacing with pain. The sweat had washed grimy rivulets
down his cheeks and his shirt clung wetly to his chest. Hearing the
strange voice, Freda and Sarah came out of the dugout.

"Mercy!" exclaimed Freda. "It's the big cowboy we met the day of the run."

Pulling up one pant leg, the man pointed. At first Fritz saw only the red bandanna knotted tightly below the knee. Then a chill knotted his stomach. On the bare flesh below the bandanna he saw the double fang marks. The area around them was swollen and black. Unless they acted fast, the wound could be fatal.

The man still had the cool, quick eyes and that no-nonsense air about him. He picked up the picket pin and handed it to Freda. "Mam, put one end of that pin in your fire and heat it. When it gits red hot, bring it back to me." Freda picked up the pin and started walking to the dugout.

"Hurry, mam!" his voice snapped crossly. "It's a hot day. I can feel the poison workin'." Freda broke into a run.

Snatching the coiled rope off his saddle horn, he limped down the canyon path out of sight of the dugout. Then he swung around, facing Fritz.

"Now lissen careful, Dutchy," he said, "build another fire right here in the sand. It don't have to be big. Jest do it quick."

Fritz jumped to obey. Returning from the woodpile with dry grass, shavings, and chips, he soon had a blaze crackling merrily.

Backing up to the only tree of any size in the canyon, a hackberry, the man thrust the rope into Fritz's hands.

"Now lissen an' do what I say," he directed, his black eyes boring commandingly into Fritz's blue ones. "I want you to snub me to this tree with my own lass-rope. Then, if you've got a rope, use it too. Tie me so tight that I can't get loose. Here—I'll show you."

Fritz was mystified. "Why?" he asked.

"So that when I beller fer you to free me, you won't pay me no heed." Quickly, he showed Fritz how to form the knots and hitches under his arms and below his knees. Soon he was trussed so securely to the tree that he looked as if he were part of its bark.

"Now go git that picket pin, if it's heated red, an' I'll show you what to do. Tell the lady she an' the kids better stay up there where they can't hear me cuss. Hurry! My leg's mortifying.''

Fritz didn't know what ''mortifying'' meant, but in a couple of minutes he was back with the fourteen-inch pin, clutching its cooler end with one of Freda's potholders. Its point glowed red as fire.

''Now jam it up against my wound,'' ordered the cowboy. ''Hurry!''

Fritz hesitated. He didn't want to burn anybody.

''Don't touch the wound,'' said the cowboy, ''jest hold it as close to it as you can without touching it. About a quarter of an inch. And don't pay me no heed if I start yellin'.''

Fritz obeyed. As the heat from the pin drew the poison out, the wound turned green and the cowboy gasped.

''It's coolin' off,'' he said finally. ''Put the pin back in the fire and git it hot again.''

Fritz did better than that. He ran to Frederic's toolbox for their own picket pin and poked it into the fire, too. Soon he was alternating the two pins, keeping constant heat on the wound. He was also blistering the man's leg, he saw.

The cowboy began to yell and swear. ''Free me, damn you!'' he cried, struggling vainly against his own knots. ''I didn't tell you to use two pins. I'd rather die from snakebite than burn to death.''

Fritz paid no attention to him. When one pin lost its strawberry glow, he'd thrust it back into the fire and withdraw the other, applying its rosy point to the fang marks.

It was hot work. With his eyes smarting from the smoke, his ears vibrating from the man's cries and threats, and the smell of singeing hair in his nostrils, Fritz felt as if he were going through almost as much torture as the victim himself. But he stayed with it, faithfully fulfilling the cowboy's original instructions.

After several applications, the wound failed to turn green. Fritz concluded that all the poison had been drawn out. He untied the man. The cowboy thanked him, rubbing his wrists to restore the circulation that had been cut off by the binding of the ropes.

A stick crackled nearby. Little Jacob stood staring. He had seen and heard it all.

"You sure can yell loud," said Jacob admiringly. "I'll bet they heard you clear to Woodward."

Fritz invited the cowboy to stay to dinner, but the man refused. Soon as his picket pin cooled, he walked laboriously to his horse, dropped the pin in his saddlebag, rewound his rope, tied it to the saddle horn, and mounted. Lifting one hand in graceful nonchalance, he rode off as coolly as if he had just come by for a cup of coffee.

"I wonder why he's always in such a hurry?" said Freda, shading her eyes with her hand as she watched him fade into the landscape. "I wanted to put some salve on that burn."

"At least we know his name," said Fritz, as he kicked sand onto the fire to extinguish it. "It's Jim Yoakum. He says that he rides for Womble."

"Womble?" said Freda, frowning. "No wonder he won't eat with us. He's probably afraid that Womble will discharge him if he does."

Flossie the hen still insisted upon spending each night within four feet of the Rombergs' backdoor. Once, just before dark, she even tried to bring her half-grown family inside the dugout, but Freda and Sarah shooed her out.

"What's the matter with you?" Freda scolded mildly. "Fritz built you a nice home, but you won't sleep in it. Maybe you'd like it better if you just tried it once."

Spreading her apron, she advanced on Flossie and her brood, attempting to herd them into the new hen house. But Flossie balked. Clucking noisily, she kept veering off to one side or the other, the chicks scurrying after her.

Finally, Fritz ran her down, caught her, and forcibly placed her inside the hen house. Then they ran after the chicks, catching them one by one and putting them inside the new domicile, too. Securing the door, they all went back to the dugout for dinner.

The next morning Fritz was carrying water to the trough for the horses, while Sarah had gone to the hen house to release Flossie and her household.

Her cries summoned the entire family. When Fritz looked through the door he saw a large possum crouched in a corner, grinning at him. During the night, he had eaten every one of the chicks and had strewn their gizzards about the floor. Flossie, frightened and distressed, had flown to the top of the perch.

"Watch him, Jacob, while I go get Father's gun," said Fritz.

"All right, Brother," said Jacob, who was barefoot. Circling to keep plenty of distance between himself and the possum, the boy stumbled across a small pile of lumber near the woodpile.

"Ow!" he yelped, "I stepped on a nail."

"We'll fix it in a minute," called Fritz. "Watch the possum."

Returning from the house with Frederic's Colt, he quickly dispatched the murderer and released Flossie. Then they went to the dugout where Freda washed Jacob's wound with soap and water and greased it with mutton tallow.

Next day they had more visitors. A horseback caravan of five riders, their animals richly caparisoned and the men wearing shoulder capes, fur caps, and long black boots, trotted into the yard.

One of the party, a man who wore his military-style trousers tight in the hips, dismounted and came forward. Halting in front of the Rombergs, he cracked his heels together and inclined his head curtly.

"This is the royal hunting party of Prince Solms of Bavaria," he said, speaking as if he were delivering an announcement of vast significance. "His Highness, the prince, is hungry. Order your servants to prepare food for us at once." His English was slightly flawed by a German accent.

Freda came forward. "We have no servants, but I can fix you something," she said. "I'd have to build a fire first. You're certainly welcome to what we have." she added graciously.

The man looked her over from head to foot. "What do you have, *frau*? At the last place we inquired, we were offered sour wild plums cooked with pie melons and a drink of creek water. His Highness is accustomed to far better fare than that.''

Little Jacob thrust out his lips in a scowl. He didn't like the man's arrogance.

"All we have to eat is dishwater and coffee grounds," he said surlily.

Freda laughed pleasantly. "Hush, Jacob," she said, "we can do better than that."

She turned again to the officer. "We're settlers and don't have much. But I can offer you warmed-over beans, fried potatoes, and bread. And if you're not in too great a hurry, we can give you fresh strawberries from our garden."

Although he frowned at the plain fare, the man accepted. They got off their horses and began to stretch and to chatter in German.

Fritz gathered a pail of fresh strawberries from the garden. He washed them and took them to the dugout. He also fetched an additional quantity for himself and Jacob to eat in the yard. But when they began eating them, the officer hurried over to him, frowning.

"How dare you eat when His Highness has not yet tasted?" he demanded.

Fritz looked at him coolly. Speaking in German, he said. "I meant no disrespect to anybody, *mynheer*. This is the United States of America, not the German monarchy. This is a free country. We have no nobility here, and want none. We aren't bound by the customs of those nations who do have a nobility, especially when their citizens are traveling in our republic."

"So!" said the man. He stamped once upon the ground. He drew in his breath. Anger flashed from his eyes. Fritz continued looking calmly at him, pleased that he had stung him out of his attitude of proud authority. The man turned on his heel, rejoining his comrades.

With his fingers, Fritz continued to put the red berries into his mouth. He was still upset by the man's superior air. He would never forget that his father's family had left Germany, then smarting under a military despotism, because they wished to live under a government that gave each citizen personal, religious, and political freedom.

Despite their haughtiness, the Teuton guests knew how to reward the Romberg hospitality. Someone among them left two silver dollars on the table.

That night Jacob tossed about restlessly. Twice he awakened crying.

"My foot's sore," he said, "where I stepped on the nail." When Freda got up and applied heat and flaxseed, the puncture looked angry and festering in the light of their kerosene lamp.

Next morning it was worse. Freda began to worry. "It's inflamed," she told Fritz. "I'm afraid he has blood poisoning."

Stroking his chin apprehensively, Fritz thought of something worse—lockjaw. Caused by the toxins of a bacillus that usually entered the body through wounds, it was often fatal. Fear, the worst of his life, twisted his insides. For a moment he stood with his back against the wall, staring at Jacob on the bed. It was a day's ride to Woodward, and the doctor might not be there when they arrived.

"I wonder if it would do any good to let the Cooper girl look at him," Freda suggested. "Daisy Patterson says she knows quite a bit about doctoring."

Ready to try anything, Fritz decided to take Jacob on Valentine. Jacob didn't want to go.

"They're Sooners, Brother," the boy protested feverishly. "I don't like them. Father said we were to stay away from them."

"I know," Fritz agreed, "but this might save us a long ride to Woodward and back to see a real doctor." He didn't want to go to the Coopers either, but his anxiety was deepening.

With Jacob in the saddle in front of him, he rode into the Cooper backyard. No horse or wagon was in sight, so he knew that Orvus was gone. Apparently they had been hoarding the wood. A fourth of the rick he had cut for them still remained.

Fritz knocked. Impatiently, he waited, wondering why they didn't come. Jacob, a forlorn figure, whimpered in the saddle, his swollen foot stuck out halfway down Valentine's bulging side.

The door opened. Mattie Cooper stood framed in it, her unruly hair falling into her eyes. Seeing Fritz, she shrank back, looking as if she would flee at the drop of an apple or the scold of a jay.

"My brother Jacob ran a nail into his foot," Fritz said. "It hurts so bad he can't sleep. What should we do?"

With the back of her hand she raked the hair out of her eyes. The declaration of his mission seemed to quiet her fears somewhat.

"Make a big bread and milk poultice," she blurted. "Put one-half teaspoon of turpentine in it. Pack it round the wound as hot as he can stand it. Keep dabbin' on the hot poultices 'til he gets shet of it."

For a moment Fritz looked at her, frowning. She looked too young and dowdy and frightened to be giving out medical advice, let alone that which might involve the saving of human life. And then he remembered.

"We have no milk at home," he said. "We have no turpentine either."

Without a word, she went back into the house. He heard her talking to her mother. Soon she returned with an old brown canvas case fastened with straps and buckles. Quickly, she opened it, and Fritz saw that it was stocked with a profusion of pills, powders, bottles, discs, everything from belladonna to goiter tablets, he surmised.

From it, she withdrew a small bottle of turpentine. She had also brought from the kitchen a fruit jar half filled with milk. It had a lid on it.

"The weather's so warm this milk may be blinked," she cautioned, "but that's all the better."

Eyes still big and fearful, she opened the door wider and handed him the articles. Gazing down, he saw that she was barefoot.

Glancing keenly at Jacob, she said, "His face looks pied. Dab the poultice on him lickety-quick. Drive the heat in by holdin' a hot smoothin' iron agin it.'' Before Fritz could thank her she shut the door.

He hoped that he had understood her queer-turned talk. Why didn't she speak so people could understand her?

Mounting behind Jacob, he was careful not to jostle the sick boy or drop the milk. He doubted if the poultice would work. All the turpentine bottle was doing was smelling up his clothing.

As they rode back he looked down at Jacob in the saddle before him, at the boyish line of the hair around the back of his neck, at his flushed cheeks, at the translucence of his big ears as the morning sun shone through them. He loved his brother very much. He didn't want anything to happen to him. And yet all that stood between Jacob and death was this barefoot Sooner girl whose dress was pale from many washings and whose speech was as hard to fathom as a foreign tongue.

Steering the horse with his knees, he fought down his fear and tried to plan ahead. Ray Patterson would volunteer to ride for Frederic at Fort Supply but could they get back in time? With a tormented shake of his head, Fritz tried to brush the dark thoughts from his mind.

Back at the dugout, Fritz punched up the fire and rekindled it. Freda prepared the poultice. Jacob was put to bed. Freda spread the hot application upon a clean cloth and tied it around the boy's foot.

''I'm all ready to take him to Woodward,'' Fritz told his mother. ''I'll fill the wagon with straw and make him a bed in it. You and Sarah can go along. I'll borrow Ray Patterson's wagon and mules. His mules will run part of the distance. It'll be a long rough ride for Jacob, but he'll be more comfortable in the wagon than on Valentine.'' Although he tried to sound cheerful, he was wretchedly afraid.

But Jacob Romberg never left his father's claim. To their astonishment, he steadily improved. The hot bread and milk poultices, invigorated by the turpentine and the heat of the flat iron, routed the infection.

With a slow crawl of shame, Fritz acknowledged to himself that he had underestimated the healing power of their mop-haired neighbor. Although the Coopers had cheated his father out of the choice farm, the Rombergs were now in debt to them.

They paid off some of it with Irish potatoes. Frederic's crop, planted in the fresh-turned sod and energized by the rains, bore so heavily that there was plenty for all. It was Freda who made the decision. Since Frederic was hauling at Fort Supply, Ray Patterson took a bushel of the potatoes to the Cooper claim. Finding them gone, he left them on their back stoop.

Back from Fort Supply, Frederic came down with the Texas slow fever, which the whole family had suffered from at times in south Texas. However, after his usual remedy, a long drink of whiskey before going to the fields in the morning, he was able to work, although he didn't bounce back with his usual vigor.

One morning he went with Fritz to the kafir field. After Sarah finished washing the breakfast dishes, she swept the dugout room. Then she went to the field, while Freda and Jacob hoed in the garden. As the sun rose, shortening the shadows and drying the dew on the buffalo grass, Sarah found a big sandstone rock near one corner of the field and started to transplant wild flowers around it.

"Father, come and see the beauty spot I'm making," she called excitedly to Frederic.

"Sarah, I don't have time for things like that," he said crossly. "I have to weed the kafir." Hurt, the girl abandoned her project. Each time he came near, Frederic acted as if he would speak to her, but she walked away from him. Fritz saw that his father wasn't feeling as well as usual. Ordinarily, he would drop anything he was doing to answer Sarah's questions or do what she asked.

In late June the wild plums along Clear Creek were ripe. One sunny morning Freda, Sarah, Jacob, and Daisy Patterson went in the Romberg wagon, pulled by the grays, to gather the plums. When they did not return by midafternoon, Frederic grew uneasy.

Riding double on Valentine, he and Fritz followed the wagon tracks and met the women, wet and shaken, returning. In the wagon was a tub two-thirds full of wild plums and on Freda's lips an exciting account of what had happened.

For three hours they had picked plums along the creek bank. The creek was running almost full. Across the stream, the plums looked bigger and redder. They decided to cross over and finish filling the tub with them. Daisy was driving.

The farther they went into the stream, the deeper the water became. They decided to turn around and go back. Then the grays began to sink in the quicksand.

Frightened, they didn't know what to do. Finally they saw a man riding a horse down a trail near the shore. Standing on the spring-seat and waving their sunbonnets, they shouted as loudly as they could, but he didn't hear them. Not until Jacob lent his shrill cries to the tumult did they get results.

The man was Jim Yoakum, the big cowboy who rode for Womble. After untying his buckskin chaps at the waist and knees and hanging them over a small mesquite tree, he waded out to their wagon to see what was wrong.

"After rains, the fine sand gets full of water and there's always danger of quicksand," he said. "If the water's low and the stream nearly dry, you don't find it. You get so you know by the look of the sand when to stay out of it. This sand's got that look."

He carried Sarah and Jacob across on his back and helped Freda and Daisy wade ashore. Then he unhitched the grays one at a time, piled brush under them and rolling them over on their sides, helped them extricate themselves. With the help of his horse and his rope, the grays pulled the lightened wagon out of the quicksand. With Yoakum driving, the Romberg rig was recrossed at a nearby ford that the women hadn't known about.

As he helped them into their wagon and headed them home, the cowboy had looked at little Jacob.

"You sure yelled loud," he said. "I'll bet they heared you clear to Amarillo."

As Fritz unhitched the team and cleaned the harness, he wished that he could have been there. Hazards were adventure. Only one percent of life is truly exciting, he reflected, as he polished a buckle. The rest of it is slog and drudge.

The Rombergs' first real crop was thirty acres of kafir corn that Frederic had planted during a spell of warm weather late in March. Everybody to whom he talked had advised him to plant kafir. It was hardy. Prolonged dry weather would not kill it. It was chiefly a horse food and could be sold to ranchers. Once they got a crop, they wouldn't have to buy any more grain for the horses. You could even make flapjacks with its round white kernels, small as shot.

The Romberg kafir did not have to prove its drought resistance, because rain fell at intervals all spring. In late July it stood as tall as Fritz himself, and the red heads, big as his fist, were eight to ten inches long.

"Abe Hooper, the implement dealer, tells me he sometimes pays two dollars a bushel for kafir seed," Frederic told them after one of his trips to Woodward. "He wants all we can give him." Excited and proud, he walked out each morning to the field to look at his crop.

In mid-August the kafir was so near the ripening stage that it had turned white. It was almost ready to harvest. On a sultry afternoon, three days later, Ray and Daisy Patterson called. While the women trimmed the wicks and washed the chimneys of the coal oil lamps, the men put a roof of logs, tar paper, and earth over the Rombergs' new sod hay shed constructed in the side of the canyon out of the wind. They had already built such a shelter on the Pattersons' place.

While they worked, a black cloud began forming in the north, illuminated by glints of jagged lightning and a distant boom of thunder.

"Looks like a storm," said Frederic, leaning on his shovel. "Maybe we'd better head for cover till it blows over."

But this storm did not blow over. It headed straight for them. Strip storms could be swift and violent, Fritz had heard. This one was conforming to the pattern. Although the sky had been sunny and blue an hour earlier, the world now grew so dark that Flossie the hen came home early to roost. Fritz led the horses into the barn, where they would be protected, and joined the others in the Romberg dugout. Then the rain came.

It swept across the land in filmy sheets. He could hear the spiteful slap of it on the prairie. The lightning darted to amazing lengths, running along the ground in fiery balls. The air grew icy and smelled like sulfur.

It was Jacob who first saw the hail. "Look, Father!" he called, pointing.

Big as the knobs on the bedposts and white as chalk, a few isolated stones began striking the wet ground and bounding high into the air. They clattered off the wagon so deafeningly that they sounded like gunshots.

Little Sarah crouched in a corner and clapped her hands over her ears. The air grew chill. For fifteen minutes the hail hammered down so hard that they couldn't see the wagon parked only twenty feet away.

Afterward, when the storm blew over and the sun began to warm the wet earth, Frederic suddenly struck the table with one hand.

"My kafir corn!" he cried. "I wonder what the hail did to my kafir corn." Clapping on his high-crowned hat, he hurried outdoors. All of them, including Daisy, big with her unborn babe, ran behind him.

At first Fritz thought they had run to the wrong field. He stood staring. Everything looked so different. Only a few unbroken stalks stood upright. The heads, hopelessly smashed, had been beaten into the soil and the dirt had washed over them. The kafir was flattened, obliterated, ruined.

"Heavenly scissors!" exclaimed Ray Patterson, his face white.

Frederic stood rigid, his eyes wide with horror, his hands knotted and shaken. A stricken wonder came into his voice.

"A man's life is like a stalk of kafir," he said in hushed tones.

Fritz stood staring, shocked by his father's face. For a moment, the tragedy of the lost crop was too great to be comprehended.

A hopeful look in her face, Freda spoke. "Now we can load up and go back home to Texas."

Frederic shook his head slowly as he continued to stare at his destroyed crop.

"No, Freda," he said, "we've come to stay."

Fritz saw her flinch and tears come into her eyes. The utter futility of their staying hurt her, he knew.

"But we're getting nowhere," she protested, spreading her hands. "We're just existing."

Nobody else spoke. But when even Sarah and Jacob stared wordlessly at her, Freda realized that her whole family was opposed to returning to their former home. For some reason that she could not comprehend, they loved this wild, treacherous land.

Touring the disaster region in the sunshine, they discovered that the hail was four feet deep in the canyon. It would stay for days.

Fritz was shaken by the disaster, but he saw no need to prolong the general grief. He remembered his parents that morning in the dripping dugout, his mother frying pancakes while his father held the umbrella over her. They needed to make the best of this situation, too.

He cast a look around him at the hail lying everywhere and felt a queer, bitter amusement twitching his lips.

"We could make ice cream," he suggested.

Daisy Patterson smiled brightly. "Let's do!" she bubbled. "I know how."

It necessitated a special trip to her dugout for the ingredients, including sugar and milk, but with Freda, who had recovered her composure, helping and the fallen hail providing the necessary chill, it didn't take long.

The cream, milk and sugar, flavored with vanilla extract, was put into a gallon syrup bucket with a lid. That, in turn, was placed in a three-gallon milk pail. The pail was filled to overflowing with hail. Salt from the nearby Salt Plains that Ray used for his cow was sprinkled on top of the hail.

Grasping the pail, Fritz turned the little bucket in the big one, slowly freezing the cream. Occasionally Ray Patterson and Frederic would spell him, dividing the labor. Sometimes they would stop to let the women take off the lid and knife the cream loose around the edges so that the middle would also freeze.

Cow-fresh homemade ice cream, Daisy called it. Fritz thought that he had never tasted anything as delicious, nor eaten it under such strange circumstances.

He grinned as he passed his plate for a second helping.

"Harvest's over," he said gaily, and everybody laughed.

That he had plowed, listed, and weeded much of the destroyed field himself he completely forgot. It was how his father took it that worried him. That beautiful patch of kafir was to have been Frederic's way of showing Sam Womble and the world that he could make farming pay in this grassy wilderness.

Frederic gradually grew a little more cheerful. After downing his second dish of ice cream, he set the plate and spoon on the window ledge.

"Well," he said, licking the tip of his thumb that had trailed in the leftover confection, "I feel like I've lost all my money through a big hole in my pants pocket."

Reaching for Freda, he set her on his knee and peered into her eyes.

"But you still like me, don't you?" he asked. Freda smiled and hid her head on his shoulder.

Two days later, after the soil had dried, he was back in the field with the grays, turning the ground with Ray Patterson's double moldboard plow.

THE BLANKET
UNDERPANTS

With the coming of the second autumn on the claim, a lack of fuel again became a problem.

When Frederic, Fritz, and Ray Patterson drove the six miles to the deep canyon where they had taken wood the previous year, a cowboy trotted boldly up to the Romberg vehicle and halted, gathering his bridle reins to his chest as he scrutinized the axes in the wagon.

"No more woodcuttin' in these canyons," he warned. "You got around us last year with your night cuttin', but we found the stumps and your wagon tracks. This year Mr. Womble is patrollin' the country night and day. If we catch you cuttin', we'll report you to the United States marshal at Woodward and appear agin' you as witnesses."

"Thank you," said Frederic politely. Without another word, he turned the wagon around and headed for home. Womble's war on the settlers, particularly the Rombergs who held a quarter section of land that he wanted to square off his range, had reached a new and ominous stage.

They tried grubbing the banks of Clear Creek for dead mesquite tree roots, but the supply was too limited and the ground too hard from a new turn of prolonged dry weather. They scouted the railroad track for discarded ties but found only a few.

Finally the problem was solved by putting sideboards on the wagon and making three weekend trips into the pastures of the nearby Texas Panhandle, well-stocked with cattle. They took a washtub, tied a short rope to one of its handles, and dragging it over the prairie, filled it with chips and emptied them into the wagon.

Back home, the Rombergs stacked their chips into a rick beneath the new sod hay shed they had built and felt reasonably secure.

Thinking of the Coopers and the previous winter, Fritz decided to tell Orvus, the father, about the new source of fuel on the Texas plains so that they could restock their own winter supply if they cared to go that far.

When Fritz rode to the Cooper claim, he found Orvus scything hay along the creek. The man paused, taking off his hat and mopping his bald head with his sleeve. Fritz told him about the Texas cowchips.

"It's a long way over there and back but we had no choice," he concluded. "Womble's riders are watching the government canyons."

Cooper laughed, a harsh laugh that sounded like a dog growling. With a long arm, he pointed to a new cord of wood piled loosely in his yard.

"Take a look at that," he said boastfully. "You don't know how to git along with Womble." Turning his back on Fritz, he resumed his scything.

As Fritz rode past the Cooper shack he saw the freshly cut pile of cottonwood and cedar and felt a rush of indignation. The explanation was as plain as the wart on Cooper's nose.

Womble let Cooper cut all the government wood he wanted in return for the exclusive right to buy Cooper's creek-bottom hay. On a ranch, horse food was important. Like most ranchmen, Womble made no effort to grow his own.

Wild grapes grew in such profusion in their small canyon that they decided to make wine in the German way. After washing the grapes, Frederic crushed them with a wooden press built from spare lumber. A layer of grapes to a layer of sugar was placed by Fritz in a barrel and pressed. When the juice arose, it was put in another barrel, more sugar added, and the bung covered tightly. Frederic had bought the sugar at Woodward.

"When it starts fermenting, it'll be good to drink," Frederic told them. "But that will take at least a year."

The drought continued into late fall. It was hard to live with. When Frederic tried to plow, the grays nearly crawled out of their collars trying to pull the implement but could break out only several large chunks of dirt. Then the plow would hit a hard place and skid out on top and the horses would start running, carrying Frederic and the plow at a trot.

"Whoa!" Frederic would yell, sawing on the reins. Dragging the plow back, he would try again. In spite of the soil's hostility, Frederic managed to sow ten acres of wheat.

"It will sprout soon as we get rain," he explained, "and we'll harvest it late next spring." The Rombergs knew all about crop failures and economic want. In south Texas they had encountered both. Hardship there had taught them that a poor year was sometimes followed by a good one. When a bad year came, you stuck it out.

While they were sticking it out in the Strip, Frederic decided to increase their dwindling cash reserves. He secured another hauling job at Fort Supply.

Before he left, he took his family to Woodward to buy supplies. They planned to arrive on a Friday evening, shop on Saturday, and return home after attending church Sunday morning.

After breakfast at Hennessey's wagonyard, they headed for the stores. To their surprise, the streets were deserted and the places of business were closed and locked.

"That's funny," said Frederic, his brow wrinkling with bafflement, "wonder what's happened?"

Walking about on the boardwalks, they finally ran into Jake Pryor, the banker, and Mrs. Pryor standing in front of the town school where the Union Sunday school met. The two families stopped to exchange greetings.

Frederic raised his gray high-crowned hat to the banker. But Jake Pryor doffed his black derby to Freda, smiling and nodding pleasantly to her; then he shook hands with Frederic. The effect of this was not lost upon Fritz who saw that in this part of the territory gentlemen sometimes went out of their way to defer to ladies. It was a graciousness he never forgot.

"Why is the town so quiet today?" Frederic asked. "I thought that Saturday was the busiest day of the week here."

"It is," said Pryor, "but today is Sunday."

It was true. Somewhere the Rombergs had lost a day.

"Why don't you come to church with us anyhow?" proposed Mrs. Pryor. "Aren't you the one who played the organ at our Christmas program last year? We'd love to have you play it again this morning, if you will. Nobody else can. It just sits there."

Freda hesitated. "I haven't looked at a keyboard since last Christmas," she warned.

"The service doesn't start for fifteen minutes yet," Fritz pointed out, "why don't you go in now, Mother, and practice?" Starved for the music, he wanted to hear her play. And it would brighten her day, too, he knew.

They went in. A few people already were seated inside, awaiting the arrival of the minister who was coming by horseback from the Curtis community.

The small chapel organ sat exactly where it had the preceding Christmas, at the end of the room near the pulpit. To Fritz, it

71

looked lonely and obscured, as if it never expected to be played again in this primitive land.

Freda seated herself at the key desk and began pulling out the celluloid stop knobs. It was warm in the room. When Freda took off her coat and gloves, Fritz saw that she was still wearing the kitchen apron she had donned at the wagonyard while cooking breakfast that morning.

Blushing, she snatched it off and thrust it into her coat pocket. She looked at Gloria Pryor sitting nearby. "I guess I was in too big a hurry to get to the stores," she laughed.

She began to play, softly at first, then with volume and feeling, using feet as well as hands. As the deep tones rolled harmoniously from the console, the little organ seemed to awaken and bestir itself as if it had been waiting for Freda all this time.

They attended the evening service, too, then shopped the following morning and began the long drive back to the claim.

"We need a calendar and a clock," said Frederic, just before he left with the wagon and the grays for Fort Supply. "It's easy to get our weekdays mixed when we live so far from town."

"We need a church and a school lots more," said Freda.

One of the items they had purchased at Woodward was an extra bottle of turpentine to replace the bottle that Mattie Cooper had given them to strengthen the hot bread and milk poultice she had prescribed for Jacob's nail wound.

"Here, Jacob," said Fritz next morning, "you take it to the Coopers. It was your foot she doctored. Be sure to thank them." He also sent along the Romberg family's copy of Mark Twain's *Roughing It* for them to read.

"I'll go with you, Jacob," said Sarah, eager to see her friend Zella.

With a maul, Fritz was breaking the ice in the trough so the horses could drink when he saw Jacob and Sarah returning. Sarah was carrying a package with a pink string wound around it.

"It's for you, Fritz," said Sarah, holding it out to him. "Mattie said not to let anybody else see it.'' Curious, he dropped the maul and took it.

While the children trailed off to the house, Fritz opened the package, which was wrapped in a three-month-old page of the *Wichita Eagle*, a Kansas newspaper. It contained a piece of blue and gray blanket, folded neatly. When Fritz lifted it out and held it up, two legs fell down and he saw that it was an undergarment for the lower part of the body. He blushed to the roots of his hair.

Why in God's world is she giving me this, he wondered. Why does she give me anything at all? Curious, he smelled it. It smelled musty. But the flannel was clean and felt soft to his touch.

A note, scribbled in pencil on the back of a baking powder label, fell out of the garment into the snow. Stooping, Fritz picked it up. Turning it over, he saw that the message was short.

''If you do not like me I shall dy,'' it said.

Exasperation flooded him. He shut his eyes and licked his lips. He tried to think of anything he had said or done that would give this gawky, tousled girl the idea that he was even remotely interested in her, or liked her.

Mortified, he flung the note into the snow. Then he picked it up again. As a matter of fact, he neither liked nor disliked her. He was grateful to her for curing Jacob's foot but that was all. He could see her now with her long neck and her thin enigmatic face that told him nothing. But her note had told him a great deal.

Returning to the house, he showed the drawers and the note to his mother. Still agitated, he sank into a chair.

Freda raised the garment so that it caught more light. In her quick deft way, she folded it neatly and laid it on the bed.

''It's an odd gift for a young woman to give to a young man with whom she's had very little social contact,'' Freda said, ''and yet all she says in her note is that she wants you to like her. She's just a little country girl who has become somewhat infatuated with the boy on the adjoining claim.''

Picking up the drawers again, she shook them out and held them up, looking at them critically. "The sewing is neat and the material durable. I've never heard of underpants made from a blanket, but in this climate it's a fabric that should give good service. I'd wear them. They'll keep you warm. Perhaps sometime you'll have the opportunity to thank her without giving her the impression that you're deeply in love with her."

Fritz looked away, flushing. Him in love with Mattie Cooper? How could his mother even talk about something so improbable? Frowning, he walked out of the dugout to do the chores, forgetting to put on his cap or mittens.

Next morning Jim Yoakum came riding up, his spurs making music in the wind. As usual, his attire indicated that he paid considerable attention to what he wore. This time it included a pair of California salmon-colored pants. His rope was suspended in a neat coil from the right side of his saddle. His oilskin slicker was rolled neatly behind the saddle's cantle.

"Hello, Dutchy," he greeted Fritz, "what's new?"

Hungry for human companionship, the Rombergs went out to greet him.

Yoakum looked with interest at the rick of Texas cowchips. "Wull," he drawled, "looks like yore gonna keep warm here all winter in spite of us."

Fritz grinned. "For several winters," he corrected, "in spite of anybody."

"Where'd you get 'em?" asked Yoakum.

Fritz didn't hesitate or blink. "From the Texas Panhandle."

Yoakum's bay horse took a forward step, and plunging his nose into the Romberg water trough, began to drink. Yoakum reached into his shirt pocket for cigarette papers and his little Bull Durham tobacco sack with its round tag dangling on the end of the drawstring.

"Womble's watchin' you," he warned. "His punchers are all takin' turns watchin' you. If I caught you takin' gov'mint wood, I'd have to run you in."

Freda said, "If you were in our place, and winter coming on, what would you burn for fuel and where would you get it?"

"I wouldn't have come here as a settler in the first place, mam," said Yoakum.

"But we are here," said Fritz. "We're here because the Federal government threw the land open to settlers. They invited us."

"I know they did," Yoakum conceded, "an' they made a big mistake. But the Federal gov'mint has also got a law that says you can't cut gov'mint timber."

"That's a mistake, too," said Fritz. "What's the good of inviting us to settle when there's nothing around here to burn when a norther blows in? Womble's got a pile of wood as big as a haystack. If you ranchers can cut government timber, why can't we?"

Jim Yoakum seemed to sense that the argument could become heated. Compassion in his face, he glanced at Sarah and Jacob who were listening with their mouths wide open. He seemed unwilling to involve or frighten them.

"Because we don't want you here, I guess," he replied honestly. "Both of us can't make it here. An' we was here first." But his voice was calm.

Fritz pointed to the Cooper claim. "They're burning cottonwood and cedar over there while we burn chips," he said. "Looks like Cooper slipped past Womble's punchers."

For a moment there was a silence filled with the scent of the sage and the crying of some crows in the small Romberg canyon below. With his back to the wind, Jim Yoakum poured loose tobacco out of the tiny muslin sack into a cigarette paper, rolled it, licked it shut, and thrust one end of it into his mouth. He nodded.

"Looks like he did," he acknowledged. "I can understand how you feel." Scratching a sulfur match off his pants and cupping both hands to protect its flame from the wind, he ducked his chin, guiding the end of the cigarette into the fire and inhaling deeply.

75

Then he blew out the smoke quietly and deliberately. Sarah and Jacob watched, enthralled.

The bay horse lifted a streaming muzzle, blowing the drops from his nostrils. Yoakum's hands tightened on the reins. His eyes on Sarah and Jacob, he told them that he had been to a store at Shattuck, a prairie village that had just been birthed over the hills eight miles southeast of them.

"I brought you a little somethin'," he said. Reaching into his saddlebag, he pulled out a small doll for Sarah and a new slingshot for Jacob. Delighted with their gifts, each child came forward to accept them.

Yoakum kept rummaging in his saddlebag. "Got somethin' else here for you all, too," he muttered, and produced a box of chocolate bonbons. He handed them to Freda.

Freda was overcome. Chocolates were a luxury. These were the first the Rombergs had ever had. "You shouldn't have spent your money on us like this," she protested. "I'm sure you work hard for it."

"Not very, mam," he said. "Anyhow, it's fun to spend it."

He swung off the bay, tied him to the horse trough, and they fell to talking. "I'll go make some hot coffee," Freda said. "It's my own make, beans roasted in the oven and ground with a hammer. My husband says it tastes better than Arbuckle's."

She walked with Sarah to the dugout, stopping on the way for an armload of cowchips to freshen the fire.

Yoakum said, "I feel like a skunk makin' you all go fifty miles for a wagon full of cowchips that yore mother has to burn to boil the coffee she's offered me," he said.

Fritz squatted on the prairie, liking the man's basic honesty.

Yoakum went on. "Of course, I can't fault Womble for keepin' you all out of the gov'mint canyons. He's fightin' fer his ranch."

Fritz shook his head and looked at his hands clenched around his knees. "We're not after his ranch," he said. "We don't want it. But he does want our claim. And to get it, he's trying to force us to give up and leave by helping the marshal police the canyons so we can't cut wood.''

With the toe of his boot, Yoakum made tiny furrows in the sand. ''There's another side to it, too. You nesters are takin' my job.''

Fritz looked up in surprise. ''How?'' he said, frowning, ''I don't understand.''

''Here's how,'' said Yoakum. ''With homesteaders startin' to come in all around him, Womble will have to shorten his range an' may soon have to fence. That means he'll need fewer hands an' the ones he keeps will have to do things like buildin' fence, plowin' fireguards, and plantin' crops. I'm not gonna do any of them. I'm a cowhand. I ride an' rope an' brand an' herd an' bust hosses. That's all I know how to do.''

Little Jacob was listening, his ears canted toward them.

''You can work for us,'' he burst out generously. ''You can sleep in our barn.''

The faint promptings of a smile touched Yoakum's lips. ''Thanks, partner,'' he said. He sounded sincere.

Fritz began to ask questions about cattle. Back in south Texas, the small farmer kept a cow or two to milk but rarely raised beef cattle because there were no railroad facilities over which to ship them to the markets. But here in the Strip, the Santa Fe's rails lay shining in the sun only a few miles southeast of the Romberg dugout. And Woodward was a thriving cattle town.

From Jim Yoakum, Fritz learned that because of their rapid increase, cattle made quick money for the ranchmen. There was practically no feeding or marketing cost. They ran wild, grazing the native grass, which was good the year round, and drinking from the creeks and rivers.

It was then that Freda called them to the dugout for coffee.

Later, after Yoakum rode slowly off, Fritz thought about it. Was the ranching industry really doomed? Farming wasn't, he was sure. People had to eat and always would.

They would always eat beef, too. And somebody had to raise it.

Could the farmer raise beef as a sideline to crop raising? How profitable would it be?

The conversation swung back to Yoakum. "He's fond of the range and very angry at anybody he thinks has a part in breaking it up," said Freda as she washed the empty cups and Sarah dried them. "We're helping to break it up and yet he brings us presents. I wonder why?"

Fritz said, "Maybe that's his way of apologizing for having to keep us from cutting timber on government land."

Jacob said, "Maybe he's lonesome."

"I think he likes us," said Sarah, hugging her new doll.

THE GUNMETAL CLOUD

Four days before Christmas Frederic and the grays rolled in from Fort Supply. With him, he brought a mysterious sack that he declined to show anybody except Freda. Fritz guessed that he had done some Christmas buying.

"I saved forty dollars from the hauling," Frederic said, "and deposited thirty of it with Jake Pryor at Woodward. I got laid off six days or I would have done better. Our bank balance now stands at sixty-three dollars and fifty cents."

"Father, at what wagonyard will we stay when we go to Woodward for Christmas?" asked little Sarah.

Frederic took off his coat and hung it on a peg in the earthen wall. "We aren't going to Woodward for Christmas this year," he announced. "The grays and I are tired. And I've got to mend the harness and soak the wagon wheels to keep the tires from coming off."

Outside, Fritz unhitched the grays and began to brush them.

79

Jacob came out and washed down their shoulders. Sarah helped her mother prepare the dinner.

"When will you get our Christmas tree?" the girl asked her father.

Frederic looked downcast. With Womble watching all the canyons, there was no opportunity to acquire an evergreen.

"I know what we'll do," said Freda, "we'll set the table for breakfast and the veiled lady wearing the blue girdle can place the presents in the plates."

Sarah began to cry. "It won't be Christmas without a tree," she said.

Frederic solved that by driving through the bitter cold five miles west, across the Texas line, where he remembered having seen a mulberry that had grown six feet high before the drought killed it. He found it, cut it down, nailed a brace across the bottom so that it would stand, and installed it in a corner of the dugout.

"That's no good," fretted Sarah. "Father, we need a cedar."

Frederic looked at her and fell silent. It was one of the few times Fritz had ever seen him dejected.

However, when Freda, Fritz, and Jacob wound narrow strips of white wrapping paper about the trunk and draped the limbs with popcorn strings and chinaberries, Sarah's eyes began to shine. Cheerfully she helped Freda assemble the ingredients for the Christmas cookies made with sugar that had been saved for weeks.

Ray and Daisy Patterson and their tiny daughter were invited for Christmas dinner at which was served fried potatoes, corn bread, navy beans, and baked prairie chickens. The fowl had been picked up by Frederic along the creek, where they had frozen to death during the abnormally cold weather. Thawed out and dressed just before the meal, they were delicious, although they tasted somewhat of the sage they had eaten.

After dinner, much of the talk centered on the new baby born in the Patterson dugout and how Mattie Cooper had presided at the birth.

"She had walked across the pastures to see how I was getting along," said Daisy. "Just as she came in, I knew that the baby was coming. Ray was still working in Kansas and I was all alone. She said she'd help me. She knew what to do. She built up the fire, boiled water, and sterilized everything she used. She even browned the gauze in the oven before she put it on the baby. She's very clean.

"She tied a sheet to the posts at the foot of the bed. When the labor pains began, she encouraged me to grasp the sheet and pull hard to help bring Carrie into the world. Then she washed her and dressed her. She got dinner for me, then walked the two miles home to tell her mother where she'd be. Then she rode back on a horse and stayed three days, doing all the cooking and cleaning and taking care of us. It was good of her mother to let her come.

"I tried to pay her for her help," Daisy went on. "I gave her a silver dollar, the only one we had. She's too shy to argue, so she took it. But after she left I found it in the pocket of one of my aprons she had washed and ironed."

Freda told how Mattie had prescribed the poultice that healed Jacob's nail wound. "She's very young and timid," Freda added, "only twelve or thirteen, I imagine."

Fritz frowned. She hadn't been timid when she sent him the blanket drawers. Abashed by all the frank talk about childbirth, he nevertheless listened attentively, wondering where the girl had got her medical knowledge.

Later Frederic read a sermon from the *Christian Herald*. After a game of euchre and a round of yuletide toddies, it was time for bed.

There wasn't room in the Romberg dugout for everybody to sleep, so Frederic proposed that he, Ray, and Fritz drive to the Patterson dugout, leaving the Romberg domicile for the others. Scowling, little Jacob liked no part of that arrangement.

"I'm not going to sleep here with all these wimmen," he protested.

Frederic looked at him. "Yes, you are," he said quietly and firmly.

"All right, Father," said Jacob. Fritz was amused at the boy's

81

sweet reasonableness. He knew that Jacob worshipped his father and always strove to please him.

Bundling up in their warmest clothing, Frederic, Ray, and Fritz started for Pattersons' dugout in the wagon. It was a star-drenched night, and so cold that they all three got out of the wagon and walked or ran alongside it to keep their feet warm. They were serenaded most of the route by the wailing of coyotes.

The dryness continued into February. Last year's tumbleweeds, bowling end over end in the furrows, scratched along the surface until they were caught on Frederic's barbed wire where they rustled futilely in the wind.

One afternoon as Fritz was plowing he noticed that the sunlight was yellowing unnaturally. The buzzards were climbing in circles as if trying to get above an approaching something that Fritz could not see on the ground. And then he saw it.

A vast cloud, stretching widely, was rising in the north. The cloud was the color of gunmetal. Moving slowly and majestically, it rolled in grayish-yellow plumes, billowing higher and higher.

Fascinated, Fritz pulled the horses to a stop and watched it. He saw that this was no rain cloud but rather a rising wall of dust, silent and sinister, that lifted as lightly as if it were a mass of feathers floating in the stratosphere. Its upper fringes were swelling and expanding in bluish whorls. The grays, hitched to the plow, also seemed affected by its mystery, tossing their heads nervously as they watched it form.

On it came, thick and low-clinging, and then it started to boil out from each side, bulging and dilating fluffily, inspiring in Fritz a vague dread.

He licked his lips and felt his scalp prickling. Everything within the cloud's interior looked black and menacing. And then he was aware that the crows had ceased their cawing and that every chirp and peep of the songbirds was hushed.

Off to the south, in the direction of the dugout, he heard his father calling, his voice strangely far-carrying. Turning, he saw Frederic standing in the yard, waving frantically for him to come.

As Fritz unhooked the horses, he saw that the advancing wall was shutting out more and more of the world to the north. His view of the Coopers' shack faded, then was gone. As he turned the team around and shot a quick look back over his shoulder, he could see only five posts of the fence line north of him.

To the south, toward the dugout, the sky was clear but tinged by a weird opaqueness. He ran the horses all the way to the barn. Working with desperate haste, he began to unharness them. Frederic hurried in to help.

"Looks bad" was all he said as he lifted the stout leather collar and hames and heaved them onto the hook in the earthen wall.

And then it was upon them. The first edges of it crept along the ground.

As Fritz slipped the bridles off the heads of the grays, he saw loose folds of dust drifting about his shoes. As he fumbled with the breeching and the traces, it was flowing around his knees. Working by feel as well as by sight, they got the harness off and left the grays in the barn.

As they ran for the dugout, where Freda had hung a lantern on the clothesline to guide them, the last of the daylight was going. A cold north wind sprang up. To the south, where the only light remained, the sky was reddish and eerie. Suddenly, that too disappeared and it seemed to Fritz that an immense drapery, dark, forbidding, and all-enfolding, had suddenly dropped upon them.

Dust was settling on his lips. He could taste its salty grittiness between his teeth, but he had no trouble breathing. A slight smarting of the eyes constituted his only discomfort.

Inside the dugout, Freda had lit the coal-oil lamp. Through the suspended dust particles that twinkled in the air like orange confetti, the lamp gave off a dreary light. Both the door and the window were tightly closed.

"Heigh-ho!" Frederic's resonant voice sang out cheerfully.

83

"I've been to two goat ropings and in under the bed after my old shoes, but I've never seen anything like this." He smiled at Jacob and Sarah. Fritz saw the fear go out of their faces.

Adopting a suggestion from Freda, Frederic brought in a tub of water from the well. Quickly Freda stripped the beds of sheets and pillow cases. Dipping them into the water, she and Frederic plastered them across the door and window without wringing them out. Water from them soon ran down the walls, forming dirty puddles on the floor.

But it worked. As they began to breathe the damp air, the storm became a frolic. While Freda cooked dinner by lamplight in the middle of the afternoon, Frederic led them in singing bits from Wagner's opera *Tannhäuser* and the southern melodies of Stephen Collins Foster, a young Pennsylvanian who had died thirty years earlier but whose music, Frederic told them, would not die while there was sorrow and pathos in the world.

Jacob and Sarah took a nap on the floor. For the remainder of the afternoon and much of the night, Frederic and Freda, with Fritz spelling them, kept dipping the sheets in water to keep the dugout fresh and much of the dirt out.

And Fritz never forgot the feeling of family warmth and solidarity and the relief from worry and fear provided by his parents during that crisis. The following morning dawned clear. There was dirt on every grass blade, on the coats of the horses, and in the feathers of Flossie the hen. But the great dust storm was over.

With most of the plowing finished, Frederic resumed his hauling at Fort Supply, taking the wagon and the grays. Hungry for companionship with others of his own age, Fritz pleaded to go along.

"I think it unwise at this time," Frederic replied. "They wouldn't pay us any more for your help, and we'd be out the expense of your food."

Fritz stepped back, feeling a twinge of disappointment. While he liked the Strip, he was homesick for the gaiety of village life at Navasota. He missed singing in harmony in the church's male quartet, the physical rivalry of the gymnastic exhibits, and the competition of the debating society that met every second Sunday afternoon. This verbal jousting with his fellows Fritz particularly enjoyed. With his powers of quick thinking, his knowledge acquired through reading, and his skill at expressing himself thoughtfully and well, he was formidable despite his youth. But that was all behind him now. Out here, he could argue only with the coyotes and the buzzards. Finally he could abide it no longer.

He discussed his plan with Freda. "Mama, if I could go to Woodward, I know I can find work. I would take good care of whatever money I earned. I would return when I ran out of a job. When my earnings and father's are added, our family income might be doubled."

"Your father wouldn't like your leaving like this," she pointed out.

"When he sees the money I can make working, I think he'd like it very much," said Fritz. If his father would give him more responsibility and permit him to make his own decisions about some things, life would be more bearable, he was sure.

Aware of his boyish longing, Freda gave her permission, although with a heavy heart. She packed food into a sack and thrust it into his bedroll. With a smile and a wave of his hand, Fritz rode off.

His first stop was Woodward. There he called on Jake Pryor, the banker, who told him that the Santa Fe railroad was hiring laborers. At the depot, Fritz found Gus Moreland, the section foreman, who took him on although his eyes swept Fritz's boyish figure warily.

"You'll have to do your share and keep up with the other hands or I'll have to let you go," he warned.

Fritz nodded. "I understand, sir," he said.

"Report here tomorrow morning," said Moreland.

At Hennessey's wagonyard, Fritz dropped his bedroll into an empty bunk. He took the saddle and bridle off Valentine, pumped him a drink, and from the feed room bought him a flake of prairie hay. In the warm camp house, he ate his own supper and went to bed early.

At five o'clock next morning he rolled out and ate a cold breakfast. As he walked to the depot, the north wind was spitting snow. Seeing nobody, he wandered about the darkened railroad yards until the agent arrived and lit a coal-oil lamp in the depot.

"Come on in," he invited. Fritz helped him build a fire in the potbellied stove, going outside to fill a flat-bottomed bucket with coal from a hamper. The fire began to glow red hot. Soon the room was warm.

Fritz explained that he had a job with the section foreman, but that the boss and the other workers had not yet reported for duty.

The agent laughed as he flicked open his telegraph key and began to transfer money from his safe to the cash drawer under the counter. "In Oklahoma Territory, men work only in the daytime, not at night," he explained. "The job will start at eight." He asked Fritz his name and where he lived. Fritz told him.

Finally the foreman and crew arrived. A switch engine chuffed busily nearby, smoke from its stack flattened by the wind. It began to move the cars about.

The laborers' first task was unloading a car of lumber. Fritz worked so fast that he cleared his side of the car while the other three were unloading theirs.

"What are you tryin' to do, show us up? Beat us out of a job?" growled one of the other laborers, a bullnecked man in a poncho, a blanket with a hole cut through its middle to admit his head.

Surprised, Fritz shook his head. "No, sir," he said politely. "I can't work slow. Besides, I keep warm working fast."

"So you think we're working too slow, do you?" snarled the man in the poncho, putting down an armful of planks and advancing threateningly. "I'll give you something to keep you warm."

"Let him alone, Pete," a voice crackled commandingly from the cab of the switch engine.

It was the fireman of the switch train. The man in the poncho took one look at him leaning nonchalantly out of the cab window, his jaw jutting out belligerently, and returned to work.

The bitter cold continued next day. They finished unloading the lumber, and the foreman assigned them the job of shoveling cinders into a cinder car in the teeth of the north wind. The man in the poncho and one of his companions quit. Grateful for the work, Fritz stayed on. Strong and wiry, he had no fear of hard labor.

The pay was $1.25 a day with fifty cents taken out for board and room. Since the "room" was a cot in a tent, Fritz was cold even under the quilts. He decided to improve his condition.

Instead of taking the railroad's room and board, he bought three meals at the hotel for thirty cents a day. He stabled and fed Valentine in the wagonyard for twenty-five cents daily, thereby earning the right to sleep free of charge in the camp house.

Hearing that buffalo bones lying on the prairie could be gathered and sold for fertilizer at five dollars a ton at Woodward, he procured a burlap sack. Each day after work, he rode Valentine onto the nearby range and collected enough of the skeletal remains to finance the new board and room arrangement and save all of his railroad pay.

Moreland, the section foreman, soon saw that in the quiet German boy he had a versatile hand as well as an industrious one. Back in south Texas, Fritz had been taught by Frederic to do some carpentry work. Soon he was assigned to a railroad bridge gang that built the first stockyards at the new town of Shattuck. He lived in a railroad bunk car with the rest of the hands.

Railroad specifications decreed that posts for the stockyards be set six feet into the ground. Because of the drought, it was impossible to dig six feet in the gumbo soil even with a spud bar.

Baffled, the construction boss thrust his hands beneath his armpits for warmth and muttered with irritation.

"Sir," said Fritz, "we could set the posts down three feet and saw them off to get the correct height. I know it violates Santa Fe procedure but this is an unusual problem. In ground as hard as this, the posts would hold like iron." His suggestion was adopted.

Meanwhile, ranchmen had begun driving their herds overland from nearby Texas and the Cheyenne-Arapaho country to Woodward to be shipped to Wichita and Kansas City. His construction duties ended for the moment, Fritz became a handyman about the Woodward stockyards.

There he had his first look at the Texas cattle being loaded in the railroad cattle cars. Their horns were so wide and their flanks so thin that they looked top-heavy. Their heads almost had to be twisted sideways to get them through the car doors.

Spring is the natural time for cows to calve, and while the herds were being held on the bed-ground, many cows gave birth to calves. Fritz was given a pistol and told to shoot the young calves found each morning, while their distraught mothers were being loaded into the cattle cars. It looked cruel but circumstances demanded it.

It was then that Fritz nearly quit his job. He wanted no part of this type of murder. Refusing to dispatch the helpless orphans, he herded them into a vacant pen and looked miserably about.

A man was sitting nearby on the top rail of the stockyards fence. At first Fritz's gaze chanced upon the man's boots. They looked familiar.

They were small and black. On each was inscribed a green butterfly with red and blue wing dots. Slowly Fritz's eyes swung upward, and he recognized Bob Quinlan, the father of Dobie Quinlan, the ranch girl he had met at the Christmas Eve party at the Woodward church.

"What's wrong, young man," asked the rancher, "do you find it hard to pull that trigger?"

Shamefaced, Fritz dropped his eyes. "Yes, sir," he said quietly.

"It seems hard, I know," said Quinlan, "but when we're shipping it has to be done. Their mothers are on their way to the butcher. The calves have to stay behind. They'd be crushed in the cattle car. They've had their last drink of mama's milk. Unless you can find some way to get milk down 'em, they'll starve.''

"I know," said Fritz unhappily. Again he looked at the gun in his hand and again he rejected it in his mind.

The ranchman was twisting a big garnet ring on his left hand. "There's a way," he said, "but it runs into work. Either you get some other cow to adopt 'em or you learn 'em to drink from a pail."

Fritz nodded. "Yes, sir. Only my father has no cows, so we have no milk. Besides, we live twenty-seven miles west of here."

The cowman peered at him keenly. "Aren't you the one whose father led the singing at the Christmas party here year before last and whose mother played the organ?"

"Yes, sir," said Fritz and was sorry that he said it. Since he was a nester and all ranchmen hated nesters, he expected hostility from this one now that he was unmasked.

Bob Quinlan jumped down off the plank fence. "Tell you what," he said, "Clay Carr, one of my hands, knows more about this than anybody. I'll go get him. Wait right here." Surprised, Fritz watched him walk away.

Soon a rangy cowboy with a sad face and a long chin walked up, carrying a bucket and leading his horse.

"I'm Carr," he said. "Now about them danged calves. One way to make a cow take a orphan calf is to pick up a handful of grass or dirt this same cow has urinated on and rub it on the orphan calf's back. Every cow whiffs a calf before she lets it suck. Cows go purely on smell."

He looked mournfully at the bucket in his hands. "Now I'll show you another way," he said.

Carrying the bucket, he approached a cow with a bulging udder. She shied off, bellowing obstinately. He got on his horse, twirled his rope, chased the cow, threw her, and with a short rope, hog-tied her two hind legs to one front. Then he milked her into the bucket while she lay on her side.

"Yore wild as a deer, ain't you?" he chided her gently. "This'll keep yore bag from spilin' fer awhile."

He carried the pail of milk to the calf pen. He showed Fritz how to teach the calf to drink by wetting his fingers in the milk and letting the calf suck them while he held them close to the milk in the bucket. Gradually he lowered his fingers into the milk. Soon the calf began to slurp from the bucket.

Fritz frowned. "I see," he said. "Now would you mind showing me that hog-tying knot? My horse knows all about roping. Before I got him, he was born on a ranch. I've roped some, but I don't know how to tie the cow down."

Patiently Carr freed the cow and stood back. Three times Valentine put Fritz right up on another running cow with a full udder. On his third cast, Fritz nailed her, and Valentine sat back, hind feet under him, forefeet braced in front, and took the shock that jerked the cow off her feet. While the horse backed up to keep the rope tight, Carr came forward, showing Fritz how to tie the hind legs to one forefoot.

Bob Quinlan walked by, watching. "My spread is located several miles east of you, just across Deer Creek," he said. "Come by sometime and I'll loan you a cow or two. It won't take you long to gentle 'em for milking."

Fritz thanked them both. Hoarding the milk carefully, he began teaching the other calves how to drink. Wet-nursing them kept him busy, but it was much better than shooting them, he thought.

Before supper that night at the hotel, Fritz met the young switch-engine fireman who had befriended him during the lumber loading.

"My name's Rucker—Patrick Rucker," the man said. "I swing the scoop on engine 90. You're famous," he went on. "Gus Moreland has been all over town telling everybody about the boy who reported for duty at five o'clock in the morning and out-worked three grown men."

Fritz didn't feel famous. Back in south Texas, everybody got up with the larks and labored until it became too dark to see. What strange customs these railroad workers had.

Rucker led Fritz into the nearby Race Track saloon and insisted on buying him a drink before supper. "Put it where the whale put Jonah," he urged.

Fritz laughed. "Wait a minute," he said, "I'm only fourteen. They'll probably kick me out." There was no trouble.

When they were served, Rucker took a long swallow. Puckering his mouth, he made a weird two-toned noise that was an excellent imitation of a railroad locomotive whistle.

"If I took another glass of this I could make my own headlight," he said, smacking his lips.

Fritz wasn't afraid of liquor, a German tradition at parties and holidays. No Romberg of his family was ever intemperate. Frederic had taught him how to handle it. He poured a small quantity into a tumbler, baptized it liberally with water, and took plenty of time to down it. And he took only one.

When his earnings had reached thirty-five dollars, the railroad temporarily suspended the employment of all its extra hands. Fritz didn't care. He wanted to see his family. Lashing his bedroll to the saddle and carrying a tie-rope and pail, he drove the little bunch of dogie calves ahead of him, traveling ten miles a day.

Occasionally, when he passed grazing cattle, he would ride boldly into them, select a nursing cow, rope and hog-tie her, milk her while she lay prone, and finger-feed his calves until they started drinking from the bucket.

When the spring weather turned blizzard-like again, he pushed the dogies into a small canyon, out of the wind, while he stayed all night with settlers in a dugout. Despite the piercing cold, he got under way again next morning.

He was approaching the east boundary of Womble's range, only five miles from home, when he met Ray Patterson on a galloping horse. Patterson curbed his mount, tightening the reins across his chest with both hands. His face looked strangely subdued.

"I'm sure glad I found you," he said. "I was prepared to ride clear into Woodward after you if necessary. Fritz, I hate having to be the one to tell you this, but I've got bad news. Your father is dead."

FREDERIC ERNST ROMBERG

Fritz's hands fell loose on the bridle reins and he got a pinched feeling in the pit of his stomach. He stared at Ray with shock and disbelief. His father dead? How could Frederic be dead when he was so alive and vigorous the last time Fritz had seen him?

Patterson's kindly crossed eyes were aglow with sympathy. "He got stuck in Wolf Creek two nights ago coming back from the freight hauling," he explained. "In trying to get his horses and wagon out, he got thoroughly soaked and walked home in his wet clothes against the cold wind. He died of lung fever and exposure."

Fritz wet his dry lips. For a moment, he sat in the saddle, trying to hold himself steady and to find his spinning thoughts. A killdeer cried piteously from a hollow nearby and the wind blurred the buffalo grass.

"He must have got so cold that he couldn't hold the lines in his hands," Ray went on, "because we found the lines wrapped around the brake lever. I think he began walking then. When the team came home without him, your mother lit the lantern and came for me. I found him a mile from your dugout. Your mother and I lifted him into the wagon and brought him home. We could hardly get his gloves off, or his clothing. They were frozen to his body.''

Fritz held his breath, wanting to sob. But the sobs wouldn't come. To Fritz, his father was perfect. When Fritz had been a little boy, there was nothing he liked better than just to walk around the Texas German settlement with Frederic, his small hand in Frederic's great one.

''We got Mattie Cooper out of bed,'' Patterson went on. ''She tried everything—hot lard poultices over his lungs, whiskey poured down him. But nothing worked. She cried when she couldn't revive him.''

''How are Mother and the children?'' Fritz asked dully.

''It was rough on them. They're all over at our place.''

On the frontier, none of the appurtenances for a funeral existed, no undertaker, no casket, no minister, no cemetery.

Fritz remembered he had heard that at the new town of Shattuck, only eight miles away, a man named Tom Miller had put up a store building of native cottonwood logs. It became the town's first post office, saloon, and grocery store. There Miller sold Arbuckle and Lion's coffee, flour, beans, dried prunes, and salt pork side meat. He also sold wagon boxes.

Fritz and Ray Patterson went to Shattuck, driving Ray's team and wagon. They bought a wagon box and built a homemade casket from it. Working on a sawhorse in the middle of the store, while business continued as usual, they painted it with shoe polish and lamp soot. The wife of the storekeeper tacked quilting cotton to the interior and black calico on the outside. Handles, originally intended for carpenters' toolboxes, were fastened to either side. The storekeeper and his son volunteered to fill the grave after the service.

In the new cemetery that had been started on a claim at the edge of town, they dug a grave. Better to put him here, Fritz thought, than on the Romberg claim where nobody would know where he was in the future. Finished, they loaded the casket in the wagon and headed home.

The sun was slanting low when they got there. To Fritz's surprise, Mrs. Cooper, the wife of Orvus the Sooner, was on duty.

"We're sorry for yore loss," she said. "Yore family is over to the Pattersons'." Fritz looked at her but couldn't speak. He went inside the dugout.

The body lay on the bed near the dirt wall that the dead man himself had shaped with his shovel. The women had laid him out and dressed him. Over his face, they had placed a wet cloth to keep it lifelike. With his own straightedge razor, Ray Patterson had shaved his upper lip.

Ray and Fritz carried the casket inside and placed it across two chairs. They lifted Frederic into it. Fritz raised the wet cloth off his father's face.

In the light of the lamp, Frederic looked composed and natural, but Fritz could think only of how cruelly his father must have suffered on the fatal night. Torn by grief, he went outdoors and wept unrestrainedly, wishing that he could hear his father's voice once more.

It was almost dusk. Ray was feeding the horses. Fritz thought of his calves in the canyon.

Defiantly he saddled Valentine and rode into a bunch of Womble's cattle. He roped, threw and hog-tied a cow, milked her in a bucket, and using his fingers, got it down the throats of the hungry dogies. This time they drank more easily and quickly. He worked automatically and in a half daze, grateful for something to keep his mind off the tragedy. He put the calves in the barn with the horses.

At the Patterson dugout, he embraced his mother, holding her tight. "You've done real well with everything, Mother," he told her. "I wish I'd been here to help you."

Sarah and Jacob ran to him and, burying their faces in his coat, sobbed softly. Fritz kissed each on top of their heads and tried to comfort them. Daisy had baked a wild turkey but Fritz scarcely touched it. For him, some of the light had faded from the world with his father's death.

Fritz insisted upon sitting up with the body during the night. Alone with Frederic, he sat with his face in his hands, thinking of all the things his father had done for him and of how little he had done for his father. Outside, the coyotes came howling down the canyon almost to the dugout door.

At midnight Ray Patterson brought in a pot of hot coffee. Together, they kept the lonely vigil the rest of the night and took turns sleeping.

Next day the glacial cold continued as they rode in two wagons with the body to Shattuck. As they passed the Cooper shack, Mrs. Cooper came out with several hot rocks to keep their feet warm in the wagon. Freda thanked her.

At the crude cemetery, they had no flowers until Daisy Patterson, voiceless with grief, handed them a small pink and blue corsage of false blossoms to place on Frederic's bier. She had cut the small garland off her only hat.

Fritz worried about his mother. Stunned, she went mechanically about with a stricken face. There was little in the brief service to give her consolation, he knew. Daisy read a chapter from the Bible. A Shattuck woman started a hymn but could not carry it through. Fritz knew the words but felt that he never wanted to sing again. The reins from the Patterson harness were used as lowering straps.

As the wagons headed back toward the claim, and the storekeeper and his son moved in with their shovels, Jacob jumped out of the rear wagon and ran back to the grave, sobbing, "Father! . . . Father! . . . Father!"

Handing the reins to Freda, Fritz went after him.

When they returned to the dugout, a wood fire glowed warmly in the little topsy stove. The floors were swept, the house cleaned, the beds made. A hot dinner was on the stove, beans flavored by side meat, canned tomatoes, fried rabbit. For dessert there was a large kettle of dried applesauce.

"Oh!" breathed Freda, deeply touched. "How kind somebody is. It must have been the Coopers."

They also found Frederic's clothing washed and ironed. Folded neatly, it lay on the bed.

Fritz smoothed it with his hand. Neighbors as thoughtful as these couldn't be all bad no matter how loosely the father had obeyed the regulations of the Strip land run.

Later, when the Rombergs were alone, they talked about their future without Frederic. Fritz was secretly downcast and heavyhearted about his ability to take on the formidable responsibility that even his father had had trouble handling. It took all his courage to conceal his fear from Freda and the children. He wanted them to feel secure.

"I know I can do the farm work," said Fritz, "because Father taught me lots about it. I'll have to get outside work to bring in the cash we'll need to operate, but I can do that too. If we go under, we can always sell the claim for something and go back to Texas. But I'd rather stay here. It's freer here. There's more opportunity. We're working for ourselves instead of for some landlord. We're learning from our mistakes."

Freda agreed. They knew that with Frederic lying in the new cemetery at nearby Shattuck, they were forever tied to this rolling sandy land.

First of all, Fritz had to have milk for his calves. Saddling Valentine, he rode the nine miles to the Quinlan ranch to get the cows Bob Quinlan had promised to lend him.

The Quinlan ranch house, built of logs, was low and rambling and ingeniously designed to provide each room with the pleasant southeast breeze. Fritz found Quinlan at the corral.

"Good morning, sir," said Fritz, swinging off his horse, "I've come for the cow you said I could borrow. I got my eleven dogies home from Woodward."

"Then you'll need more than one cow," said the ranchman. He

came forward, his brown face grave and compassionate. "We just heard this morning about your father," he said. "I'm sorry."

Fritz, distressed by the grief that still welled up in his throat every time he thought of Frederic, could say nothing.

"You're wanting to borrow cows tells me that your family is going to try to stick it out," said Quinlan, as they walked toward a corral.

"Yes, sir," said Fritz.

"I honestly think you'll find it very hard to make a living farming these uplands," Quinlan said. "Grass is the best crop this land will ever produce." He looked sideways at Fritz while they walked. "Maybe we can make a rancher out of you, now that you've started in the cattle business. Many people who have small bunches of cattle loose-herd them on the untaken land."

"I'm like my father," said Fritz, "I still think we can make it farming."

At the corral, Quinlan bridled a horse and swung a blanket and saddle on him. They rode out onto the range. Finding the cattle, Quinlan cut out three cows with calves.

He said, "After you get 'em gentled and located, they'll stay with you. Be sure these calves get plenty of milk. I don't want 'em scrawny at weaning time. You need a brand, don't you?"

"Got one," said Fritz. "It's a capital 'R' for Romberg. The letter leans and looks like it is walking, so I call it the 'Walking R.' I had it made by a blacksmith at Woodward. Got it registered there, too."

Surprise and respect showed in Quinlan's eyes. "You've come a long ways since refusing to pull that trigger back at Woodward."

Quinlan's daughter, Dobie, was visiting at a ranch near the new town of Gage. "Come on up to the house an' we'll get some dinner," Quinlan invited. Fritz thanked him but declined.

"Thank you, sir, for the cows and everything," he added. "It'll sure be nice to have milk again. My family hasn't had much since we left south Texas."

With Ray Patterson helping, Fritz branded the dogies, dragging them to the fire, flanking them, jerking them upward and then down on their sides, and burning the Romberg "R" into their hides with the branding iron. On an unowned sweep of land behind Patterson's claim, Ray dug a hole in the sand of a dry creek bed. When he had deepened the hole to two feet, water began to seep out. It was warm from being in the sand but tasted soft and good. They widened the hole to four feet square and curbed it with rock. They damned up a small ravine, one hundred yards below it, and started a pond.

The small flow trickling down the stream bed furnished adequate water for Fritz's calves, now also learning to nibble on grass. Soon the cows loaned to Fritz by Quinlan permitted themselves to be milked and the Rombergs had cream and fresh-churned butter.

Needing supplies, the Pattersons and Rombergs went together in one wagon to Shattuck. Ray drove. Daisy and Freda sat on the seat beside him. Fritz sat on the floor in the back with his arms around Jacob and Sarah. The children were taking their father's death stoically, their grief showing in uncommon spells of silence.

Freda had written the news of Frederic's death in a letter to her relatives back in Texas. They mailed it at the Shattuck post office. It was convenient, Fritz thought. to have the railroad close by so that its new post office could be utilized to keep the channels of communication open to distant kinfolk and friends.

At Miller's cottonwood log store they saw Jim Yoakum. He was standing at the counter purchasing sacks of Bull Durham tobacco.

He came over to Freda, sweeping off his big hat. "I just heared, mam, about yore loss," he said. "I've been line ridin' over in the sand hills and jest got in. I'm sorry."

Leading Jacob and Sarah to the candy counter, he bought each a sack of horehound squares and old-fashioned Arabian gumdrops. Their faces brightening, each thanked him.

Fritz went by the new cemetery to plant a sandstone marker at his father's grave. With his pocketknife he carved "F. Romberg" upon it. Freda knelt to pull a weed and tidy up the turf. Jacob and Sarah stood silently nearby.

Both families purchased their supplies. Just before they started home, Fritz saw several wooden kegs on the floor.

"What's in them?" he asked the storekeeper.

"Salt whitefish," Miller replied. "They've got a great flavor. Shipped in on the railroad. Look here." Stooping, he lifted the lid of a keg. The fish were large, eighteen inches long and an inch thick. Pickled in brine, they would keep in hot weather, requiring no refrigeration.

Tempted, Fritz thought it over. The Rombergs needed cheering up. And the Pattersons had stayed by them faithfully during Frederic's death. Better buy the fish now while he had the cash. He wanted to give them all something. Everybody was tired of fried rabbit.

He purchased a forty-pound wooden tub and divided the fish with the Pattersons. Freda knew how to cook them. Slow-fried after soaking, they were delicious. Again Fritz had to admire his father's good sense in taking a claim so near the Santa Fe tracks. Living near the railroad meant living near the new country's commercial pulse. It could be helpful in many ways.

"Do you recken we ought to give some to the Coopers?" asked Fritz.

"I think that's a good idea," said Freda. "They've been very kind, too."

Fritz blushed, dropping his eyes to the floor. "If we do, Mother, could we let Sarah and Jacob deliver them?" he asked. Still thinking of the blanket drawers and the older girl's romantic note, he was reluctant to go near that family.

"Why, I think we should all call on them together," said Freda. "They were very decent and neighborly during Father's death. When Mattie failed to bring Frederic back to life, she cried. I think she cried because she was afraid you'd blame her because she failed. I think your good opinion is important to her."

The blood ran hot under Fritz's skin. What he wanted most was not to have any contact with the girl while she harbored this strange attraction toward him. But obedience to his mother's wishes ran strong within him.

They went in the wagon. Freda knocked. Zella opened the door and drew back until she saw Sarah. Then her eyes kindled.

"Our cow has got a new calf," she announced proudly.

Sarah giggled. "Oh, Zella, that's not very many. Our cow has eleven calves."

That required explanations. Inside the Cooper shack Freda made them while they all sat down.

Mrs. Cooper got up, moving toward the stove. "I'll parch some coffee," she said, her voice a singsong chant. "Wait'll I take off the stove-eye and put in some wood." From a nearby box she lifted out several sticks of cedar. Fritz winced, knowing that it probably came from the government canyon near Womble's.

"It was kind of you to wash and cook and tidy up for us while we went to the funeral," said Freda.

"It was a bad time fer you-uns," said Mrs. Cooper as she put water on to boil and began to rattle cups and saucers. "We's glad to help you. Mattie cooked yore supper while Zella and I cleaned up." She sat down and took up her knitting.

Mattie sat quietly behind her mother with eyes averted. With a sharp knife she was peeling potatoes from a pan in her lap.

Mrs. Cooper knitted with uncommon celerity, the orange needles in her hands clicking softly and busily. The house looked clean.

"Are you knitting socks?" asked Freda.

"Yes," Mrs. Cooper replied. "I learnt to knit as a little girl back at Fayetteville"—she pronounced it "Fed-vil"—"during the war. We all knitted socks fer General Sterling Price's home guards. I soon got so I could rib 'em, turn the heel, and toe 'em off in the dark."

She raked a wisp of hair out of her eyes. "Mattie, here, is the best seamstress of our family," she added. Fritz, thinking of the blanket drawers, felt his face flushing. He could attest to that.

101

Mrs. Cooper went on. "The day I had her I canned thirty-six quarts of green beans. She started sewin' when she was very young. Orvus worked fer a cotton mill then and we got cloth free. She was makin' her own clothes by the second grade, but of course we didn't let her wear 'em out of the yard. Now she kin make a gathered skirt in fifteen minutes. She sews fast and does it without patterns."

She looked around at Mattie as if for confirmation. Red-faced, the girl seemed to shrink within herself.

Fritz sat on a stool by the door, his back straight as a hoe handle. He felt stupid at being so tongue-tied before a girl as plain and frumpy as this one. Then he realized that he and she were the only stiff ones in the room. Neither of them had spoken a word.

In his hands, he held the package of salted whitefish.

Freda looked at it. "We brought you something from the store at Shattuck." She looked at Fritz and smiled. "It was my son's idea." She took the package from Fritz and opened it, showing them the fish.

"We's obliged," said Mrs. Cooper, her eyes widening at the size of the fish. "We's been hard run fer vittles lately," she added. "Orvus is bull-whackin' outa Fort Supply an' he ain't brought us nothing."

Rising, she put the package of fish on the table. "We'll have plenty to eat after our hay cures," she said. "Last year Orvus sold his hay to Sam Womble and it paid fer nearly a year's provisions."

Fritz clenched his jaws and the old anger filled him as he thought of his father's dream of growing hay on that same land. For the remainder of the visit the day seemed sour and the room chilly as he sat hunched in the corner, brooding.

Next day the weather moderated. Fritz began to plant kafir over the area destroyed by hail the previous season. He also planted sorghum. From it they would make syrup with which to season the sand plum jelly Freda would make if the plums didn't freeze.

Now that he was usually alone while working in the field he missed his father sorely. For several minutes that first day he sat under a mesquite tree reflecting on the future, while the grays stood idle in the traces. What did he know of himself out here where loneliness was a fact of life and a man—or a boy—must rely solely upon himself?

He tried to temper his sorrow with hard work. He tried to plan the sowing and the cultivating as Frederic would have wished him to. He had plowed a garden, which Freda and the children planted in vegetables. He helped Ray Patterson break out more prairie, harrowing the grass roots from it with a big brush dragged back and forth by the grays. Frederic's winter wheat, sowed the preceding fall and protected by a fence, was six inches high and greening.

They all worked with energy and enthusiasm. Each morning long before daylight Fritz would rise and build a fire, then go to the barn to clean the stalls and feed and harness the horses. Freda and Jacob milked the cows, while Sarah, back in the dugout, had the table set, the coffee made, and breakfast started. When they milked they were careful not to strip the cows, remembering Bob Quinlan's stipulation that his calves get plenty of milk, too.

"If I had some way to keep our milk and cream cold, I could make butter and sell it," Freda said.

"Hang it in the well," Daisy Patterson suggested. Freda did. Later they hauled the butter to Shattuck and Freda bartered it at twelve cents a pound for coffee, rice, and sugar.

At Miller's store Fritz encountered a farmer who had lost his two workhorses to Strip outlaws and needed to sell some of his stock to get funds to purchase another team. Fritz bought six skinny heifers from him for one dollar each and proudly drove them home. The Romberg herd was growing.

It grew still more in the days that followed. Early one afternoon Fritz saw dust coloring the sky to the west. Before he could identify it a cowboy came riding up. His jaded horse headed without invitation to the Rombergs' stump trough and buried its nose in the water. The cowboy slid off his mount, spanking the dirt from his clothing with his gloves.

"My name's Mogford—Mitch Mogford," he said. "I ride

point for the K.H., south of Beaver City on Kiowa Creek. We're on our way to the railroad at Woodward with nine hundred head. This is about as far as we can trail 'em today. They're due here in about two hours. We'll try not to let 'em damage anything.''

At first, Fritz fought to hold himself calm. Range cattle on a drive usually ate all the buffalo grass, trampled the plowed space, and drank the small creeks dry. Then he remembered where he was and that hospitality was expected in this country, even to a trail herd.

Introducing himself, he shook hands. ''This is our third season on this place,'' he said. ''Let's walk up to the dugout and my mother will fix you some coffee. Then tonight we'd like to have you eat with us.''

The cowboy shook his head. ''I'll gladly drink coffee with you but our chuck wagon will be here tonight. I'll eat with them.'' He tied his reins to a post and followed Fritz to the dugout. ''Glad to see you've got your garden fenced strong.''

''We have no water for cattle on this quarter,'' said Fritz, ''but Sam Womble, the rancher, who lives just northeast of us''—he pointed toward Womble's holdings—''has a creek nearby. If you talked to him, I'm sure it would be all right to water your herd in his creek. They could graze on the prairie between us. We're neighbors.''

Fritz introduced him to his mother. Later, when the herd arrived, Mogford brought the trail boss, Dick Conger, to the dugout. Freda received him cordially.

''Give me your soiled clothing and I'll wash and iron it for you,'' she insisted. ''You probably need some buttons sewed on, too, and maybe some other mending done.''

''Send your chuck wagon by and get a barrel of our spring water,'' Fritz invited. ''We just hauled some fresh from the Pattersons'.''

Later, when Mogford rode off, Jacob thought of another reason the visitors would be welcome. ''Brother,'' he said, ''think of all the cowchips those nine hundred cows will leave on our land.''

They also left something else valuable, seven new calves born that day on the bed-grounds.

"You can have 'em," Conger told them over a cup of Freda's dried bean coffee. "They're too weak to travel and we ain't got no calf wagon to haul 'em in. We usually have to shoot 'em." He also gave them a cow too lame to continue the trip. She was mothering a calf, too.

Thus Fritz's dogie herd increased still more. And he had learned from Dick Conger as well as from Bob Quinlan that not all cowmen came from the Womble stamp.

Freda gave the trail boss his clothing freshly washed and ironed. Conger left them a hindquarter of beef that had turned an unappetizing black but was aged and air-cured just right. It had been a mutually profitable encounter.

At night Fritz was never too tired from work in the field to read to the children as his father had done. Sarah listened with sparkling eyes, but Jacob just sat quietly staring at the fire and poking aimlessly with his foot at the cowchip box, which it was now his duty to keep filled.

One night Jacob didn't come home for supper. Fritz searched for him until dusk without result. Then he heard the cry of a wounded rabbit in the long grass growing along the creek on the Orvus Cooper place.

Moving quietly and staying out of sight, Fritz stole closer, coming up behind Jacob who lay concealed in the grass.

"What in the world are you doing?" Fritz asked.

Jacob leaped to his feet and turned around. "Baiting coyotes," he said. "I hide in the grass and squeal like a rabbit, or cluck like a scared chicken, until the coyotes come up within five or six feet. Then I jump up and throw rocks at them. It's fun, Brother. Sometimes I almost hit them."

They began walking back together. "If this is all you've got to do, I'm going to put you to work in the field," said Fritz.

"Can I plow?" asked Jacob eagerly.

"We'll see," replied Fritz. To himself, he thought, Jacob is almost big enough. He controls horses well. Plowing would give him something to do.

Next day they tried it, but the boy wasn't tall enough to reach the plow handles. Fritz had to lower them for him and help him heft the harness. Jacob's first rows were far from straight. But he was learning.

Sarah played constantly with Zella Cooper now that the Rombergs had accepted their Arkansas neighbors. Soon the little girls were stringing the bright green pods of the canyon cottonwoods for beads and lining their doll beds with the soft fuzz that blew from the tree. Fritz did not interfere.

THE RANGE DANCE

Robbery in the Strip began to occur in isolated cases that spring. Country stores occasionally were hit. Farmers also were victimized and their horses stolen.

On a morning in April, the menace struck at Ray Patterson's claim. Daisy was alone with the baby. Ray and Fritz had driven to Shattuck to buy supplies.

Two shabbily dressed men, wearing battered felt hats and pistols at their belts, rode up. One had bright, alert eyes that kept peering at everything that moved on the distant skyline.

"We'd like to buy some breakfast and some horse feed," the other said. "We'll pay you for it."

"The breakfast will be free," said Daisy, tying an apron around her waist. "I'll let you pay for the horse feed since it's corn and corn's very dear. My husband has to buy ours at Shattuck."

She cooked breakfast for them, then got several ears of corn for their horses and a sack to put them in. The bright-eyed man tendered a twenty-dollar bill.

"I can't change that," said Daisy.

"What change do you have?" he asked, pocketing the twenty and producing a five.

Daisy got her purse and, opening it, began to count the change. "I have only two dollars and seventy cents," she said. She placed it on the table.

"That's all right," said the man. "We'll jest take the rest in corn."

Reaching out, he swept the coins from the table into his hand, then thrust it and the five-dollar bill back into his pocket. Meanwhile, the other man began filling the sack to overflowing with corn from the Patterson bin.

Daisy saw what was happening. Alone and unarmed, she stood silently at the dugout door, holding the baby, and watched them mount and ride away.

Then she saddled Ray's pony and, with the baby in her arms, rode to the Rombergs. She related the incident to Freda.

"There's nothing we can do but wait until Fritz and Ray return," Freda said. "I don't think the outlaws will bother us. We're out of corn, and Fritz took all our change to buy some for our horses. The outlaws wouldn't get anything here."

"Oh, yes they would, Mother," said Jacob. "They'd get this." He came out of the dugout lugging Frederic's revolver. In his chubby hands, the loaded weapon looked like a small cannon.

Freda carefully took it from him, scolding him. When Fritz and Ray Patterson returned, Fritz also reproved the boy.

"You're never to handle this gun, Jacob, until you're much older, and not until you've asked me first," he said sternly. "We appreciate you're wanting to protect us, but you might have shot some of the family accidently. Do you understand?"

Jacob blinked, then dropped his eyes contritely. "All right, Brother," he said.

"The thieves are getting bolder and bolder," said Ray Patterson. "Three men stole Orville Burns' horses, then two days later rode back on them and made Burns feed his own stolen stock. Then they got on them again and rode off."

The dry weather of April persisted through May. Ordinarily these were rain months. Although the orchard lay close enough to the well to permit watering the seedlings by hand, most of the garden was cooked by the drought and the wheat lost all inclination to grow. Only the kafir corn and the sorghum defied the aridity.

Once when Jacob was pouring water out of a bucket onto the roots of the fledgling fruit trees, a bee stung him. It made him sick to his stomach. Sarah, who was playing nearby, took him to Mattie Cooper.

Mattie daubed mud on it, rubbed it with a freshly scraped potato, and applied soda.

"The soda felt the best," Jacob told them later at supper. "It sure stopped the stinging."

Fritz grinned. He had been helping Ray Patterson repair a fence.

"Wonder why she didn't use turpentine?" he said. "I thought she used turpentine for everything." After that, he called her "the Turpentine Doctor."

Next morning, while all four Rombergs worked at hoeing the garden, Sarah called excitedly, "Mother! Fritz! Come here!"

They hurried to her side. The girl was standing near the flat sandstone rock at a corner of the garden, her face transfixed with excitement and joy.

"Look at the flowers Father planted," she said, smiling through her wet eyes. "He planted them for me!"

Fritz remembered the scene the preceding year when Sarah, building a beauty spot in the corner of the garden, had called to Frederic to come and see it. Tired and weak from the attack of Texas slow fever, Frederic had refused. "Sarah, I don't have time for things like that," he had said. Hurt, she had abandoned the project.

Now there was an orderly design of color about the stone as blossoms of briar rose, Indian blanket, and sand daisy flashed in the sun. And Fritz knew his father had brought the wild flowers from the prairie and transplanted them around Sarah's stone. All winter, they had lived beneath their coverlet of snow.

Money became more and more of a problem as the drought continued. Early in June Fritz cut the wheat with a scythe, then threshed it by placing the heads in the wagon bed and flailing the grain out with the broom. The entire crop made only three bushels to the acre, enough for their seed wheat and, with the help of the coffee mill, for a coarse but usable flour that gave Freda's home-baked bread a nutty flavor. But that was all.

Discouragement ate at Fritz's vitals. He recalled something that Frederic had once told him on the trip from Texas to the Strip. "Remember, Son. A farmer depends on himself and the land and the weather. You raise most of what you eat. You work hard, but you work as you please and no man can tell you to come or go. You'll be free and independent on a farm."

Yes, thought Fritz—and poor. I'm going to get us some more calves.

Sam Womble seemed to know all about their misfortunes. On the morning they got their first rain in months, a light sprinkle that helped nothing beyond spreading its welcome odor over the prairie, he rode up to their dugout door on his gray mare, sitting deep in his Apple Horn saddle. His thin lips were sucking on a cigarette. Fritz could smell the burning tobacco.

His hostile eyes raked Fritz. "Where's your mother?" he asked.

"I'll get her," said Fritz. "Won't you get down and have a cup of coffee?"

Womble shook his head impatiently. In his yellow slicker he looked wet and waspish. Fritz brought Freda. Womble took the cigarette out of his mouth and flipped it behind him onto the prairie.

"I'm Sam Womble," he began in his raspy voice. "I've come to make you a decent offer for this claim." He did not take off his black hat.

"Why, Mr. Womble, we haven't put up our claim for sale," said Freda. "Had you heard it was for sale?"

Womble ignored that. "I'll give you two dollars an acre," he said doggedly. "That's a good price fer land as cloddy as this."

Freda smiled. "Thank you," she said, "but we aren't selling."

Womble's look became openly insolent. "You're not doing very well," he pointed out. "Hail got yore kafir last year. Drought jest got yore wheat."

Freda's smile went out.

"We're staying anyhow," she said.

Womble twisted his hands and scowled. "This land's treacherous," he said. "It won't raise nothin' but grass. Times is hard. You ain't got no man now."

Fritz stepped up beside her. "She's got me, Mr. Womble," he said.

Womble glared at him. "I'm fixin' to buy three hundert head of yearlins soon," he said. "When they see yore kafir, they ain't gonna hold back. A one-wire fence and a dog won't stop 'em."

Fritz held up two fingers. "Two wires and no dog, Mr. Womble," he corrected. He was proud of that fence. He and Frederic and Ray Patterson had worked hard building it.

Womble turned again to Freda. "You'll change yore mind, soon, mam," he told her gruffly. "When you do, let me know. The longer you wait, the lower my price is gonna be." Turning his horse, he rode off, his yellow slicker squeaking.

"He wants our claim so he can balance his range," Fritz told Freda. "He'd like to buy us out cheap." He remembered that when Frederic had died, this man, one of their closest neighbors, hadn't come on the place.

In spite of the dry weather, Fritz continued to buy calves whenever he could get them at a favorable price. He heard at the Shattuck store that a farmer living northwest of Gage was selling out and leaving the Strip. Saddling Valentine and taking along all their ready cash in Frederic's buckskin pocket bag, Fritz found the farmer and bought several calves and two older cows.

111

"Why are you leaving?" he inquired, pulling the pocket bag's drawstrings to close it.

Frustration and anger came into the man's face. "Life is too damned hard here," he said. "The land's got too much power over you. It hasn't rained since Noah, and Sam Womble's herds are always in my feed patch. The only law out here is Womble law."

As he herded them home, Fritz thought that the time would soon come when he and Womble would have a showdown. He also knew that despite the cattle bargains he was driving, he had spent most of his and Frederic's cash wages that had originally been deposited with the banker Jake Pryor at Woodward.

Next morning Jim Yoakum, Womble's cowboy, rode up on his bay horse. In his lavender shirt and the purple silk bandanna tucked neatly inside his open collar he radiated a splendor that would have shamed a peacock. Purple was his favorite color, it seemed to Fritz. Even his buckskin chaps were embroidered in purple thread with the ends fringed.

"Hello, Dutchy," he said. "What's new?"

"Get down," Fritz invited.

"You been workin' too hard, Dutchy," Yoakum said as he swung off his mount. "You need some fun. There's a shindig tonight at a ranch over on Skeleton Crick. Come an' go with me." He had a pint flask thrust into one boot, Fritz saw.

At first, Fritz decided not to go. His clothing was old and patched. The sole of one boot had started to flap. He didn't like to leave his family so soon after Frederic's death.

"My boots are so frazzled that I can't strike a match on the soles without burning my feet," said Fritz.

"You won't need to strike no matches," said Yoakum. "I'll do the smokin' fer both of us."

Fritz grinned. "Will there be girls there?"

"Shore!" said Yoakum. "Bound to be."

"Why don't you go, Fritz?" urged Freda. "It'll do you good. Jacob and I can do the chores."

Hearing Jacob's name, Yoakum snapped his fingers. "Dawgone," he said, "I almost fergot."

Looking mysteriously at Jacob and Sarah, he reached into his saddlebag. Sarah smiled shyly. It wasn't a surprise to her that he had brought them something. He almost always did. This time it turned out to be a sack of Mexican candy. Both children thanked him.

He also held out something to Fritz, a blue silk neckerchief.

"Here," he said, "let's dude you up a little. I'll loan you this."

"You said ranch," said Fritz, "I'm a nester. They'd probably run me off."

"Naw," scoffed Yoakum, "everybody invited, nobody slighted."

Fritz decided to go. "If you'll cut my hair, Mother," he told Freda, "and find me a clean shirt." He accepted the neckerchief and tied it around his neck.

"I'll cut it," offered Yoakum. Walking back to his horse, he pulled a pair of scissors from his saddlebag. That saddlebag is full of surprises, thought Fritz.

With short quick strokes, Yoakum snipped around Fritz's ears, while Fritz sat in a chair in the yard with the wind blowing the cuttings off him in small clouds. As Yoakum worked he explained that no formal invitations were sent to a range dance. Anybody who heard about one was automatically invited.

"There you are, all trimmed up," said Yoakum, backing up and cocking his head to study his handiwork. You ain't got no chin bristles to shave off, so guess I'm through."

Fritz saddled Valentine, Yoakum rolled a fresh cigarette, and they started.

"How far's this place we're going?" asked Fritz as Valentine and the bay began to strike off the miles, traveling east.

"Oh, about twenty miles or so," said Yoakum.

"How will you ever find it?"

"We'll cut across the hills and river bottoms," said Yoakum. "At night we'll be guided by the stars."

Yoakum was a unique character, different from anybody Fritz had ever known. He told Fritz that when he was riding night watch on a herd he didn't need a timepiece, that he could tell time within twenty minutes by watching the swing of the Big Dipper's pointer stars, or if it was daytime, the rider on guard counted time by cigarettes.

"I've counted land measurements that way—so many cigarettes north, so many east, meaning the distance a man would ride while rollin' and smokin' that many," the cowboy explained.

In midafternoon they rode into a part of the prairie that had been graced by light rains. The green shortgrass had taken every square foot of terrain. Even the gulleys were so grassed over that the land looked dimpled.

Fritz told Yoakum about the two outlaws taking Daisy Patterson's change and a sack full of Ray Patterson's precious corn.

Yoakum snorted. "They're jest sneak thieves," he said. "They jest hit farms and country stores."

They talked of the daring holdup of the Woodward depot by Bill Doolin, the premier highwayman of Oklahoma Territory. Soon they were discussing all outlawry. In the Strip, cowboy conversation was full of the doings of outlaw gangs, Fritz discovered, probably because nearly every outlaw had first been a cowboy.

To Fritz's surprise, Yoakum had known Bill Doolin when Doolin worked on the Halsell ranch on the lower Cimarron.

"You wouldn't catch Doolin robbin' people like those two men who robbed your friends," said Yoakum. "He's got too much class."

Fritz laughed. "I wouldn't catch him anyhow," he said, "because I'd be going in the opposite direction." He wondered what Yoakum meant by class?

"Doolin will fool you," Yoakum went on. "He's got plenty of gravel in his gizzard an' he's cool with a gun. But he's likable. An' peaceable. Reads everything he can get his hands on. Buys oysters and crackers fer the country dances. Always pays fer his meals an' fer his horse's food. He pays fer everything he needs."

Fritz laughed again. "He's probably paying for it with that six thousand dollars he stole from the Woodward depot. That was the Fort Supply payroll. Part of it belonged to my father. He hauled for the fort. He had to wait another month for his pay."

Ahead, the land seemed to roll away in receding areas of flatness. There was nothing on the horizon, not even a house, just gentle topography mellowing into the distance.

"Why do cowboys like Doolin and the others go bad?" asked Fritz. "Aren't cowboys paid pretty well? Thirty dollars a month seems awfully good to me."

Yoakum switched his weight in the saddle and considered it.

"Life gets dull," he said. "You get restless an' start junin' around. You want a lot of money an' workin' seems a slow way to get it. Love of excitement an' adventure sways you, too. The tales you hear of Jesse James an' the Youngers fires you up. It seems so easy to try it out in a new country, like this one, where fear of the outlaw paralyzes everybody." It seemed a subject about which he was singularly well informed.

Toward evening they forded a creek that to Fritz's surprise had water in it. Under the oblique rays of the sun the water shone like glass, hurting his eyes. Looking east, the grass was a light-bluish haze and the trail ahead seemed to bound over the slopes like the rise and fall of a running hound's back.

Although Yoakum wasn't chattery, he asked his share of questions. He wanted to know all about the German settlements in south Texas.

"I may not stay here much longer," he revealed. "Womble knows I'm good with an axe. It's gettin' so all he wants me to do is swing it, buildin' corrals an' fence. I'm a cowboy, not a lumberjack." A defiant, rebellious expression had come into his face.

"Why don't you work for another spread?" asked Fritz.

Yoakum gave him a long, slow look, points of flame in his eyes. "Because there won't be no other spreads in a few years," he said. "When this country loses the wide open ranges an' the happy, carefree ranch life and gets civilized"—he spat out the word venomously—"it will take somethin' away that won't never return."

Fritz glanced down the trail between Valentine's ears. Ride fifteen miles with a man and you got to know him pretty well. But something was agitating this one. And then Yoakum told him point-blank what it was.

"The banks an' the railroads is what's breakin' up the range," he said bitterly. "Them an' the big mercantile stores."

Surprised, Fritz felt a faint line of perspiration on his upper lip. Yoakum had it pegged about right. The banks, the Santa Fe, and the big stores were promoting immigrations of homesteaders, he knew. But there was a world of room for the ranchmen, too. They just had to be shown that they couldn't have it all.

They kept riding. The sullen look had lifted from Yoakum's face. He did not smile but his anger had cooled.

Suddenly he looked roguishly at Fritz, his tongue between his teeth. "Doolin an' Yoakum" he said, "that'd be a hell of a combination, wouldn't it?"

Dusk had fallen. Behind them, it seemed to Fritz that everything was hidden in dark shadows. The tops of the little knolls were etched black against the orange glow of the skyline.

"We're gettin' close," said Yoakum. "Wish I had me a big ripe persimmon. After I smoke or throw out my chaw of tobacco they sweeten my breath. Then the wimmen have a big hug an' kiss fer me." His tension was entirely gone.

Ahead of them, lights gleamed from a bend in the road and Fritz saw buggies, wagons, buckboards, and saddle horses everywhere. The smell of a wood fire and of roasting meat was in the air. Dogs rushed out, barking excitedly. A horse neighed shrilly.

But the sound that thrilled Fritz to his toes was the squeak of a fiddle, the rhythmic thump, thump, thump of cowboy boots on a board floor, and the loud calls, delivered in a monotone, of somebody who seemed to be directing the whole procedure. And it was all tied together in perfect beat and tempo.

116

They got off, stretched, and tied their horses to a corral fence. A savage dogfight erupted under their feet but nobody paid much attention. Every vehicle, it seemed, had been followed by the family dog. The dogs have to have fun too, Fritz thought.

They went inside, Yoakum leading. The hostess came forward with a smile. Yoakum saw her coming and, reaching into his boot, surrendered his flask.

"Write your name on it," she directed, tendering a pencil. Yoakum did. Others were doing likewise.

She looked at Fritz. "Where's yours, young man?"

Grinning, Fritz raised both arms, shaking his head. "They won't sell it to me, mam," he joked. "I'm too young."

From a table behind her, they were served cups of eggnog flavored by the confiscated liquor.

Yoakum turned to Fritz, hoisting his cup. "Here's to you, at you, an' fer you," he said, downing it. Fritz tasted his, running it over his tongue. Good.

The crowd was just arriving but the dance had already begun. The interior was lighted by kerosene lamps in wall brackets, shaded by tin reflectors. Through a bedroom door, Fritz saw girls and women piling their wraps on a mahogony bed with head boards reaching almost to the ceiling. As he and Yoakum moved from group to group, they were greeted by "Hello there!" from perfect strangers.

A fat, old puncher recognized Yoakum. "Howdy, Jim," he drawled, putting a world of meaning into that "howdy."

Yoakum shook hands and flashed one of his rare grins. "Step aside, Ab, an' let two gentlemen pass," he replied.

By the time supper was served, almost a hundred guests had arrived. Yoakum led Fritz outside where a barbecued calf was simmering over mesquite-root coals. Dutch ovens filled with sour-dough biscuits, pots of red beans, and skillets of potatoes fried with onions lay all about. A tub of doughnuts had been fried. Great coffeepots sat in the outer edge of the fire. To Fritz, it all tasted so

117

good that when a roving current of wind blew wood ashes into his plate, he didn't care.

"Git yo podnuhs fo' a quadrille," bawled the square-dance caller from inside. In the general outburst of good-natured excitement, girls giggled happily and married couples stole each other's mates and raced for the last place in the sets.

Fritz became so engrossed watching everything that he soon lost Jim Yoakum who went inside to dance. Shy, Fritz stood outside and watched the action through a window. He strained to hear the caller's words that despite their ambiguity seemed to guide the dancers.

"Ladies to the center, how you do?
Right hand across, an' how are you?
Chicken in the bread tray kickin' up dough,
Granny will yo' dog bite? No by Joe!"

Most of the women had come in bright calico dresses with long sleeves and high necks. Brooches and lockets were worn at the throat or bosom and bits of ribbon were ingeniously stuck here and there. Most of the men were shaved and clad in the best they owned with new neckerchiefs and shining boots. Here and there could be seen a white buckskin vest decorated with Indian beadwork or a watch chain woven from the hair of a sweetheart or a young wife.

The fiddler tapped his foot and nodded his head. Violin cupped beneath his chin, he sawed fast and frisky, bending his ear to his instrument as if listening to and admiring what he heard. While his fiddle moaned and wailed, the dancers stomped and the caller chanted his calls with the singsong cadence of an auctioneer. Fritz listened and looked, drinking it all in.

Emotions were unbridled, he discovered. New friendships were being forged as the dancers began to mingle. "My dreams will be only of you, baby, until we meet right here next summer," he heard one cowboy say.

The floor shook, the lamps trembled, and the tin reflectors

threatened to fall. Fritz had never seen anything like it. At the German frolics he had attended in the piney woods of south Texas, the dancers were just as animated and the orchestras—cornets, flutes, trombones, and bass violins brought from the old country— were better, but the speed, pace, and jollity of this range dance were a revelation. And the hospitality was unsurpassed. Fritz vowed someday to bring his whole family.

As the dance gained momentum through the night and the dust and tobacco smoke began to haze everything, Fritz forgot his shyness. The clapping and the whistling got into his blood-stream.

He edged into a set and found that he had to think faster than he ever had in his life before. Twice he became confused and the caller, without losing a syllable, joined him on the floor to demon-strate the step. Light-footed and graceful, Fritz gradually caught on. Soon he was darting and whirling to the fiddle's tantalizing tones.

"Hello, Nester Boy," said somebody at his elbow in an agree-able, low-pitched voice.

Wheeling, he looked into a pair of eyes that were as gray as thimbles. If somebody had whopped him across the face with a big western hat, he wouldn't have been more surprised. It was Dobie Quinlan, the ranch girl.

Her blonde hair was caught in a braid that trailed down her back. She was dancing in an adjoining square and he didn't see her again until that square ended. Then he found her at the water bucket.

"You've still got that white hair, haven't you?" she teased. "White as the foam on fresh-whipped milk."

"It's good to see you again," said Fritz, and he meant it. She was the only female on the premises that he knew and he didn't know her very well. But her manner was so friendly and open that he felt as if he had known her much longer.

"Let's see," he added, "it's been about a year and a half, hasn't it?"

She raised her blonde brows and looked at the ceiling, calculating. "Something like that, I guess," she said. She was wearing a dress of green calico print with long sleeves and a high neck and a black velvet band around one wrist.

"Why don't you be my partner in this next set?" he suggested. "Of course, you'd have to steer me. I never saw this kind of dancing until tonight."

"All right," she agreed. Fritz's fingers curled around hers and he led her into a new set being formed. For a moment they just stood in the middle of the floor holding hands, looking at each other and laughing happily. She's prettier than ever, Fritz thought. She's as soft and pretty as a young calf's ear.

"We were sorry to hear about your father," she said.

"Thank you," he replied. Then he felt the corners of his own mouth twitching. "Where's your father?" he asked. "I'll bet he's not very far away."

"Standing right over there," she returned, pointing with her head and eyes, "and he's watching you, too." Again they both laughed.

"I like him," said Fritz. "He loaned me three of his cows."

They danced two sets together. "You're doing good," she complimented him. "Looks to me like you've danced yourself right out of the church. You'll have to be saved all over again at the next revival."

They danced seven more squares together and then Dobie said, "Let's sit out one, want to? My feet are tired."

She led him outdoors to the corral where half a dozen young ranch people like herself were sitting or leaning on the plank fence talking. The boys wore boots and hats and unbuttoned vests well supplied with pockets. The girls were smartly fashionable in calico.

"This is Fritz Romberg," Dobie said. They looked him over.

Fritz knew what they saw. His clothing was clean but faded, beat-up and sun-weathered. Nothing he wore was new save the blue neckerchief that Yoakum had loaned him.

"What spread you work for?" somebody asked after hellos were said all around.

Dobie rescued him. "Mr. Romberg's in agriculture," she said, eyes twinkling.

Fritz chuckled. "What she's trying not to say is that I'm a nester," he said. He turned to Dobie whose ears were turning pink. "It's better to have agriculture than no culture at all," he told her. They all laughed, Dobie more merrily than anybody.

"I'm hungry," she said. Fritz escorted her to the barbecue pit and filled two plates. Leaning against a buggy, they began eating and talking.

He told her about his family, his dogies, and the claim. He showed her his horse Valentine. She told him about her horse. "He's a grulla, mouse-colored," she said. "His name is Duke. He's so gentle you could stake him to a hairpin."

Jim Yoakum's gaunt figure loomed by the fire, a cup of coffee in one hand. Fritz brought him over to meet Dobie.

"This is Dobie Quinlan," he said. "She's been teaching me how to dance." Then he looked at Dobie. "And this is my friend Jim Yoakum."

Jim bowed. "My pleasure," he said, his grave eyes full upon her.

Fritz added, "He brought me here tonight so everybody could see how greatly he outdresses me."

Jim looked once at Fritz, then down at his own finery. "Wull now," he told Dobie, "when I go dancin' I like to wear full war paint." Dobie laughed heartily.

Behind them, the crowd was gradually thinning out. People were yawning and taking more time between dances. The caller was getting hoarse and the fiddler sounded squeakier than ever. The sweetest music of all, Fritz thought, was the grinding of the stone coffee mill. He got them each a cup that was strong and fresh and hot. Soon it was time to say good-bye.

"When will I see you again?" asked Fritz as he walked her back

121

to her parents. "I sure hope I don't have to wait another year and a half."

"Come over any time and I'll show you my horse," said Dobie.

"I don't want to see your horse," said Fritz. "I'd rather see you."

In the orange light of dawn she reached into the surrey for her straw hat. "We're located only nine miles east of your claim," she said. "Come over and we'll feed you good. You ought to taste the cobbler Mom bakes in our old fireplace. It's usually apple or peach from our orchard. We'll want you to take some home with you."

She looked sleepy as she pushed back her blonde hair and pulled the hat on crookedly. And Fritz wished that he had her in a buggy, his arm around her, driving her home, her head cushioned against his shoulder.

Relinquishing his dream, he helped Bob Quinlan hook his team to the surrey and then he met Dobie's mother, a quiet, brown-faced woman with an appearance of health and endurance. She looked at him, an interested, summing look.

"We've been having a bragging match, Mrs. Quinlan," said Fritz. "I bragged about my mother's *Scharzsauer*—that's a German dish, a jellied pigs' feet salad. Mother puts dumplings, prunes, and spices in it. Your daughter's been boosting the fruit cobbler you bake in your fireplace. It came out a draw. Neither of us gave in."

After a final cup of the fresh-ground coffee, Jim and Fritz started the long ride home in the crisp, biting air. Awash with dew, the prairie looked enameled in the early morning sunshine, a halo of light green.

"Wull," said Yoakum resignedly, "dance all night an' nod back home."

Fritz yawned widely, like a young bobcat, and thought about it. Why had he ever hesitated to come with Jim? He needed more social contact with young people of the area. He had liked the dance, the people, and the cordiality. He had especially liked the thrill of being with a nice girl. Now he understood why Jim had insisted that he go, that the event truly would be worth the forty-mile ride.

To the cowboy, the range dance was probably the most important social event of his life, Fritz surmised. It was something to look forward to, a place to go. It afforded an opportunity to see old friends and meet new ones in this big lonely land.

A VISIT
WITH DOBIE QUINLAN

———————————•—•—•———————————

With no forests to clear or rocks to move, Fritz, like all Strip farmers, had periods of idleness. Unwilling to squander them, he persuaded Ray Patterson to join him in building a sod house on each of their farms, all of it above ground. The habit of constant diligence was so deeply instilled within him that he found it hard not to make a steady effort at improving some part of the claim.

They started on the Patterson homestead, taking sod from the open prairie to the south where the soil was less sandy and the buffalo grass better matted. With the sod plow they turned over long strips and used shovels to cut them into individual building blocks eighteen inches long, ten inches wide, and two and one-half inches thick. Hauling these back to the Pattersons' in a wagon, they laid them grassy side down along Ray's carefully computed dimensions, overlapping the joints like brick.

Wanting two ten- by twelve-foot rooms, Patterson built his outside walls with two thicknesses of sod, which would add strength to the structure and insulate it no matter what the weather. Rafters of cedar were run from wall to wall to support the weight of the low roof.

Trying a new tack, they took the cedar logs at night from the brakes of Beaver River to the north. They were not challenged.

An acre and a half of sod was needed. Between each plowed segment long ribbons of open prairie were left, permitting the scarred strips to heal back. When each night came, both Fritz and Ray realized they had done a full day's work.

It was surprising how fast both houses went up. Fritz staked out a larger house, two twelve- by fifteen-foot rooms, and added a fireplace and chimney for cooking and warmth.

That required special planning. First he built a mold in which to form the homemade brick. He mixed prairie grass into a plaster he had contrived from nearby gypsum beds and pressed them together to harden. He was pleased with their strength and solidity.

Then he burned a quantity of gypsum in a fire and, mixing it with creek sand and water, made a crude concrete with which he coated the floor and the walls to keep the insects out. Openings were left for the doorways and windows, materials for which they could not then afford.

Honeysuckle and trumpet vine were planted by Freda and Sarah to cover the porch. A sweetbriar rose was put into the ground by the front step. In the backyard Fritz set out a red mulberry tree to attract songbirds. All of this was within watering distance of the well.

"Even when the hot winds burn everything brown, we'll have an oasis here," Freda enthused.

"A tree full of singing birds will soften our feelings and warm our hearts," added Fritz.

On the afternoon they finished the Patterson soddy, Ray and Daisy walked to their garden to gather vegetables, leaving Fritz in the dugout to watch the baby.

Taking off his shoes, Fritz lay on the bed reading a copy of the *Woodward News*, a weekly newspaper.

The baby had just learned to crawl. She kept peeking over the edge of the bed and laughing. Fritz held on to her dress with his left hand while holding the newspaper with his right.

A loud thump sounded on the floor. Fritz sat up, pulling the baby back on the bed. He looked over the side of the bed. What he saw chilled him to the marrow.

A large rattlesnake, with diamond-shaped blotches running the length of its back, was coiling on the dugout floor around Fritz's shoes. Apparently, it had tried to crawl onto the bed but had slipped off. The baby had been reaching toward it and playing peekaboo with it.

Grabbing the baby, Fritz leaped off the end of the bed and out the open door into the sunshine. For a moment he just stood there, gasping and trembling. Then he realized that he had to find the snake.

Looking around, he saw Ray's wagon. He placed the baby in it. Heart thumping, he picked up a shovel and returned to the dugout door. The snake was nowhere in sight. Behind him, he could hear the birds chirping and Daisy's mother hen clucking busily as she helped her brood find food on the ground.

Fritz caught the hen, a Rhode Island Red, and carried her squawking into the dugout. He tied her to the leg of the table. Then he went back for her yellow chicks and put them with her. Picking up the shovel, he stood quietly against the wall, waiting.

Soon, he heard a sliding along the floor as if somebody was dragging a burlap sack. From underneath the stove, the snake thrust out its head, watching the chickens. Then it moved stealthily toward them.

When Fritz raised the shovel, the snake saw him. He heard the deadly singing of its rattles. It hissed and blew at him, swinging its head from side to side. It exuded a musty odor, as of rotting cloth in a damp cellar.

With the flat of the shovel Fritz killed it, took it outside, and buried it. With water from Ray's wooden stock tank, he returned to the dugout and washed the floor.

126

As he went back to the wagon for the baby, he still felt perspiration beading on his forehead and the back of his neck. If the snake had bitten the infant, it would have meant certain death. They were twenty-seven miles from the doctor at Woodward.

The dry spell hung on. Their food supply dwindling, Fritz occasionally shot rabbits or prairie chicken. They had little else to eat. Freda was baking bread from kafir corn seed ground in the coffee mill. Coffee was brewed from roasted okra seeds.

Soon they had little left to eat but the last peck of seed wheat. Freda ground that in the coffee mill, mixed it with water, and made a delicious brown soup.

"Mother, a good cook is one who can make a meal out of nothing," Fritz praised. "Looks like I'm going to have to shoot another rabbit."

"Or go fishing," said Jacob. But there was no water in the creeks. The dry stream beds all lay panting in the sun. It seemed to Fritz that almost the only things growing besides the shortgrass were the weeds, grass, and wild flowers that adorned the dugout's sod roof.

Drought did not deter the wild things. Most of them took it in stride or made adjustments. Like the quail.

One Sunday morning Fritz heard a quail whistling peculiarly outside the door. Investigating, he saw a mother bobwhite proudly leading her brood of fourteen downy chicks past the back step. With her beak, she began thrashing out a sprig of chickweed and calling for her babies. The most active ones rushed in, scrambling greedily for the seeds.

Fritz awakened Jacob and Sarah. Barefooted and still wearing their sleeping garments, they slipped quietly out the back door and sat on the step watching. The quail mother twittered with alarm and rushed toward them, fluttering wildly in the dust at their feet in an effort to distract attention away from her family. The baby quail froze, squatting motionless and sticking their necks out parallel to the surface of the ground.

127

An angry whir of wings sounded and the chestnut-breasted quail father, his feathers puffed out aggressively, zoomed in from behind and chirping wildly ruddered to a stop within four feet of the Rombergs.

"Don't move!" whispered Fritz. "Be still!"

The excitement subsiding, the mother emitted a soft, plaintive call that seemed to say, "Follow me as fast as you can go." It was exhilarating to see her move out of the yard at a gliding pace with the chicks, some with pieces of their natal shell still sticking to their backs, following on the run, tiny feet blurring, bodies moving as smoothly as if drawn on invisible wheels. And the vigilant cock brought up the rear.

"They're probably only a few minutes old," Fritz said. "In time of drought, Father once told me, the mother will lose no time teaching them to run. She'll have to this year because the dryness has left them so little cover. But no matter how fast they run, most of them will lose their lives to coyotes, blue jays, hunters, hawks, and sometimes snow and ice."

One day a familiar figure rode up on a bay horse, his spurs with the daisy-shaped rowels jingling merrily. In front of him across the saddle he held a mysterious something wrapped in an old feed sack.

"Howdy," drawled Jim Yoakum, "brought you somethin'."

It was a quarter of fresh-killed beef. Never was a gift more enthusiastically received. Steaks were cut off for immediate eating. Jim showed them how to cure the remainder, cutting it into strips one and a half inches wide and a foot and a half long. These were salted and hung on strong cord extending from the wagon tongue. Smoke from a fire of cowchips kept the flies away. After three days, Yoakum told them, it would be dry and keep.

"Christmas is quite a way off and I've no idea what we'll have to eat, but you're invited to come anyhow and have dinner with us," Freda told the cowboy.

He stayed for dinner, visiting with the children, too. For each of them he had brought a toy from the Shattuck store. He looked without emotion at the new sod house Fritz had built.

"Looks like yore startin' a town out here," he said laconically. "When you gonna move in?"

"Soon as we can afford to buy a door and four windows," said Fritz.

When Yoakum left, Fritz rode with him as far as the pasture to show him how his calves were putting on poundage despite the drought.

"We're not completely destitute," said Fritz. "I'm holding the heifers for breeding. The steers aren't big enough yet to sell."

"Lots of strength in this old grass," said Jim Yoakum, as he lifted two fingers in farewell and rode off, the reins held gracefully in one hand.

Fritz wondered if the beef he had brought them came from Womble's herd? Ray Patterson had told him that fifteen minutes on a cloudy night was all anybody needed to kill and dress a beef and cut the brand out of its hide so proof of ownership would be lacking.

Next day, he harnessed the grays to the wagon and drove to Woodward, stopping at the depot to get more seed wheat.

While he was gone, outlaws made their second visit to the area. Wide-eyed and fearful, Freda and the children told him about it when he returned.

Two riders had trotted up to the Romberg claim, revolvers at their belts and rifles thrust into carbine saddle scabbards. One, a small, sway-jawed man, looked mean and ruthless. He wore moccasins and chewed tobacco. The other was a big, smiling fellow with the personality of a hotel greeter.

While the big man walked to the dugout to ask Freda to get them something to eat, the small man turned their horses over to Jacob in the barnyard.

"Here, boy!" he ordered roughly. "Give each of these horses twelve ears of corn."

Jacob stared at him defiantly. "Do you know how much that corn cost?" he asked. "My brother had to pay twenty-five cents a bushel for it. Corn doesn't grow wild on the prairie, you know." But he did as he was asked.

Freda, from the door, stiffened at the boy's boldness. Sarah stared with fear at the rifle the big man stood against the dugout wall.

But nothing happened. Although the food was commonplace, except for the steaks, it must have been typical of the area, for the big man left a one-dollar bill beneath his plate. Outside, he tossed a silver half-dollar to Jacob and stationed him on a box by the horse trough.

"When the marshal or his posse gits here, tell 'em which way we went," he said, chuckling. They rode leisurely off. When the posse arrived, Fritz learned that the men were Dick Yeager and Ike Black, well-known Strip outlaws. Both would later die while being pursued by officers.

At Woodward Fritz had traded the grays for two young saddle ponies and fifteen dollars in cash. He spent part of the fifteen dollars for a stock of groceries. The ponies were also broken to work in harness and, while they were small compared to the grays, they would dig in and pull hard, Fritz knew. And they didn't tire on long trips. Besides, they were used to rustling their own food from the buffalo grass and required only a little grain.

On his way home, Fritz stopped at the Quinlan ranch to inquire if the rancher had any work. He was promptly hired to plow fireguards and to build fence around stackyards. He labored four days, boarding with the ranch hands in the cookshack and sleeping in the bunkhouse at no extra charge.

"The job pays a dollar and a half a day," Quinlan told him when he started him off.

"Pay me in calves, sir, if you wish," said Fritz. Thus he built his small calf herd still larger. Where was Dobie, he wondered?

At the end of the second day he found out. He was getting a drink at the well when hoofbeats and a whirring of wheels sounded and the Quinlan surrey, driven by a cowboy, approached from the trail. Riding alongside it on the mouse-colored grulla was Dobie. She and her mother had been visiting in Woodward. It seemed that the girl had brought back something for everybody in her family.

Tying her mount to a gate, she dug out her bundles from beneath the surrey seat and began distributing gifts. There was a pair of earrings for each of her two aunts, who had stayed at home, and candy for the children.

"Brought you something, Dad," Dobie said to her father, handing him a package, too.

Awkwardly he undid it, revealing a bottle of perfume.

"She knows I don't use perfume," he laughed. "She knows she'll get it back."

Then Dobie spied Fritz at the pump.

"Well!" she said, coming over to him. "If it isn't Fritz Romberg. If I'd known you were here I'd have brought you a gift, too."

Fritz glanced at the bottle of perfume in the ranchman's hands and laughed. "No thanks," he said. "It would probably have been a lady's parasol or a flannel underskirt, neither of which I need."

What he really needed, he knew, was a bath. Ashamed of his shabby clothing, he backed off a bit. "Don't get downwind from me," he warned. "I smell sweaty. I've been digging postholes. I'm the one who needs that perfume."

Dobie halted, aware of his sensibility. "Come to the house after supper," she invited, "and I'll show you our new parlor organ. Five octaves, eleven stops, and one set of melodia reeds—only none of us can play it."

"I can't either," said Fritz, "but my mother can."

"Yes, I know," said Dobie, remembering the Christmas program at Woodward.

After he had eaten with the cowboys, Fritz went outside and in the darkness took a quick bath in the horse trough. Letting the wind dry him, he donned his one change of clothing. Old and patched, it was clean-smelling from a washing he had given it in the wagonyard at Woodward. He knocked on the Quinlans' door.

The ranchman's wife admitted him. She showed him into the parlor. There Quinlan sat in his favorite chair, an ancient Morris recliner. Dobie was nowhere in sight.

Quinlan fell to describing his start in ranching. Quickly, Fritz saw that the cowman liked to talk about the days of his youth when he rode for another man's outfit and listened for horse bells and bawling calves not his own. The boy was fascinated with the telling. As a cowboy, Quinlan had helped trail Texas cattle across the Strip on the way to the Kansas markets. So lush was the Strip greenery that the ranchmen liked to linger there, fattening their herds before pushing on.

"There's never been a finer cow country than the Strip," said Quinlan, "and it was all being wasted. From the tops of the little hills to the bottoms of the draws there was buffalo grass, grama, and curly mesquite with plenty of sage for the older cattle to eat in dry years. There was shelter. And it was close to the markets. Without asking anybody, we took it over, established our herds, built our ranch buildings and settled down for a last stand against the nesters."

From a leather pouch on a stand-table, Quinlan filled his pipe. Lighting it, he blew the smoke out thoughtfully, looking straight at Fritz.

"This will surprise you," Quinlan went on. "Some ranchers favor the settler who is an honest law-and-order man. But many ranchers despise him no matter what he is. If a nester is a good citizen, I like to help and protect him. He's needed for the development of the country. But the good ones are few and far between. And good or bad, they all starve out in these uplands."

Fritz wondered in which category Dobie's father rated him. He wished that Quinlan could have met Frederic, his own father.

Dobie came in then, wearing boots, a skirt of brown denim, and a red polka-dot waist. The ranchman, his wife, and the rest of the family retreated to the coolness of the porch.

"I've been trying to bake you some cookies but I burned them," Dobie said. "I don't cook very good."

She led him into what she called the music room and showed him the new organ. They began singing together some of the old favorites, "Lorena," "Bell Branden," "Faded Flowers," "Jesus, Lover of My Soul," and the rollicking "Oh Lord Gals One Friday." Dobie knew them all and so did Fritz. She sang the melody, Fritz the tenor. Her voice wasn't trained but she stayed on pitch.

They began talking. She told him more about Duke, her horse. "He has to be disciplined all the time," she said. "If he sees he can get away with something, he's going to do it. He just tries you."

Absently she sat down at the organ and, pumping one of the pedals at her feet, pressed lightly on a key. The note purled out high and thin and reedlike.

"Some boys are that way," she added, throwing him a quick sideways glance.

Fritz grinned. Who could blame them?

They began talking about cattle and farming. It was then Fritz found out that Dobie Quinlan wasn't wholly ignorant about the subject of homesteading versus ranching. She had probably heard scores of ranchmen discussing it with her father.

"When Dad told you that grass was the best crop this country would ever grow, he was merely voicing the belief of every experienced farmer who has come out here from the east or the north and looked the land over," she said. "Since the coming of the first white people, this has always been cow country. Only those who don't own farms in a proven agricultural region would come here and try to make farming pay. The drought always gets them."

Fritz's smile went out. It wasn't going to get the Rombergs. "I think we can make farming pay," he said with quiet stubbornness. "Crop growing has never been given a real try here."

"Why don't you become a cowboy?" she asked.

Still a bit miffed, he wiggled his toes in his ragged shoes. "Because I want more than just a job working for somebody else," he replied quietly. "Few cowboys can support a wife. I want to own my own land, and my own home. When I propose to a girl, I'd like to be able to give her something besides just my name.''

Dobie looked at him mischievously, the little wrinkles crinkling around her eyes. "Are you proposing to me?" she asked.

Fritz felt his face go crimson. For once, he couldn't think of anything to say.

"How old are you?" she persisted.

"Fifteen."

"When's your birthday?"

He told her.

"Jeepers!" she exclaimed, her eyes as round as cinch rings. "You're six days younger than I am."

Leaning forward, she blew dust off the organ's case of solid oak. Then she told him something that surprised him profoundly.

"We're poor, too," she said, "although we don't let on. The cattle business is carried on mainly through borrowed capital. We borrow all our money, much of it at eight percent interest. We borrow mostly from livestock commission houses located at the markets where we sell our herds."

Fritz blinked and wet his lips with his tongue. He had never heard of this kind of borrowing. He had believed all ranchmen wealthy.

Next morning he returned home, driving his calves and another borrowed cow in front of him. He would like to have stayed longer but now that he was his family's only support he had no choice.

Summer was passing. The kafir harvest was next and since only this hardy crop had survived the drought, Fritz was looking forward to it. But he had no cutting implement.

To make one, he fastened an old crosscut saw four inches off the ground to a homemade sled or leveler. To the front of this he attached a singletree so that a horse could draw it. The saw mowed down the stalks and Fritz, riding the sled, caught them in his arms and laid them in rows. Later, he and Jacob headed the severed stalks, stacking them in the field to await ripening by the first frost.

Meanwhile, Fritz drove the family to Shattuck so that Freda could trade her butter for staples. With Frederic lying in the new cemetery there, they felt a bond to the place. Every time he went to the new town, Fritz visited the little cemetery, cutting out the dandelions with his pocketknife and tidying up the grass. He longed for the money to purchase a proper tombstone.

Jacob walked into the Miller store with an air of great assurance. He took Sarah with him.

"Give us a half-dollar worth of that," he said, proudly tossing his silver half-dollar on the counter and pointing to the rock candy.

Amused, Mr. Miller gave them some candy but wouldn't take the money. Jacob was determined to spend it anyhow. He walked into the implement store.

"Give me that pair of spurs," he demanded, pitching his silver piece on the counter with a loud ring. Although the spurs were priced at seventy-five cents, Mr. Rose, the proprieter, sold them to him for fifty. During the remainder of their stay in the new village, Jacob proudly walked the streets to their clinking music.

"All you need now is a bridle, a saddle, and a horse," Fritz told him as they loaded for home.

With the nights becoming colder, Fritz had to look about for winter fuel. For a while, they could use the dried chips left by their own calf herd. One morning when Fritz and Jacob were collecting these, they learned that danger sometimes lurked beneath them.

When Fritz picked up a large one, he was bitten by a scorpion, an insect with a front pair of nipping claws and a jointed tail terminating in a curved stinger. It had been lying under the chip.

Having heard that the bite of one was deadly poisonous, Fritz ran to the dugout. His finger was swelling and the pain came in waves. All he could think about was Freda and the children trying to get back to Texas alone.

Freda took one look at the bite. "We must do something right away." She looked wildly about, her face flushed with fear.

135

"Wait," she said suddenly, "Mattie Cooper might know what to do. Let's go see her."

Since there wasn't time to saddle Valentine, grazing a quarter of a mile away, Fritz began running toward the Coopers', followed by Freda and the children in order of size and speed.

Mattie was bent over a small fire in the yard, making soap. She was barefoot. As Fritz ran up, she raised her head, then whirled around, looking startled, and again he got the impression that she would flee the premises if he wrinkled an eyebrow or drew a quick breath.

"I just got bit by a scorpion," Fritz blurted out, displaying the wound and its ugly swelling.

Instantly she changed from a startled moppet to a cool practitioner. Concern in her face, she dried her hands on her apron and came up to him, taking him by the wrist and peering down at the swollen finger. She made no effort to hide her bare feet beneath her skirt.

"You sure it was a scorpion and not a snake?" she asked, staring up at him anxiously. "Did it have a long jointed tail?"

Fritz scowled, nodding wildly. "I'm sure," he said roughly. "I know the difference between a scorpion and a snake. Its tail was half a foot long. It stung me with the tip of it." By this time the other Rombergs were arriving, one by one, panting breathlessly. Mrs. Cooper and Zella joined them in the yard.

Mattie looked at the finger again. Then she released his wrist and blew out her breath in relief.

"The sting of a scorpion ain't much worse than the bite of a bee," she said matter-of-factly. "Smarts at first, then goes away. Wait a minute, I ken fix it." She went into the house.

Ashamed of his panic, Fritz stood with his mouth open, his chest rising and falling from the fatigue of his dash. He had run almost half a mile, and his family with him, only to be told by this slip of a girl that it was all for naught. Why did she have to be the one to expose his stupidity?

The excitement over, Mrs. Cooper invited Freda inside to look at a spread she was quilting. Sarah and Jacob wandered down to the spring with Zella. Fritz was displeased with his mother for leaving him alone with Mattie.

Mattie returned in five minutes, bearing in her hands something that smelled of turpentine. Fritz wrinkled his nose. He might hve known that she'd use turpentine. She bent over his hand and the breeze ruffled her dark hair. He looked at her.

She looked different. He saw that her breasts were forming and that her hair was neater. She still talked in the back of her throat with a slight lisp, but she didn't sniff and tweak her nose as she once had.

"This here's May butter," she said. "Only we churned it in October. It's fresh. I put turpentine with it."

She rubbed some on his finger, coating it thoroughly. She wrapped it in a clean cloth. Her movements were quick and deft. While she worked, there was silence between them and Fritz was conscious only of the scent of the sage and the worrisome crying of killdeer near the Cooper spring.

He kept gawking at her. Although still a bit on the skinny side, she had fewer freckles now across the bridge of her nose. Her dress with the brown apron over it, which she had probably made herself, looked fresh and clean. But he couldn't forget that this was the same girl who had sewn him the blanket underpants and had written that silly note.

She tied the bandage. She handed him a dish filled with the rest of the May butter and turpentine.

"Carry this home with you," she directed. "Dab it on three times a day. Between dabs, rub on some bakin' sody and leave it on fer a half hour. Sody's good fer stings. So's tobaccer juice, only my father's gone to Kansas and you don't chew."

As she tied the bandage tighter, she stole a curious little glance at him, while the killdeer swung and tilted, crying on the wind. A ghost of a smile came to her lips.

"You looked so pale an' come on me so sudden while ago that I almost thought you was a sperret," she said.

Fritz bristled, regarding her remark as a slight upon his manhood.

"I don't care what you thought," he burst out crossly. "Coming here was my mother's idea, not mine."

For a moment she looked as surprised as if he had slapped her. Then her nostrils flared and her small chin lifted higher and higher as it had that time she had come to their dugout begging for fuel.

"Why do you hate us so?"—her voice trembled with passion— "I know it was wrong fer my father to sooner this place, but he didn't know that you-uns, or anybody, was after it too. Likely, we'd a beat you-uns here anyhow. Even if we'd awaited til the day of the run."

Fritz said sharply, "It's just as likely that you would not have. We'll never know, will we?"

Dumb wonder and pain came into her eyes. Recoiling from him, she ran swiftly into the house.

Remorse gripped him. His heart beat faster and he felt his throat tighten. In spite of his disinterest in her, she had treated his finger expertly, as she had Jacob's rusty-nail puncture. And she would have accepted nothing for doing either even if he had made the offer.

Carrying the dish of May butter, he began walking home, not waiting for the rest of his family. As he walked against the north wind that cooled his anger, he thought about it. He seemed to regard all the Coopers with the same aversion he felt for Orvus, the father, forgetting that they all had a personality and being of their own.

Could he ever forget that they were Sooners?

THE ROAD TROTTER

When they were down to their last armful of cowchips and again everybody was going to bed at sundown to save fuel, Fritz hitched the ponies to the wagon. Taking Jacob, he again drove north to the Beaver River brakes to cut a load of firewood. It was land obviously not filed on and didn't seemed guarded by any ranch.

For three nights they worked like beavers, cutting by lantern light and sleeping by day in the sand hills. While Fritz hewed down the trees, Jacob trimmed the smaller branches off them with a hatchet.

On the fourth day they loaded the wood and headed home, a brisk north wind rippling the ponies' black manes. They stopped near a wash for lunch. Fritz had finished eating and was sitting on the load driving wooden pegs into the disintegrating soles of his shoes when several men rode out from behind a small sand hill and approached at a gallop.

The leader, whose graying red hair fell to his shoulders beneath his black hat, fascinated Fritz. He had only one arm but below his right hand, easy to draw, was a revolver in a holster. A rifle swung in the saddle scabbard near his right boot.

With falling heart, Fritz knew that he was Jonas Ritter, a United States Army scout stationed at Fort Supply. Pat Rucker, the fireman, had once pointed him out at Woodward. A well-known frontier figure, Ritter had served heroically as an army scout in the Indian wars and afterward had married the daughter of a Cheyenne chief. The men riding with him were probably Cheyenne deputies. They all wore faded army regalia of dark blue coats and light blue pants.

"Where's your dad?" snapped Ritter. A small man, he had the face of an angry dwarf.

"We have no father," said Fritz. "He died last year. We live in a dugout about ten miles south of here."

"Throw off that wood," snapped Ritter.

"If you want it, throw it off yourself," retorted Jacob.

But Fritz jumped down and began unloading the wood on the prairie.

"Come on, Jacob," he said quietly. "He's from the army. Help me." Jacob crawled down off the wagon and began to help, although unwillingly. Ritter and his Indian deputies just sat their horses in stony silence, waiting.

When all the wood was on the ground, Ritter spat his cud of chewing tobacco into his hand, threw it behind him, and wiped his wet palm on his greasy trousers.

"Git up in your wagon and les go," he said.

"Yes, sir," said Fritz. Jacob climbed up with him. Downcast, Fritz expected no mercy. Ritter was paid a fee out of the fines levied for each arrest, he knew.

"Sir, where are we going?" Fritz asked.

"To see the judge," said the scout.

As they drove off, Fritz saw that two of the deputies had stayed behind. They began separating the wood, stacking the cedar in one pile and all the other varieties in another. They'll probably sell the cedar, Fritz figured.

Ritter took them to Woodward and filed charges against them. Freda was notified. Ray Patterson brought her to Woodward. The trial was short.

"Don't you know it's against the law to steal wood from government land?" scolded the judge. His name was Wheelock. His dark double-breasted coat was bedraggled and his black bow tie obviously needed scrubbing with benzene. He looked as if he would decide in favor of the man who was strongest and had the most friends.

"Yes, sir," said Fritz, "but it seemed to me, sir, that it was a question of who needed the wood the worst, the government or the Romberg family. Winter's coming, sir, and we have nothing to burn. There are very few cowchips left in our country. For us, it was steal or freeze."

They were fined forty dollars. It took the last of their deposit in the new John J. Geist bank located in the front corner of a frame mercantile store. Geist had bought out Jake Pryor. It was a mortal financial blow to the Rombergs. They barely had enough left to pay for their stay in the wagonyard with the few pennies left over.

As they walked cheerlessly out of the court, Pat Rucker, the railroad fireman, accosted Fritz in the chilly air. He looked resplendent in a new tan business suit and a black derby hat. He was now an engineer and it was his day off. He had heard about the trial.

He took them all to dinner, Ray Patterson too, in the dining room of the Central Hotel where Fritz on previous trips had only dared to stick his head inside to see the white cloths on the tables and smell the appetizing odor of vinegar and roast beef.

"How far is the railroad from your claim?" Rucker asked.

"About seven or eight miles," said Fritz. "Shattuck is the closest town."

"Tell you what I'll do," said Rucker. He looked around him

141

conspiratorially. "There's a coal chute at Waynoka. We fill the engine tender there. For some distance out of town the coal always falls from the tender. I'll see to it that none falls until we get about three miles northeast of Shattuck. Then you can drive alongside the tracks and take it home in your wagon." He winked at Fritz broadly. "It's the Santa Fe's policy to help settlers. I'll start spilling the overflow tomorrow."

He did, too. Soon, lump coal from the Santa Fe's deluxe passenger train would lie in a heap in the sod bin on the Romberg claim. Fritz would divide it with Ray Patterson.

Rucker's kindness bucked Fritz up, giving him courage to meet his other problems. When you're up against the wall, it's great to have friends, he thought. Money is important but friends are the finest thing in the world.

Before they left Woodward, Fritz told Abe Hooper, the implement store owner, about his excellent kafir crop.

"I need kafir seed badly," Hooper replied. "I'll pay two dollars a bushel for it and take all you can bring me."

But when the Rombergs arrived home they discovered that bad luck had outrun them. Clouds of wild prairie chicken rose and wheeled above the kafir rows. Most of the kafir seed had gone down their destructive throats.

Swallowing his distress, Fritz fought back by mowing them down with bird shot from Ray Patterson's shotgun. But most of the crop was lost. The whole family worked diligently to save what they could.

The heads, thick as a fist and eight to ten inches long, were shelled by rubbing them on the washboard. The grain had to be free of husks to be suitable for feed and this was a problem until Freda suggested that they soak it for an hour in tubs of water. This freed the husks, which floated to the surface and were skimmed off. Then the whitish grain was poured on a sheet and placed in the sun to dry.

For three days Fritz and Freda labored until midnight, but when the supply was exhausted, the proceeds were too slight to be of much help, although every cent was managed economically.

At the Miller store in Shattuck three days later, when Fritz tied Valentine to a hitching post, Tom Hess, a tall young ranchman, spoke from the porch.

"If you ever want to sell that horse, I'll give you fifty dollars cash for him," he said.

Shocked at the thought of parting with his pet, Fritz shook his blond head vigorously. "Thank you," he said, "but I'd have to be awfully desperate ever to let him go."

Inside the store, he heard two interesting bits of news. Jim Yoakum had quit Sam Womble. Nobody knew where he'd gone. Also, a four-month subscription school had been organized in a small frame building in Shattuck that was then vacant. Eleven students had been recruited but they represented only four families. Since the teacher would be paid thirty-five dollars monthly, more families were needed.

Each family sending students had pledged twenty-five dollars annually to pay the teacher. Fritz bit down on his lower lip. At that moment, he would have had trouble finding twenty-five cents. And yet remembering his joy in his own school back in south Texas, he wanted very much for Jacob and Sarah to go.

That night, when Fritz mentioned the subject at supper, Sarah was eager to go but Jacob refused.

"I already know everything anyhow," he argued.

Fritz grasped him by both shoulders, shaking him vigorously. "You don't know anything," he said angrily, "and you won't unless you go to school. I want no more talk like that out of you or I'll blister your bottom."

Jacob looked as surprised as if Fritz had struck him. Seeing the astonishment in Freda's face, Fritz swallowed his temper and walked to the water bucket for a long drink. As he slowly drained the dipper, he was sorry for his action. I've got to stop taking the skin off other people's backs, he told himself. I've got to stop acting like my Teuton ancestors.

Back at the table, Jacob fixed him with a cool, challenging look. "Brother," he said, "you haven't got the twenty-five dollars to send us."

Frustrated and speechless, Fritz could only stare at the floor.

Freda spoke from the dishpan on the stove. "Maybe we ought to wait until next year," she said. "Both children need shoes badly, too. Both are practically barefoot and winter is coming on. Both have outgrown the clothing I last sewed for them and no new cloth is available."

Sarah began to cry. "No, Mama," she sobbed, "I want to go to school. Zella and Mattie are going."

Surprised, Fritz looked at Freda for confirmation.

She nodded. "They've signed up," she said. "Mrs. Cooper says Mattie will review her schooling she began back in Arkansas. She wants to take the examination for a teacher's certificate so she might help out with the family income."

Next day was Sunday. A new Baptist church had started in the same frame building in Shattuck where the school was to be held. Although they were Lutherans, the Rombergs arose early to attend. Twice a month, the minister came on horseback from Higgins, Texas. Fritz drove the family in the wagon behind Jack and Joe.

All the way to Shattuck and all the way back, Fritz sat tight-jawed and silent, fighting it out in his mind for the hundredth time. He was thinking hard and sweating hard. His hands were shaking as they held the reins. Half a mile from home, he let out his breath slowly in one long weary exhalation. He had finally made up his mind.

After the milking next morning, he saddled Valentine and set off for Shattuck, leading Jack behind on a rope haltar. He didn't tell anybody what he was going to do.

At the Miller store, he found Tom Hess at the tobacco counter.

"Well," said Fritz unhappily, "I finally got desperate. Do you still want to buy him?"

Hess pulled out his wallet and extracted five ten-dollar bills. He handed them to Fritz. Although Fritz had investigated him with the storekeeper and had been assured that Hess would use the horse kindly, he felt wretched. His grief was so sharp that he almost wished he could ride off some place alone on Valentine and leave the whole miserable mess to stew in its own juice.

Nobody will ever know what this horse means to me, Fritz thought as he took the fifty dollars. A special gift from his father, Valentine had carried him all the way from Texas. He was his friend and constant companion. And all I ever gave him in return, Fritz thought, was some shelled corn and a dry place to sleep. And now I'm selling him off to a stranger.

When Fritz took the saddle off the buckskin, the horse arched his neck around and bunted Fritz affectionately with his nose. Fritz gave him a final pat and, leaving him with his new master, rode off with blurred eyes on Jack. Valentine looked around at him, flattened his ears and nickered softly as if asking, what's going on here? You'll come back for me soon, won't you?

In spite of the dull misery in his heart, Fritz felt calm and relieved as he rode back to the farm. He was glad to have the struggle over with. I had no choice, he told himself. It was either sell my horse or keep Jacob and Sarah home from school. Every child is entitled to its chance to get an education.

Riding double on Joe, the other pony, Jacob and Sarah would take the sixteen-mile round trip daily to the Shattuck school. Each student brought whatever textbooks were available at home and these were so varied that each received almost individual attention. Each brought his own chair to sit on, too. Some of the older boys were almost as tall as Clifton Powell, the teacher, but he had played football at the state university at Norman, so he had no discipline problems.

Drawing a long breath, Fritz thought about the fine for timber stealing that had taken all their cash, the loss of the kafir to the prairie chickens, and the selling of Valentine. I'm becoming used to adversity, he told himself. I'm getting so I can adjust to anything. Each new setback seems just half as bad as the last one.

As he rode north, he saw that some of the trail had been closed by the new fences that were starting to be built along the section lines. Twice he had to pull the staples and take down the barbed wire, drive across it, and then nail it back up. It was after dark when he neared the dugout, but Freda had tied a lantern to the clothesline so that he could find his way.

Next morning, after a breakfast of kafir flapjacks and molasses, Fritz was just starting for the feedlot to turn his calves in on the kafir stalks when a man rode up on a sorrel horse. He was a big thick-chested fellow, muscled like a bull. Inside his belt, he wore a revolver, the butt protruding.

"What are you doin' on my claim?" he demanded, his eyes darting vigilantly about the premises.

Instantly Fritz knew that he was a "Road Trotter," a new species of outlaw spawned by the Strip. He had heard settlers camping in the Woodward wagonyard talking about them. They would ride up and state that they had staked the claim first and that the only way they could be dispossessed was to pay them a sum of money, which they named.

"My father took this claim two days after the Run," said Fritz, calm-voiced. "We have his filing papers and application to homestead inside. We also have the receipt from the government land office showing he paid his filing fee. They told us nobody else had filed on it."

The stranger switched the bridle reins to his left hand, while his right hovered over his revolver, which Fritz saw was to be the man's Blackstone.

"That kind of talk won't wash," growled the big man. "This claim's mine. An' yore goin' to have to pack up and git out, or pay me fer it."

Fritz stayed cool. In the dugout, they still had the fifty dollars received from the sale of Valentine. The fellow might try to take that, too.

"How much are you asking?" inquired Fritz. Inwardly, he felt his temper rising. Adversity had made him reckless. He was sick and tired of all the misfortune that was plaguing the Rombergs.

"Twenty dollars."

"I'm sorry we trespassed on you," said Fritz. "Perhaps our application called for us to settle someplace else. Wait right here and I'll go get it." Out of the corner of his eye he saw that Freda and the children had shrunk back, dismayed at his surrendering so passively.

In the dugout, Fritz reached up on the shelf and took down Frederic's Colt. All the chambers were loaded, he knew. Holding the weapon in his right hand with a newspaper over it, he went back outside.

His first bullet thudded into the prairie beneath the sorrel, which leaped and reared, whinnying in fright. The big man shagged his head wildly about, sawing at the reins as he fought to keep his seat in the saddle.

Fritz's second bullet went past the outlaw's ear. With a bawl of rage and panic, the big man dug his spurs into the sorrel and they fled south down the trail.

Fritz blew the smoke from the chambers and looked around at his family. "I'm sorry if the gun frightened you," he apologized. "There wasn't time to warn you. I wanted to surprise him." Reloading the two empty cylinders, he saddled one of the ponies and rode to both the Coopers' and the Pattersons' to warn them.

As he rode, he marveled at how easy it had been. He had disliked firing on another, but the man and the circumstances had given him no choice.

Next morning Fritz counted his little herd and discovered a calf missing. Saddling Jack, the other pony, he found the lost animal in the heart of the Womble range on the prettiest tract of land he had ever seen. The grass looked as if it hadn't been pastured for years. Not only was it natural cow country but a safe retreat and a hallowed spot as well. For half an hour, Fritz pleasured himself riding over it and looking.

Not only did the land sink away in a long sweep, but a canyon full of cedar sealed its south border, making a fence there unnecessary. The cedars were festooned with wild grapevines, and Fritz could imagine how his mother would exclaim over the picture the clusters of grapes would make in spring against the background of dark green verdure. The only thing it lacked was water but since Womble had so much of that on his other ranges, that should be no problem for him.

But it would be for us if we owned it, Fritz realized. Our cows would get awfully thirsty waiting for Womble to let them drink from his streams.

Fascinated, he decided to investigate the spot, despite the long odds against their ever owning it. The time was coming when they'd need self-curing buffalo grass to carry their little herd through the winter. Also, he planned to expand their cattle holdings and someday would need more range.

The next day he drove his family to Woodward. While Freda bought new shoes and school books for the children and purchased calico and denim from which to sew their school clothing, Fritz visited the government land office.

"That's a school section," the clerk told him. "The law says that two sections of land in each township are reserved for the benefit of the public schools. These are territorial lands, not subject to public entry. However, anybody can lease a school section for grazing or homesteading, or both, for thirty-three dollars cash rental per year."

Cash rental? Fritz's mouth twisted in disappointment. That eliminated the Rombergs.

"I suppose Sam Womble holds the lease to it, doesn't he?"

The clerk scanned his ledgers. "No, sir. He's been in and talked about leasing it, but he's never put up his thirty-three dollars.

Guess he's too tight, or thinks nobody else knows about it. He owns land on three sides of it."

Fritz grinned. "We own the claim on the fourth side," he revealed.

The clerk closed his ledger, nodding. "That's Womble, all right. Thinks he's a cattle baron. Tries to take over all the vacant public lands and use 'em for himself. He strings his fences across public roads, too, and won't build gates."

Fritz turned to go. "The first one posting the lease money gets it, doesn't he?"

"Yes, sir," replied the clerk. "He puts up his money at Guthrie, the territorial capital, with a legal description of the land. But I think I should warn you that the Strip cowmen are leasing every acre of school land in the western third of the Strip. Governor Renfrew of Oklahoma Territory met with the cattlemen here two years ago and promised them he'd do all in his power to protect them from the trespassing of the settlers. That's a tough combine to buck."

Fritz asked for the legal description of the land and wrote it down.

"Thank you," he said. As he walked out he thought, where could I get thirty-three dollars even if I was reckless enough to take this on? And then he thought of his dogies who now weighed approximately four hundred pounds each.

As he walked down Woodward's business district past bags of stock salt, cans of calf vaccine, and coils of linen lariats in the windows of the ranch supply stores, he saw that these establishments had also begun to exhibit a few plows, horse collars, and even a baby buggy or two. Looks like we nesters at least have a foot in the door, he thought with satisfaction.

It was Pat Rucker's day off and Fritz decided to find him and thank him for the coal. As he walked along the tracks to the depot, he passed the railroad water tower. Above it he heard a strange squeaking in the wind. Looking up, he saw an odd flat wheel containing several oblique blades spinning round and round in the breeze.

"What's that?" Fritz asked Rucker, leading him outside and pointing aloft.

"That's a windmill," Rucker answered. "It pumps water out of the ground into the railroad water tank. Then we bring that same water into the engine tender to make the steam that runs the locomotive. They're economical gadgets. Require no labor to operate, and no fuel. The railroad bought a bunch of 'em just to keep their water tanks full."

Fritz gawked in awe, listening to the rattle of the whirling blades. "How does it keep from wrecking itself in the wind?" he asked.

Rucker laughed. "That's the genius of the thing, me lad," he said. "The inventor worked out a simple method of reefing the blades so as to keep the speed of the mill uniform during irregularities in the force of the wind."

Fritz's young face tightened and his eyes were alive with thinking. I wish I had that big thing out in our pasture, he thought, pumping water out of the ground for our cows. But he knew that was almost as improbable as wishing that the railroad itself was out there, and the depot, and the water tank, too.

All the way home Fritz thought about the school section. If I'm ever going to lease it, now's the time, he told himself—before Womble or somebody else wakes up and posts the money. I'd have trouble with Womble over it, but I'd wrestle that when it got here.

He sat up straighter on the wagon seat. The big ranchmen, he knew, still retained the grip of an octopus over all the Strip land that had not been preempted for homesteading. But why give them all the school sections, too?

Shaking out the lines, he explained the situation to Freda and the children. They agreed that he should buy it.

When they crossed Wolf Creek, Fritz turned north, off the trail, to a barren canyon near a sand hill. He stopped the ponies. A medium-sized cedar tree grew nearby. Handing the reins to Jacob, he got out. Then he lifted Sarah out.

"Think this one's about the right size, Sarah?" he asked, squinting calculatingly at the tree, then at her.

The girl clutched her hands together and laughed aloud.

"Christmas!" she shouted joyfully. "This year we're going to have a real cedar for Christmas!" She began jumping up and down.

Fritz cut down the tree and put it in the wagon. All the way home Sarah sat near it, stroking its scalelike branches and smelling its aromatic fragrance.

A week before Christmas, a cattle buyer in a buggy came by the Romberg claim and had dinner with them. Jim Yoakum had told Fritz about cattle buyers. They knew the different ranchers, big and little, and tried to buy a cow, calf, or bull here and there, estimating the weight. When they got enough for a carload, they'd send a man on horseback to herd them to the nearest railroad stockyards. If a stockman needed money, the cattle buyer might pay him half the total amount when the agreement was made, the rest on surrender of the calves. His word was good.

Fritz sold him the nine biggest dogie steers for forty-five dollars. He sent thirty-three dollars of it by Railroad Express money order to the State School Land Department at Guthrie with a letter of explanation and a legal description of the land. Then he settled down to wait.

He was convinced, now, of the wisdom of raising cattle as a sideline to farming in the Strip. With settlers starting to come, legal ownership of the range was vital. The mile-square school section could provide it when they could afford to fence it. Finding water for the cattle to drink would be the most vexing problem.

The first Christmas without Frederic started gloomily. A star, cut from cardboard and wound with foil, hung from the topmost branch of the cedar. But one look at that foil, which Freda had saved from Frederic's pipe tobacco wrappings, was too poignant for her. Dropping her face into her hands, she burst into tears.

While Fritz tried to cheer her, Sarah began crying softly. Then Jacob walked to the door and turning his back on them began sniffing and wiping his nose with the back of his hand. Although Fritz himself felt like bawling, he was so busy comforting the others that there wasn't time.

"Go ahead and cry all you want," he soothed, trying to put his arms around first one and then another. "I'll probably join you in a minute. I, too, loved our father and wish he was here." Then he thought of the wild grape wine.

While the others composed themselves, he rolled out the small barrel. He opened it and sampled the contents, which had aged for fifteen months. The taste was excellent.

"It's kind of strengthy," he warned them as he poured small quantities in four tin cups.

Jacob downed his, then smacked his lips and blinked. "Makes me feel like my head's full of bees," he said and they all laughed. Sarah only tasted hers. After an hour of card playing and a round of singing, they had family prayers and went to bed.

The next day was better. When Fritz and Jacob walked out at dawn into the crisp white world to do the chores, frost had turned the heads of the tall Indian grass into a lace of glistening diamonds. The cowchips were coated with sparkling sequins. So deep was the silence that when Fritz broke the ice in the horse trough with blows of his hatchet it shattered as noisily as breaking glass.

After breakfast they opened their gifts. They weren't elaborate, a string ball, a rag doll for Sarah, and other trifles. But the tree was lovely. Fritz read a sermon from the *Christian Herald*.

The next day long drifts of clouds blew in like flotillas of gray geese. It snowed three inches and stopped. Ray and Daisy Patterson and their infant daughter, Carrie, came for Christmas dinner. The wild grape wine was served. Fritz said grace. Then Freda served the food.

"It's not fancy," she laughed, "but there's plenty. A German cook wastes nothing. She makes something out of everything."

There was liver dumpling soup, *Schmierkase*, a dry crumbly cheese, and *Sauerbraten*, a cut of Jim Yoakum's beef marinated and so tender that they could cut it with a fork. But Jim himself did not show, despite Freda's invitation.

Afterward, Ray, Fritz, and Jacob put on their coats and gloves and played horseshoes in the snow, while the women washed the dishes and Carrie took a nap.

Later Fritz hitched Jack and Joe to his homemade sled and with the snow coming down afresh took them all sleigh riding. A meadowlark flew leisurely through the whirling flakes, its black and yellow underparts brightening the scene.

Thus passed their third Christmas in the Strip. Fritz wondered how Dobie Quinlan had passed hers.

BOX SUPPER
AT SHATTUCK

———————◆—◆—◆———————

Early in February Fritz resolved to break fifteen additional acres of prairie sod on the Romberg quarter. To make the plowing easier, he decided to burn off the grass first.

"Never fire a range when it's windy or too dry," Frederic had warned. "After a rain, when the grass first dries out, is the best time."

But there had been no rain. Wanting to get started with the plowing, Fritz decided to burn the grass anyhow. As a precaution, he first plowed an eight-furrow fireguard entirely around the area to be burned.

Waiting until late afternoon, when the south wind became almost calm, Fritz started the fire upwind. It burned slowly, with a gentle crackling and an acrid smell, laying a carpet of black velvet over the earth as it passed. With wet sacks and brooms, Freda, Jacob, and Sarah were posted just beyond the plowed fireguard to beat out any side fires ignited by the embers.

154

Just as the new field was nearly burned off, the wind switched to the north and began to blow hard.

"Careful!" Fritz yelled to his family. "The wind has changed! Watch out for sparks jumping the fireguard!"

But they jumped too fast and in too many places. Fritz leaped to help but all around him the flames tossed their red flowers into the dry grass which burst into roars of heat, cracking and popping like a thousand whips. Fritz and his family fought the blaze like demons, trying to contain it before it engulfed the winter range he had saved for their calves. But it was useless.

"Go to the dugout!" he yelled. "I'm going for help."

Saddling Jack, one of the ponies, he rode hard for Womble's ranch. There he found Womble leaning with folded arms on a wooden gate, one calfskin boot with its green mule-eared tug lifted lazily to a lower bar. He was watching the conflagration.

"Come and help me!" Fritz called. "That fire jumped my fireguard!"

With an upward lift of his head, Womble laughed derisively. "You set it," he shouted back hoarsely, "now let's see you put it out."

This lack of friendliness so angered Fritz that he let the fire go. Turning back toward the dugout, he saw Ray Patterson's wagon coming from the southeast on the run. Patterson had seen the smoke.

"What can I do to help?" he shouted, pulling his team to a stop. "It's headed for our winter grass."

Fritz licked his lips and tried to control his panting. "Nothing now, I'm afraid," he said. "She's gone." He told Patterson about Womble refusing to help. Together, they stood and watched helplessly.

Suddenly a moving wall of flame, fanned by the gale, jumped the east fireguard and, curling a hundred fiery tongues around the bunchgrass, ignited Womble's south range. The evening sky was livid from the glow, which lighted up the front of the Romberg dugout in reflections that rose and fell across its sod face.

Fritz spun round, throwing a look at the Cooper house. It might soon lie squarely in the path of the blaze. He turned to Patterson.

"Lend me your team, Ray," he said. "I'd better cut a fireguard around them or their wooden shack could burn like somebody had poured kerosene on it."

Quickly they uncoupled Patterson's team from the wagon and hitched it to the plow, which was dragged on the run to the Cooper boundary. Around and around the Cooper home and outbuildings the plow ripped up the earth with Fritz trudging behind it and remembering with nearly every step Orvus Cooper's unlawful seizure of the same land he was now sealing off from the flames.

Every time he passed the Cooper home, Fritz could see the Cooper females staring out the window with wide eyes and frightened faces.

Afterward, while Fritz and Ray with soot-blackened faces supped the hot coffee Freda had prepared, there came a drumming of hooves and a roll of wheels and Womble came storming up in his buggy. Leaning over the side with the reins in his left hand and a buggy whip in his right, the ranchman glared at Fritz, his face livid with hate.

"I'm going to sue you for damages and take every damn cent you've got," he threatened, flicking the whip along the grass near Fritz's feet. "I know you haven't got much, but whatever it is, I mean to have it. Your fire destroyed a section of my cured-out grass and burned my fence posts to ashes."

Fritz wiped his hand across his cheek and looked at him coolly. "I'm sorry you were damaged," he said. "You might not have been had you helped me when I asked you to."

Ray Patterson moved up beside Fritz. He said, "I doubt if the judge would sympathize with a man who builds fences on government land. That's dead against the law."

Womble's face drained and turned a sickly yellow. His breath came in little wheezing gasps and his hand shook so much that he almost dropped the whip.

"I'll get you damn churn-twisters yet!" he growled. "I know a dozen ways to get you.'' Touching the tip of his whip to his horse's back, he moved out of the Romberg yard at a brisk trot, raising in his wake twin dust funnels of defeat.

Later, the burned area turned easily with the sod plow and Fritz broke out the fifteen acres to be sowed to kafir in March.

On a Saturday afternoon at the post office in Shattuck a registered letter was given to Fritz. It was from the government land office at Guthrie. After signing for it, he slit it open with his pocketknife.

"We got the school section,'' he told Freda, who was standing at the dress-goods counter. However, with his elation came the sobering realization that in twelve months from the date on the receipt he would be expected to pay another thirty-three dollars to hold it. Where was it coming from? Fritz wondered.

A surprise awaited them when they returned home. A small range saddle with a deep-dished cantle and a high slim horn lay on the back step where they'd be sure to see it. That it was for Jacob there could be no doubt because the rawhide-bound stirrups had been adjusted high enough for his feet to reach.

A note scribbled on a cigarette paper was anchored to the step by a rock. It said, "Remember, kid. The seat of a saddle is the easiest thing to find but the hardest to keep.'' They knew that the giver was Jim Yoakum.

Jacob thought that saddle was the prettiest thing in the Strip. Fritz fastened it on the wooden corral gate. Jacob would climb on it, then get off and look at it, then climb on it again. That night, he wouldn't leave it long enough to go to sleep. Finally Fritz brought it inside the dugout, placed it near the boy's bed, and Jacob dozed off with his hand on it.

Next morning Fritz put the saddle on Joe, the smaller pony. Jacob was too small and inexperienced to mount the horse unaided, so Fritz gave him a boost, planting him in the seat and helping him place his feet in the stirrups.

"Now, Jacob, don't get off that horse until I tell you,'' admonished Fritz. But every time Jacob saw a rabbit, he'd slide off and throw rocks at it. Then, leading the horse to Fritz, he would have to be helped back on again.

Finally Fritz showed him how to maneuver Joe alongside the corral gate, climb the gate, grasp the saddle horn, and vault into the seat. Later, Jacob improved even on that. Shucking off one shoe, he would thrust his toes in the dimple of the horse's front knee, clutch the saddle horn, and leap aboard.

"You should have seen him this afternoon," Freda told Fritz that evening. "He put on your big hat and rode around in the sunshine, looking at the shadow of himself sitting in that saddle on Joe."

Spring came. The prairie turned as green as the top of a billiard table. Farming began. Jacob's riding had improved so greatly that Fritz set him to herding their calves on the open range, taking them off the wheat pasture. Fritz borrowed four more fresh cows from Bob Quinlan to feed the new dogies he had begun acquiring. The few hens they obtained began to lay and the garden to bear.

Fritz replowed the fifteen acres he had burned off so it would not sprout into grass after the first rain. He also plowed the original cropland that he and Frederic had broken out after their arrival from Texas. He would sow both plots to kafir.

He sang as he plowed. He yelled at Jack and Joe and whistled piercingly between his teeth to keep them going. He liked the feel of the ponies' mouths in his fingers and of his walking feet sinking into the pulverized soil. He liked the sound of the blade hurling the dirt off the moldboard and the smell of the fresh earth and the sight of the dewy prairie lying jeweled in the morning sunshine.

Despite the dryness, their wheat was not a total loss. Busy as bedbugs, Fritz and Ray Patterson worked fourteen hours a day early in June harvesting it. First they cut the wheat by hand with a scythe, then placed the stalks on a clean sheet in a wagon bed and flailed the grain out with tree branches. Then they cleaned it in the wind.

Traveling together so that they could double their teams and help each other's wagons up the hills and across the dry stream beds, they hauled the wheat to the railroad at Shattuck. There were no grain elevators there so they had to scoop the grain from the wagon into the railroad car assigned to the buyer by the depot agent. The buyer's station consisted of little else than scales for weighing, a grain tester, and two scoop shovels.

Fritz's share was enough to replenish their low stock of grocery staples and buy more clothing for his family. Splurging a bit, he purchased a bridle and saddle blanket for Jacob. He also obtained four heifer calves from a discouraged settler who was selling out.

Although he had enough seed left to plant more wheat in the fall, he was torn with discontent. They still had not been able to purchase glass and frames for the doors and windows of their new sod house or to acquire the materials needed to fence the school section.

The kafir was Fritz's special pride. Although the vegetation around it drooped in the general dryness, the kafir stood two feet high in late May and was growing vigorously.

And then one morning much of it lay in ruin. Fritz had ridden out to look at it and was appalled by what he found. A section of his fence was down. Womble's herd was devouring the kafir. Most of it was eaten to the ground.

After he had driven the cattle from his field, Fritz stood amid his severed stalks, a growing fury filling him as he noted the devastation. *What am I going to do,* he asked himself with sick bitterness. *We needed the kafir. We were depending upon it.*

Ray Patterson rode up on a horse, surveying the damage. "Those cows had to have human help to breach your fence," he said. "It was tight as a banjo string."

With the hammer and staples he carried in his saddlebag, Fritz repaired the fence. Then he and Patterson rode to Womble's ranch. Fritz knocked on the door.

Womble opened the door. A shrewd, exultant look was on his face and Fritz knew that the cowman had planned the incident.

"Mr. Womble, I'm here to warn you," said Fritz. "Keep your

cattle off our land and don't damage our fences or crops again—or I'll be forced to retaliate.''

Womble laughed. "This is free grass country. My cattle will graze where they please.''

Fritz felt his insides chilling. "We had the free grass law back in south Texas, Mr. Womble. My father always respected it and fenced his crops. And the Texas cattlemen honored the fences. When you tear down our fence so your cows can destroy our green feed you commit a criminal act. Now I want an explanation. Why did you do it?''

Womble came out on the porch, softly closing the door behind him. His small hands were shaking.

"All right," he said, "I'll give you a explanation. Yesterday I went to the land office in Woodward to put up the money for that school section''—he pointed to it on his left—"that lays right in the middle of my range only to find out that you'd gone behind my back and leased it. You think you're gonna plow it but you ain't.'' He was almost choking on his ire. "War's what you want and war's what yore gonna git.''

Afraid he couldn't control his own temper, Fritz rode off, Patterson with him.

As they rode, Ray's idly roving glance suddenly sharpened. "We've got to figure where he'll strike next," he said, "before he strikes. About all you've got left is your garden and your calf herd. And the rest of your kafir. I think some of the kafir his cattle ate will come up again. Kafir's pretty tough and hardy.''

For a week Fritz slept in the wagon in the midst of the kafir, guarding it with the Colt. Nothing happened.

Meanwhile, another letter arrived at the Shattuck post office. Addressed to Freda, it was from her sister in south Texas. "If life gets too hard for you there without Frederic, come back to Texas and live," she invited. "We'd love to have you.''

Freda handed the missive to Fritz. "I want to stay here," she said, "but it's nice knowing that if we don't make it here, we've got a place to go and relatives who want us.''

Fritz felt a nagging displeasure but tried not to show it. He'd rather they had no place to go if they failed. Then they'd try harder and work more energetically here.

Two days after Fritz stopped sleeping in the kafir and returned to the dugout, Womble and his cowboys struck a second time. Fritz awakened before daylight to find his kafir field full of cattle wearing the Womble brand. Throwing on his garments, he drove them beyond his wrecked fence.

Womble's bull, a big brown beast with horns as wide as the antlers of a moose, turned and charged him.

Fritz ran into the dugout, grabbed up the Colt, and returned to the field. When the bull circled for another charge, Fritz shot him in the flank. Enraged, the animal lowered his horns and made another rush.

Fritz fired twice. The second bullet dropped the beast. He rolled over, got up and headed for Womble's. He died within a quarter mile of Womble's barns.

Fritz walked numbly about, assessing the damage to the field. Three-fourths of the kafir had now been eaten. Staring down, he tore the spent cartridges out of the Colt and felt a nervous sickness starting in his stomach. Womble's motive was plain.

He's determined we're not going to make a feed crop, Fritz thought. He's going to starve us out. And the only restraining force in the land is the United States marshal twenty-seven miles away at Woodward.

Again Fritz repaired the fence. With every chop of his hammer, his eyes stung and he felt the wrenching pangs of anger and vexation. He nailed a warning sign on the restored fence, "Keep Cattle Out."

Afraid he would not have enough feed for the horses, Fritz resorted to an unusual tactic. He had noticed his livestock eating the green Russian thistle that grew in thick mats before drying out in autumn and being blown about the countryside as tumbleweeds. Jack and Joe relished it.

With scythes, Fritz and Ray Patterson cut down the green thistle before it became dry, stickery, and windblown. They piled it and let it cure, then tromped it and stacked it near their barns. It made good horse feed.

It also served another purpose. Sarah went out into the field and picked up a small thistle. Returning to the dugout, she pretended that it was a doll, laying it tenderly in a cradle she contrived out of grass and tying ribbons of colored string in its hair. Then it became in turn a cat and finally a dog that she drew about the yard with a string leash tied to her waist, pretending that it followed her.

"*Ach*, mother!" Fritz sighed, shaking his blond head in bafflement. "We're so poor that my little sister has a tumbleweed for a pet."

At supper that night Freda said, "Daisy Patterson came by for a while this afternoon. She says they're having a box supper next Tuesday night at Shattuck to raise money to buy blackboards, erasers, and supplies for the Shattuck School. I think we ought to go."

"So do I," said Fritz, "but what's a box supper?"

Freda explained. Daisy had told her. Each woman or girl brought a box containing supper for two. The boxes were auctioned to the highest men bidders. The men weren't supposed to know who had brought each box, although there were ways of finding out. After each box was sold, the buyer found the lady whose name was on it and they ate the supper together.

Fritz was surprised at the good attendance. The town's only street was crowded with buggies, wagons, buckboards, surreys, and saddle horses. Every hitching post was festooned with bridle reins and hitching ropes. Even people living outside the school district came. They wanted to help the new school as well as satisfy the general yearning for human companionship.

And then suddenly Fritz felt the blood pounding in his veins. Bob Quinlan entered with Mrs. Quinlan. And with them was Dobie, her long blonde braid dangling down the back of a freshly ironed yellow dress.

She stooped and placed her box with all the others. Eager to eat

162

with her, Fritz tried to memorize the color of its wrapping paper. He didn't get a clear view of it, but he thought he would recognize it when the auctioneer held it up.

Fritz liked the friendliness and democracy of the gathering. Like the range dance, social equality prevailed. The homesteaders were in the majority here, but ranchmen and their families attended as well. A spirit of good fellowship reigned. Neighbor introduced himself to neighbor and each seemed interested in the other.

With half the Romberg family enrolled in the Shattuck School, Fritz was pleased that they all had come. He was proud of the appearance they made in the new clothing Freda had sewn from cloth purchased with the wheat money. Jacob wore short-length trousers and button-down suspenders, Freda and Sarah white caps, white aprons, white shoulder kerchiefs, and skirts that reached to their shoe tops.

When Fritz introduced them to Dobie and her parents, Sarah made a polite curtsy to each, bending her knee and dipping her body. Fritz could tell that the Quinlans were charmed with the little girl's old-world manner.

Soon he was able to maneuver Dobie beneath a sputtering coal-oil bracket lamp bolted into the wall.

"What color is your box?" he whispered.

Her gray eyes widened and the corners of her mouth crinkled. "I didn't bring a box," she teased. "I brought my food in a water pail. You can't miss it. It's got three nickel-plated hoops around it and a lid to keep the ants out."

Provoked, Fritz frowned at her. "Please, Dobie," he pleaded, "tell me."

She came closer, and there was the clean scent of lavender about her. She lowered her voice.

"It's red," she told him, "same as your face."

Fritz was confused. He had thought it purple. Two ranch boys who obviously thought well of themselves entered just then. They looked like brothers. Each wore a white shirt, black string tie, vest, striped pants, and boots. Each carried a big western hat with buckskin bonnet strings dangling. They began talking loudly to Dobie. Fritz felt left out and wandered away.

Another girl came into his line of vision. She was wearing a blue dress that was pale from many washings and darned around the sleeves, but she was extremely pretty in spite of it. Slim as a willow shoot, she wore her dark hair coiled in a soft bun at the nape of her neck.

She was looking up at Clifton Powell, the schoolteacher, who was muscled like a wrestler and farmed his own claim over on Hand Pull Creek. She was talking to him and smiling. Fritz stared at her. Something about her looked familiar, something that made him feel uneasy.

He tried to move closer but the room was packed. Then her gaze swung around and for a moment fell full upon him. It was a straight, surprised look with the wonder not quite gone from it. And then he recognized her.

Mattie Cooper!

Her hair had fooled him. No longer an untidy mane, it lay in soft waves close to her head. The bun at the base of her neck made her look more composed and mature. She was as tall as the schoolmaster's chin and leggy. Fritz heard her call him "Mr. Powell." She wasn't stiff, or shy, or scared with the teacher as she had always been with him.

Fritz blinked. After all, he reflected, I haven't seen her for eight or nine months. She was barefoot the last time I saw her. Barefoot and bent over a fire in the yard, making soap.

Beyond her, he saw Mrs. Cooper talking to Freda, while Orvus Cooper stood unsociably to one side. Sarah, Zella, and Jacob were chatting like sparrows.

And then everybody sat down and the selling of the boxes began. Fritz, seated with his family, saw that the auctioneer was the cattle buyer who had purchased his dogie steers. He looked around, searching for Dobie.

One by one, the boxes were lifted and praised lavishly. Then the bidding on each began. One by one they were sold, and the successful bidder and the lady whose name was on his purchase found a place to sit and eat together.

And then Fritz's lips tightened and he took a deep, steadying breath. In the auctioneer's hands was a box tastefully wrapped in red paper. Or was it purple? In the weak incandescence of the bracket lamps, the box assumed an orangish cast.

Sure that it was Dobie's, he began bidding. Vanquishing opponent after opponent, he bought it for forty cents and went up to pay the clerk. The auctioneer recognized him, smiled, and handed him the box.

But the name on it, written in a small neat script, wasn't Dobie's. Fritz looked at it twice, his temples throbbing. He could hardly believe his eyes.

The name on the box was that of Mattie Cooper.

When he found her sitting with her family in the back of the room, she drew away from him, her lips parting, and searched his face quickly and desperately. She can't run from me this time, he thought wildly. There isn't room. He kept looking at her. In spite of himself, he found her singularly attractive.

The burden of reconciliation was his, he knew. Recalling how rude he had been when she treated his scorpion bite and remembering her other kindnesses, he experienced that worst of all mental sufferings, remorse for his ingratitude toward one who had befriended him and his family in time of distress.

For a moment, he stood upon his dignity, feeling awkward and ill at ease. *It's nothing but words,* he thought. *I've got to say them.* He took the plunge.

He looked at her. "It's a pretty box," he said. And it was.

"Thank you," she replied, her voice as hushed as a dying breeze. She still watched him warily.

He led her to a corner of the room, away from both their families, and placed the box between them on a bench. She sat primly, her hands gripped in her lap, the muscles of her throat quivering. Fritz knew that it was all his fault. In the three years that

165

he had known them, he'd never shown her a courtesy or even been polite.

He began pulling the violet crepe paper off the box. A pleasant fragrance emanated from it. There were sandwiches of home-baked bread and butter wrapped in wax paper and six pieces of fried chicken. There was a wedge of yellow potato salad, two small jars of canned apricots, and a pint fruit jar of sweet milk that had probably been cooled in the Cooper spring. And the climax that truly excited his taste buds, half of a small white coconut cake.

As if stimulated by the need for domesticity, Mattie roused herself. Reaching inside the box, she brought out napkins, small plates, knives, forks, and spoons. Timidly, she handed him a setting.

Then she began to serve the food and Fritz began to eat it. After only three bites, his German astuteness in matters regarding cooking told him that this was superb.

Immediately, he forgot all his former standoffishness.

"Did you cook this?" he asked incredulously, his mouth full of chicken. He suspected that her mother had helped.

"Yes," she answered, wide-eyed and breathless. "Why? Don't you like it?"

He gave her a buttery grin. "I'd like it if it had bugs on it," he said. "It's great." His disappointment over not getting to eat with Dobie Quinlan was becoming more and more bearable. Dobie can't cook like this, he consoled himself, remembering her burnt cookies.

As they sat there, a settler and his wife stopped. The woman came up to Mattie.

"You look so different," she said, "but ain't you the girl that worked on our Bessie's leg? Don't you remember us? In the dugout over on Sand Creek? Daisy Patterson sent you to us."

Mattie's face brightened. "I'll be jimmyjohned," she said with surprise and pleasure, "you're Mrs. Cunningham. Sure I remember you. How is she?"

"Jest fine," beamed the woman. "She jest goes a skimmin' on that leg." They moved on.

Through the forks of a wishbone held in both his hands, Fritz saw the girl's eyes gradually lose their fear of him. She began nibbling timidly at the food. Slowly and self-consciously, like two enemies who have discovered each other during a truce, they began talking.

"Where'd you learn all you know about medicine?" he asked, consuming his second sandwich.

"We got a copy of old Doctor Chase's doctor book at home," she replied. "I read it so I could help take care of our family if the need ever came. That book was about all I had to read at night—it and the Bible—and the Sears Roebuck catalogue."

"Sears Roebuck?" he repeated. "What's that?"

Unscrewing the lid of the fruit jar, she began pouring him a glass of the cold milk.

"You kin borry it sometime if you want," she said shyly. "It's a mastrous big mail-order catalogue that shows pictures of every-thing they got for sale. You order things from it by mail—if you got the money."

Fritz nodded, reaching for the milk. "We Rombergs know all about not having money," he said grimly. Before he realized it, he was telling her about selling Valentine to put Jacob and Sarah in school. And she was telling him the true reason why she attended the Shattuck School.

"I'm learnin' to talk better," she said. "Mr. Powell is helpin' me."

Conquering her diffidence, she put up a question of her own. "How did you like living down in Texas?"

"Fine," said Fritz, "only the mosquitoes were bad. If you killed one, a million came to the funeral."

She laughed, a bashful, throaty little laugh that ended almost as soon as it began. It was the first time Fritz had ever heard her laugh. Then she became silent and reserved again, and sat back, eyes wide, watching him demolish her food.

"We like it much better here in the Strip," he added, as he spooned the apricots from the can to his mouth, savoring the juice. "We like it in spite of the drought."

She nodded and began slicing the cake. "I know," she said. "It lightnin's in the north an' the tree frogs sing but still no rain."

By the time he was biting a half moon out of the cake, he was telling her about seeing the windmill owned by the railroad at Shattuck. "I'd sure like to have that big thing out in our school section," he said. "It would water all the cattle we could put over there. But it costs too much."

Her eyes became as big as the saucers in which she had served the potato salad. "I know where there's a small windmill that don't cost very much a'tall," she said.

Fritz sat stiffly erect. "Where?" The word exploded from him.

"In our Sears Roebuck catalogue."

He gaped at her. "Can I come over tomorrow and see it?"

She nodded. "Call by if you want to."

Later, when people were leaving, Mattie began stacking the dishes in the box and folding the napkins and wax paper. She saves everything, Fritz thought, as, wordlessly, he handed her his napkin. Looking for their families, they began moving through the crowd.

The two loud-spoken ranch boys came by just then with Dobie Quinlan. Now they were wearing the western hats and had tied the buckskin bonnet strings beneath their chins. They didn't see Fritz and Mattie.

One of them was talking guardedly and confidentially to Dobie but his voice was so audible that Fritz and Mattie heard him plainly.

"We saw your friend Fritz Romberg," he said to Dobie. "He ate with Mattie Cooper, that Sooner girl who lives on the claim above them." Then he saw Fritz and Mattie. Flustered, he fell silent.

Fritz looked at Dobie. "I want you to meet my friend Mattie

Cooper. Mattie, this is Dobie Quinlan." Dobie smiled and nodded.

She said, "And these are my friends, Ben and Bill Hornaday. They live on the ranch next to ours."

Gravely, Fritz shook hands with each. But Mattie Cooper, he perceived, had drawn herself tautly together. Her small jaw set firmly and her eye darkening, she faced Ben Hornaday.

"I couldn't help hearin' you call me a Sooner girl," she said, her gaze fastened steadily on him. "That was an unthoughted remark. The first Sooners of all was you cowmen who had only cattle. You beat us here ten years or more."

Surprise flooded Fritz, then admiration for her spontaneous wit. There had always been a quality of spunk and directness about her that came out when you least expected it, he reflected.

Dobie grinned, respect for Mattie Cooper showing in her face. "It's good to meet you," she said. "You must ride over and visit me sometime."

Ben and Bill Hornaday looked down their noses and said nothing. Although Fritz was careful to keep his face straight, he was inwardly laughing all over the place at the way his companion in the old blue gown had washed Ben Hornaday down the drain.

JOHN J. GEIST

Next morning after chores, Fritz saddled Jack and rode to the Coopers. Tying the horse to a post in the yard, he knocked on the back door. Mrs. Cooper opened it.

"I've come to look at the Sears Roebuck catalogue," he said. "Mattie told me about a small windmill it has for sale."

Mrs. Cooper invited him in. "She was brinin' the cabbage a while ago," she said, "but now I think she's out behind puttin' fresh hay in her bedtick. Sit down. I'll call her."

After being called, Mattie did not come in immediately. Instead there was a whispered consultation at the back door and Mrs. Cooper returned to pick up the girl's shoes and carry them to her.

Amused, Fritz thought, that's a switch. Now that she's growing up I suppose she'll think she's half undressed every time I catch her barefooted.

When Mattie entered, she was again clad in an old patched gown, but she had her shoes on. She still wore her hair in the bun and this time she did not look as if she would vanish toward Kansas City if he wiggled his nose at her.

"It wasn't hay I was stuffin' in the bedtick," she said. "It was bufferlo grass."

Seated shyly side by side, they explored the fattish volume that listed a dizzying variety of merchandise and recorded the technological advances of the times.

"The windmills is jest apast the pony plows and sickle grinders," Mattie said. In spite of the fact that her mother had gone to the garden and they were alone in the house, she was natural and friendly and trusting.

Fritz chuckled at item No. 24813, a lady's corset. Another advertisement said, "If nature has not favored you with that greatest charm, a symmetrically rounded bosom, full and perfect, send for our Princess Bust Developer."

With quick flips of her small thumb, Mattie bypassed that to scrutinize the patent medicines, twenty pages of elixers, specifics, boluses, capsules, chemicals, tinctures, and granules that would undertake to combat any malaise on earth.

They giggled together at the advertisement for obesity powders that guaranteed to reduce the flesh of corpulent people but warned them not to look for immediate results. They tittered at the German Liquor Cure that "stimulated the entire system without after-prostration," offering special prices to temperance societies. Finally they located the section picturing and describing windmills.

After ten minutes of careful reading, Fritz found that Mattie was right and the price was reasonable, despite the fact that he could not begin to meet it. Quickly he decided that the most practical mill for the Strip was the small self-oiling size. Complete with curved steel blades, it had a ten-foot wheel, long bolts to secure it to the top of the tower, and forty feet of pump rod. The purchaser could build his own wooden tower or buy a steel one for forty cents per foot.

The price of the mill itself was twenty-four dollars and after advancing transportation charges both ways the customer was permitted to examine the mill at his local railroad freight depot before accepting it and paying the agent the total price, minus the return freight fee.

His eyes alive with thinking, Fritz said, "With this windmill and a stock tank, I could water all the cows our land would support. I could soak the orchard and irrigate the garden, selling truck from it and making it yield a profit as well as food for our table. With a windmill and a bunch of good cattle, I could take a lot of the treachery out of farming this old droughty land."

"Yes," said Mattie, "and you could pipe water through a springhouse and let it cool the butter and milk on its way to the stock tank. You could pipe it into your new sod house and have a bathroom, flower beds, and a lawn sprinkler."

He looked at her, surprised at her awareness and comprehension. Then his mouth quirked in a bitter smile.

"But where am I going to get the money to pay for all this?" he asked.

"You'll get it," breathed Mattie quietly. "You'll find a way to get it, I know." Fritz looked at her oddly, wondering at her confidence in him.

Twice after that he had to sell steers from their dwindling dogie herd to buy the most necessary supplies. Half of the money went to purchase additional seed wheat, for he was still resolved to try wheat as a supplement to kafir.

In late summer Frtiz and Jacob plowed the wheat land, then sowed fifty acres. A fall rain invigorated the new wheat so greatly that Fritz knew he could turn his cattle in on it to graze in October. On the day after, he was standing at the pasture gate, Jacob by his side and mounted on Joe, when a dozen riders approached in the distance.

"I don't like their looks, Brother," said Jacob, squinting. "Do you want me to ride to the dugout and get the Colt?"

"No," said Fritz. "I'm afraid we'd be outnumbered." He saw no reason for alarm.

Jacob's concern was justified when the group rode up and Fritz identified the leader, a one-armed man whose graying red hair fell beneath his hat to his shoulders. Behind Jonas Ritter rode his Indian deputies. All were heavily armed. What have I done now, wondered Fritz, while the horses fidgeted and bits and spurs jingled in the crisp fall air.

With his lone arm, Ritter pointed to the saddle that Jacob was straddling on Joe's back.

"Where'd he get that saddle?" he demanded of Fritz.

"A friend left it for him while we were in Shattuck buying supplies," said Fritz. "We found it on the back step when we returned. He left a note. The note wasn't signed."

Ritter laughed, a harsh laugh. "So!" he grunted, and Fritz knew that he wasn't believed. When the scout moved his horse closer to Jacob to inspect the saddle, he smelled as if he hadn't bathed for a month.

"Sir," said Fritz, "I can show you the note, if you wish to see it. It's at our dugout. It's written on a cigarette paper. It said that the seat of a saddle was the easiest thing to find but the hardest to keep." He looked at Jacob for confirmation. Jacob nodded his head.

Ritter wanted to see it. Fritz vaulted into the saddle behind Jacob and with a multiple clopping of hooves they all rode to the dugout. Freda and Sarah were visiting Daisy Patterson, but Jacob found the note thrust beneath the nickel alarm clock sitting on the shelf. Ritter looked at it quizzically, then grunted again and thrust it into his shirt pocket. He looked at Fritz.

"Who do you reckon wrote it?"

"We think it was Jim Yoakum, a cowboy who used to work for Sam Womble," Fritz replied. What's all the fuss about, he wondered.

They all went back outside. Ritter and his deputies mounted. Jacob backed Joe against the wagon and, crawling into it, jumped onto the horse's back. Fritz, standing in the yard, was the only one dismounted.

Ritter spat his cud of chewing tobacco into his hand, flung it behind him, and swiped his wet palm across the seat of his pants.

"That saddle was stole from the depot freight room at Whitehead," he told them. "The thief also got seven hundred dollars. We're lookin' fer him. An' we're takin' the saddle back with us."

Without any warning, the biggest of the scouts spurred his horse up to Jacob and jerked the bridle reins out of the boy's hands. He started leading Joe down the trail.

"Stop that!" shouted Jacob, glaring at the man. Fritz took a step forward, looking around at Ritter. Surely the government's chief of scouts would not permit Jacob to be harmed. But Ritter made no effort to restrain his man.

Suddenly the big deputy drew his heavy rawhide quirt and began to lash the horse across the rump with heavy blows. Joe jumped out from under Jacob, spilling him from the saddle. As he fell, the boy caught one foot in the stirrup and was dragged a few feet before falling free. The entire scouting party whooped and roared with laughter at the rough prank.

It was then that Fritz lost control. He ran to the big deputy, leaped upon him, and with both hands jerked him off his horse. As the man was falling, Fritz drove his right fist into his face and, staying on top of him, punched him all around the yard. Then he felt a shattering blow at the base of his skull.

When the world came back into focus, he was on his back with his head in Jacob's lap. Water was running down his neck. A brilliant flame of pain lanced like a scalpel through his head. Jacob was crying.

"Don't die, Brother," Jacob pleaded as he poured water from an old tomato can onto the bump behind Fritz's ear.

"That's enough water," said Fritz. "Thank you, but it's running down my back." He sat up, blinking. His knuckles felt as if they had been driven down into his hands, which indicated that Ritter's deputy hadn't escaped unscathed. He looked dazedly at Jacob. The posse had gone.

"While you were whipping that big one, another slipped up

behind you and busted you with the butt of his gun," said Jacob.

His head still aching fiercely, Fritz walked to the well and, with Jacob working the pump handle, thrust his head beneath the stream of cold gyp water. He also held his bruised knuckles under the flow. He began to feel better.

"Brother, they took my saddle," sobbed Jacob. Regret twisted Fritz's insides. It hurt not to be able to do anything about that.

He stood, shaking his head. "I'll get you another someday," he promised. "But it's going to take time. Meanwhile, I'll share mine with you. And we can both do more bareback riding."

That night they all lay awake trying to solve the puzzle of why Jim Yoakum had given Jacob a stolen saddle.

"Jim didn't know it was stolen," Jacob insisted.

"Perhaps he bought it from the man who stole it," suggested Freda.

Fritz shook his head, then winced. His head was still sore. "I doubt if this was the stolen saddle," he said. "I think Jonas Ritter and his deputies got Jacob's saddle mixed up with another that looked just like it."

Three nights later the riddle was solved. At midnight Fritz was awakened from a sound sleep by a man's voice calling softly from outside the dugout.

"Dutchy, Dutchy," came the voice over and over.

Fritz got up, rubbing the sleep out of his eyes with the heels of his hands. Dressing quietly, he went outside. A tall figure emerged from behind the wagon, holding his left arm unnaturally.

"Hello, Dutchy. What's new?" said Jim Yoakum, talking low so that he wouldn't awaken the rest of the Rombergs. His voice seemed edged with pain. In the moonlight, Fritz saw that Yoakum's shoulder was crudely bound with the remnants of a shirt.

"Jim," blurted Fritz, "you're hurt. What happened?"

"Been in a fight and got winged," said Yoakum. "Took a bullet through the shoulder." He looked emaciated and exhausted, thoroughly down and out.

Immediately, Fritz thought of Mattie Cooper. "Wait right here," he told Jim. "We've got a doctor who lives just up the road. I'll go get her. She'll know what to do."

Riding Jack bareback and leading Joe, saddled for Mattie to ride, Fritz galloped to the Cooper shack and awakened them. Mattie could handle this if it could be handled. He had seen her react coolly and skillfully in a crisis, a trait he admired.

In five minutes Mattie came out with her brown canvas kit, blinking sleepily and dabbing at her hair.

"Who's hurt?" she asked.

"Friend of ours," Fritz replied, "a cowboy named Jim Yoakum. He got shot."

Fritz took the kit from her and laid it on the ground. Crouching a little beside Joe, he cupped his hands low.

"Here," he said, "take hold of the saddle horn and put your foot in my hands. I'll boost you onto his back."

Obeying, she sprang into the saddle and her skirt twisted upward around her thighs. She stood in the stirrups, pulling it down as best she could. Fritz leaped astride Jack and in ten more minutes delivered her and her medical kit into the Romberg yard.

"I never worked on a bullet wound before," she warned him as he helped her down. "It's kinda misty-moisty out," she added. "We'll need a good light."

Fritz got the lamp out of the dugout, lighted it, and turned up the wick. Awakening Freda, he told her what had happened. Jim Yoakum walked out of the shadows, all bent over with pain.

The minute she saw the shoulder, Mattie Cooper forgot her abashment. "That's a whizzing big hole," she said and went to work.

When Jim Yoakum's cool eyes fell upon her and he saw that the doctor was a girl, and a young one at that, his mouth fell open. It was plain that he figured he was a goner with only a girl in charge of his treatment. But the girl went right ahead.

"Hold the lamp globe closer," she directed, as with a pair of scissors she cut the bloody shirt off the wounded man. "That bullet had a bitter farewell to it," she added. "It went high, probably through the muscle. Bone must be all right. That's lucky."

Yoakum flinched a little, his face glazed with pain. He still wore his pistol in a holster on his right hip and in keeping with his love of ornamentation a purple silk bandanna, the knot of which had slipped behind his neck. Carefully Mattie untied it and took it off.

"There's no bullet in you 'cause the shoulder's got a hole in both front and back," she said practically, "but there's some infection." She looked at Fritz. "We'll need a fire an' some kerosene to disinfect the wound. We'll need pulp scraped from the leaf of a prickly pear cactus fer a dressing. I'm plum out of turpentine."

They moved the whole procedure into the new sod house so Fritz could build a fire in the fireplace. At Mattie's direction, he got a kettle from the dugout, filled it with water, and put it on the fire to boil.

While Mattie dissolved table salt and sulfate of zinc in cold water and bathed the wound thoroughly, Fritz went to the pasture for the cactus pulp. From the buffalo grass, the katydids were singing their sad, bittersweet songs as if lamenting the passing of summer. Fritz wondered who had shot Jim and why they had quarreled. He hurried back.

With the kerosene, Mattie had doused both sides of the wound, while Jim, at her bidding, lay first on his stomach and then on his back so that the kerosene could penetrate. Gently she smeared on the cactus pulp, pressing it in deep. Jim moaned once. He looked feverish.

"I'm sorry if I hurted you," Mattie apologized. "I didn't go to." Then she looked Jim Yoakum squarely in the eye. "I'm sorry if I seem anxioused up," she added, "but I never worked on a outlaw before."

Fritz recoiled with shock. Jim Yoakum an outlaw? The girl was too free-spoken. He started to protest, but Yoakum laughed easily, beating him to the punch.

177

"I haven't done nothin' wrong 'cept nighthawk a store or two," he said. "I can still sleep when the wind blows."

He shot her a defiant look. "The store I hit when I got this has been helpin' break up the ranches by sellin' supplies to the nesters," he went on. "The railroads and banks are jest as bad. They're tryin' to change this whole country into farms. They're tryin' to destroy the range."

Dismayed at the disastrous turn his friend's life had taken, Fritz ran his tongue over dry lips. The picture was clearing.

A stricken wonder came into his voice. "Then the saddle you left for Jacob *was* stolen," he said. "Why did you do it, Jim?"

Yoakum's face twisted wryly. "Because that was the only way I could get it just then," he said. "There wasn't any clerk there to take my money. Besides, I was too busy takin' their money. It happened at night. The saddle was jest the kid's size. I looked fer a bridle too but there was none in sight."

Through stiff lips, Fritz told him of the visit of Jonas Ritter and his posse and of its painful aftermath.

A steely look came into Jim Yoakum's face. "I'm sorry for that, Dutchy," he said. "I'll get him another saddle."

"Get me another head while you're at it," said Fritz. The lump on his skull still gave off a dull ache.

He put his hands on his hips and looked at Jim with exasperation. "Jim, you won't last fifteen minutes leading this kind of a life."

As well as he could with a crippled shoulder, Jim shrugged, puckering his lips and spreading the fingers of his right hand. "If a trail is smooth where you're travelin' why worry about the fords ahead?"

Fritz pointed at the shoulder to which Mattie was now affixing the cactus-pulp poultice. "Looks like you've already fallen in one ford," he said.

"Jest a little nick, Dutchy," said Jim Yoakum. A stoic look came into his melancholy face. "Everybody dies," he added.

"Tell 'em to bury me in hard ground, so the coyotes can't scratch out my bones."

Fritz knotted his hands together, feeling a compulsion to stop all this gloomy talk.

"Tell 'em yourself," he said. "Where have you been hiding all this time?"

"Been bunkin' with a line rider friend," said Jim Yoakum. But he didn't say what line rider or what ranch.

Freda was dressed. Lighting a candle, she had begun to cook and pack a lunch for Jim to take with him.

Mattie was buttressing the shoulder poultice with bags of hot sand heated in the fire. Jim winced, then sighed. His forehead was filmed with sweat. He looked at her gratefully.

"Feels good," he said, his voice low. She tied the poultice to both sides of the wound, binding it with part of his shirt, which she had browned near the fire, sterilizing it.

"I'd like to take a smoothin' iron to that shirt," she muttered, "but there ain't enough of it left."

Fritz went back into the dugout for one of his own shirts and got as much of it as he could on Jim. Mattie made a sling of the silk bandanna and showed Jim how to wear it.

She said, "Keep heatin' these bags an' dabbin' 'em on your wound. Maybe your line rider friend can do it for you."

When Jim reached into his pocket to pay her, she shook her head. "I won't take money for doin' this," she said simply. "I like to nurse my neighbors. We're all pore together."

For a moment, Jim looked at her peculiarly. He didn't reply.

Freda came out with the food in a sack. With a courtly gesture, Yoakum touched his forefinger to the front brim of his hat. "Sorry I had to bother you all, mam," he said, "but I had no place else to go."

"You're always welcome here, you know that," said Freda. "But I hope you'll stay out of trouble."

Gripping the cantle with his right hand, Yoakum mounted the bay. Freda handed him the sack.

179

He looked at Mattie. Then he looked at Fritz.

"So long, Dutchy," he said.

Fritz felt a deep commiseration for his poor, hurt, mixed-up friend. Eyes wet, he couldn't speak. But he could remember. He remembered how Jim had brought the quarter of beef when they were half starving and how he had helped Freda and Daisy Patterson out of the quicksand. He remembered how Jim had taken him to the range dance and of his many kindnesses to Sarah and Jacob.

As Jim rode off, his arm in a sling and his long body slumped forward, he didn't look as graceful as usual. Every jolt of the horse hurt him, Fritz knew.

Fritz turned to Freda and Mattie Cooper. "He'll never be able to adapt to changing conditions in this country," he said. "That's why he turned against society and did what he's done."

"He's a good man inside," said Freda. "He always did think twice before he spoke once."

"That's right, Mama," said Fritz, "but his thinking on this is all twisted."

Mattie had her kit packed. Fritz looked at her and a singing started inside him. She just keeps doing things for us when we need her, he told himself. Now that he had achieved a toleration for her uniquenesses—her dialect, her joy of going barefoot, and her gift of healing with eccentric remedies—he found that he liked and respected her very much.

In the glow of the glass lamp held by Freda, she looked weary. Fritz put his arm around her and she gave him a smile so sunny and warm that he was surprised at its intensity. He hadn't known that she could smile like that.

"How can we thank you?" he said. "You're always so good to help us. You must be dead tired." Again he cupped his hands low to help her into the saddle.

"I'm all right," said Mattie Cooper. "I'm glad you came and got me." And he knew that there was friendship between them now, formed without words and needing none.

*   *   *

The surprise of the summer was the rally made by the kafir Sam Womble's cows had not eaten to the ground. Although there was only a little of it left, on August fifteenth it stood three feet high. By September it was as tall as Jacob's chin and its white heads were eight to ten inches long. After the shooting of his bull, Sam Womble had kept his cattle away from the Romberg fences. Freda and Sarah built scarecrows to frighten off the prairie chickens.

Electing again to sell it as seed to Abe Hooper, Fritz kept out barely enough for horse feed. Once more the Rombergs worked until midnight to shell the heads on the washboard, soaking the husks loose from them in tubs of water and pouring the whitish grains on a sheet in the sun to dry.

It came to only fourteen bushels, but at two dollars per bushel, they realized enough to buy a few supplies and provide a modest Christmas, which this time was spent at the Pattersons. And, Fritz thought, if we can ever keep our kafir out of the calamity column—hail, prairie chickens, Sam Womble's hungry cows—we might make a considerable profit on it. It's an obstinate, plucky crop. It's not afraid to put up its dukes against this climate and it should be winning.

After cold weather set in, they just hung on "beanless and broke" as Ray Patterson put it. Freda boiled the same coffee grounds so many times that they wouldn't even color the water. We're touching bottom, Fritz told himself, but he was afraid to seek steady employment at Woodward or Fort Supply; he wanted to stay near the claim so that he could guard his wheat pasture from Womble. The wheat looked unbelievably good.

Twice during a spell of warm weather in January and February, Fritz took Jacob and the team and they combed the prairie for buffalo bones, hauling them to Woodward and selling them.

On another occasion they made the long drive to the Salt Plains, near the Salt Fork River, to get salt. Clean and pure, it accumulated on sand bars. When the water was low, it could be shoveled into the wagon and sold for seven dollars a load. But that was the extent of their earnings.

In March Fritz took his cattle off the winter wheat and, with Patterson and Jacob guarding both their fields, went to Woodward so that he could sell the last of their buffalo bones, only a third of a wagon full. Freda went along. Sarah stayed with Daisy Patterson.

At the Woodward post office he found a disquieting letter from Freda's sister in south Texas.

"Misfortune has been our lot," the letter revealed. "We've tried to open new fields, but plowing is difficult because of the stumps which broke our plow. Also, we have no wagon now and must haul our grain and wood to market on crude sleds made from local trees and drawn by oxen." As Fritz washed his hands at the wagonyard, he frowned as he considered the bad news. The doors were closing behind them as well as in front.

On his way back, he passed the big frame building that housed the Geist Brothers mercantile store. On a front window in gold-leaf lettering was printed, OFFICE OF THE GEIST BANK, JOHN J. GEIST CASHIER. And below that a single word, LOANS.

Loans? For a moment, Fritz stood and thought about the word. It undoubtedly referred to loaning money. "Probably to ranchers," he reasoned. Then he remembered Dobie Quinlan telling him that most ranchers did their borrowing from Wichita and Kansas City commission houses. To whom did banks lend money?

Since he could think of nobody who needed it worse than the Rombergs, he decided upon a bold move. They can't do any worse than kick me out, he thought. The name of the cashier gave him hope. Geist, like Romberg, was a German name.

He went inside. A smell of gingersnaps and pickle brine was in the air. Everything from tobacco and sulfur matches to dried apricots, Bibles, and bolts of dress goods in gay colors was being sold over the counter, while clerks and customers mingled and chatted in friendly concourse.

"Where's Mr. John Geist?" Fritz asked a clerk.

"Up front in the Hole-in-the-Wall," the clerk replied, gesturing with a shirt-clad arm.

In one corner of the store's front, partitioned off for privacy, Fritz found the bank. And behind a rolltop desk sat John J. Geist, its cashier.

"Hello, young man," he said. He had straight black hair and keen judging eyes. His white shirt was clean and freshly ironed and his green four-in-hand necktie neatly knotted. In his own ragged attire, Fritz felt shamed and inadequate. He was surprised at how young the banker appeared.

"Mr. Geist, I'm Fritz Romberg," Fritz began. "We live on a claim twenty-seven miles west of here. We've been there since the run of ninety-three. Much of what we've done is right on the verge of making a profit, but if we had some financial help, we would make it lots faster. I don't know anything about banking, but do you ever lend money to homesteaders?"

Geist's black thatchlike eyebrows tufted upward. "Please sit down," he invited, designating a chair. "Yes, we occasionally make loans to settlers. The settler we want most is the one who has saved a few hundred dollars when he gets here and will roll up his sleeves and produce something—stock, feed, grain—a man who will have his family, his home, and his interests here. We aren't looking for city people or professional men—they'll come later. We prefer farmers from the populous rural districts of the north and east."

For a moment Fritz stared at him, feeling as if he'd been hit and floored by a sandbag, but at least he was no worse off than he had been before he walked in.

Drawing a long breath, he stood, shaking his head and grimacing with resignation, a boy beset by trouble.

"I guess I'm in the wrong place," he said. "Mr. Geist, we're not from the north or the east. We're Germans from south Texas. We've been living on kafir pancakes and dried beans. We're about droughted out. We've got only about a dollar and a quarter cash to our names and a little bunch of calves. But I'll tell you one thing. Even if nobody helps us, we're going to stick. We like this crazy country even though it's got us by the throat."

Compassion in his face, the banker stood and said, "Don't go. Sit down. Tell me about it."

Fritz sat down again. He told him about their Texas background, about Frederic's death, and about the various disasters to the kafir corn. He related how he had been forced into the cattle business by accident because he had been reluctant to shoot the newborn calves, and about the difficulty of getting wood or cowchips for fuel.

He told him about leasing the school section in the heart of the Womble range, about trading off the grays, and about selling Valentine so Jacob and Sarah could go to school. He told him what he thought he could do if he had a windmill and materials for fencing.

"What merchants here are carrying you?" the banker asked.

"Sir, we've never borrowed a penny from anybody," said Fritz. "My father always had a mortal fear of going in debt. In south Texas, none of our group could borrow money from the banks."

John Geist picked up a glass paperweight on his desk and moved it three feet to the right. "Are you married, young man?"

"No, sir," said Fritz.

"How old are you?"

"Sixteen, sir."

John Geist's black brows shot upward like spring-rollered shades. "Who do you know around here that might serve as a reference?" he asked after he got over his surprise.

Fritz plucked a sandbur off his pant leg and lifted his chin. "First I'll give you the names of two who won't recommend me," he said. "Sam Womble, the rancher, and Jonas Ritter, the government scout." And he told Geist why.

Then he told him of his association with Bob Quinlan, the rancher; with Pat Rucker, the railroad engineer whom Geist told him had been transferred to Newton, Kansas, and with George Rourke, the Santa Fe railroad agent. He told him of their dealings with Abe Hooper, the implement man, Tom Miller, the merchant at Shattuck, and Jake Pryor, the banker before Geist. He told him about Ray Patterson, his neighbor.

"I don't know him," said Geist. "I do know the others."

"I wish you did know him," said Fritz. "We pool our work, help each other in everything. He's back home now guarding my wheat from Womble. He needs help, too. We're both right on the brink of moving over the hump."

He pushed back his hair and sat forward, hands on knees, the yearning still strong within him.

"If I had a windmill at home, we could raise a truck garden. We could irrigate our orchard and shade trees until, in a few years, their roots reach the underflow of water and they wouldn't have to be irrigated."

He hesitated, the unshed tears aching behind his eyes. "If I had a windmill on our school section, I could bring our water and grass together. I could keep forty cows and their calves there the year round. And if I could fence it, and get one of those Hereford bulls Mr. Quinlan was telling me about, I could grade up our little herd, going for bigger, beefier animals."

At the mention of Herefords, the banker's eyes shone. "Herefords are a fine breed," he said. "They're great hustlers. They graze farther from water and find fresher grasses. They're the first to fatten in spring. They stand storms and blizzards better. At the first indication of snow, other breeds will hunt for a haystack, but the Herefords will be right out in the weather hustling for grass. They're just getting started in this country. I was just beginning to find out about them when I sold my ranch in Hemphill County, Texas."

Fritz saw through the window some new farm machinery displayed on the boardwalk in front of the store—mowers, binders, plows. He stood so he could see them better.

"Sir," he said, "I wish I had some of those implements. I've never seen them before."

"We've just become agents for them," explained Geist. "We're agents for John Deere plows and Aultman-Miller Buckeye mowers and binders. And for Daniel Halladay windmills, too.''

Fritz craned his neck, looking for a sample windmill. There was none. "Sir," he said, "every farmer in the Strip ought to have a windmill, plenty of fence, and farm machinery like this. Nobody's got much, and nobody can pay you now. But after they got their first good crop, they could. It would speed the development of this country by two or three years.''

"We don't have a salesman yet," said Geist.

Fritz moved his hands. He tried to make his voice natural and persuasive but inwardly he was scared to death.

"Sir," he said, "I could call on homesteaders all over the western half of the Strip and sell these implements to them if I had some samples to show them. I could sell windmills and barbed wire to the ranchers. I could do this, and farm, and run cattle, too. A Strip farmer's got lots of extra time, you know.''

Geist looked at Fritz's ragged clothing and at his blucher-cut shoes run over and split around the soles.

"Sir," said Fritz, reading that look in a flash, "if I was dressed like the homesteaders themselves, I could come nearer selling them your machinery than if I were all togged up like a traveling drummer, don't you think?''

John Geist's judging eyes softened. "Tell you what I'll do," he said; he moved the glass paperweight back three feet to the left, where it was originally.

"I've got a new Halladay windmill, steel tower and all, on order from the factory at Kalamazoo, Michigan. When it gets here, I'll credit it to you at cost if you'll take it and erect it on your place so you can bring the settlers and ranchers in to see it. I could ship it prepaid on the railroad to you at Shattuck and you could haul it the rest of the way to your claim. Meanwhile, I'll need a little time to go over your references. Next time you're in town, stop and see me and we'll talk about the rest of it.''

Elation leaped through Fritz. He could hardly believe his good fortune.

A stranger was trusting him with the thing he wanted most, the backing to buy a windmill. It probably wouldn't lead to more help, but it could. It would depend upon how he handled this. And just think, he told himself, I almost decided not to come inside this store.

"Thank you, sir," he said, standing. They shook hands.

"You said you were German," said Geist. "My father came from Hanover in Germany. He was a contractor."

"My people came from Saxe-Meiningen," said Fritz. "My father was a farmer. He always longed to be a farmer, own land and have a good house and barns. He wanted to prosper. I'm the same way except I want a bunch of cattle, too, to help carry us over the lean years."

"The Lutheran Church Synod will soon start sending a minister to Woodward," said the banker. "He'll be searching for Lutheran homesteaders. I'll tell him about your family."

Fritz hurried out of the store to find his mother. He had exciting news for her now.

THE WINDMILL

In April third the spring blizzard blew in.

Fritz, warm and snug in bed with Jacob, was faintly conscious
of the wind rising in the night and of the increasing cold in the
dugout. However, he slept so soundly that he knew nothing of
conditions outdoors until he heard Freda rousing him in the
morning.

"Fritz, Fritz," she was saying, her voice low and urgent, "take
a look outside."

Squinting through the glass door, which was partly frosted over,
he saw snow falling in wind-slanted lines and fast burying everything. The sky was filled with a gray drabness that obscured the
sun.

The storm's intrusion was sudden and unforeseen. The day
before had dawned clear and winey. The Rombergs had packed a
picnic lunch, embellished it with radishes and onions plucked from
their early garden, and had driven across the prairie seeking
cowchips. And now, this.

Instantly Fritz thought of their cattle. The danger lay in the cutting wind that would drive the cold, like icy daggers, through their bodies. At the first sign of it, cattle instinctively hunted for a thicket at the bottom of a canyon. But there were no canyons near the Pattersons' range where they grazed their small herds.

Dressing as warmly as he could, Fritz hastily swallowed Freda's meager breakfast and went out into the wintry weather.

"I've got to find our calves," he said before he left. "I've got to get them to shelter or they'll freeze to death."

Outside the wind gusted so strongly that his hat blew off. Going to the barn, he found a strand of baling wire. Pulling it down tightly over the crown of his hat, he bound the brims over his ears, twisting the ends of the wire together beneath his chin. It was so cold that he brought Jack's bridle into the dugout so the bit could be warmed before it went into the horse's mouth.

On Jack, he rode toward the Pattersons. Half a mile north of the Patterson dugout he met Ray, also on horseback, looking for the cattle too.

"This weather would fool the oldest goose a flyin'," Ray shouted. "Whoever heard of a blizzard in April? On my thermometer the temperature tumbled forty degrees the first hour. It's already down to seventeen."

"Seventeen's not so bad," yelled Fritz. "It's this wind." The snow was crusting on them. Several times they dismounted, stomping and flailing themselves with their hands to brush it off and keep warm.

There was not a cow or calf in sight. The only things moving were a few tumbleweeds somersaulting across the ice-bound range.

"They've drifted south somewheres," Fritz said, pulling the collar of his jacket higher. "I think my two cows are leading them, hunting for the brakes." Fear clutched his heart. There were no brakes. Out there somewhere in the barren desolation were the fourteen head that comprised the Romberg herd.

All day they searched. In late afternoon, when the drifts were so

189

deep that only the tops of the fence posts showed, they found half the herd huddled forlornly against a Womble fence. They stood before the taut barbed wire like gray ghosts, icicles dangling from their eyes, ears, and muzzles. But where were the others?

And then Fritz saw them. They lay on their sides, half a dozen or so silent mounds encrusted with snow. With a full heart he realized that they would never drift again.

For a moment Fritz sat numbly in the saddle, shocked by his loss, feeling that part of himself had died with these frozen brutes. He thought of how patiently and with what labor he had taught many of them to drink from a bucket, or from a recalcitrant cow.

In this setting, the rigors of blizzard feeding began. The cattle were too weak to walk the eight miles to the home pasture.

Back at the Patterson dugout, Ray harnessed his mules. "This flatbed wagon'll bog down in those snowdrifts," he said. "How we gonna get the feed to 'em?"

"Let's take the wheels off the wagon and sled it to them," proposed Fritz. That's what they did. Loading the wagon with kafir heads, they took the feed to the beleaguered animals.

It wasn't a time for range custom niceties. Cutting Womble's fence with his pliers, Fritz swung Frederic's maul, breaking the ice in Womble's creek so the survivors could drink. Then he repaired the fence.

After the sun came out and they got the cattle back home, Fritz hitched Jack and Joe to his sled and dragged the snow off the grass in spots so the remaining cattle could feed. When he returned home, he found Freda and Sarah rolling snowballs and lifting them into a tub so they'd have soft water for cooking and washing their hair.

Later, in the dugout, Fritz pulled off his wet shoes and, sitting on the floor, elevated his cold feet to the fire in the topsy stove.

"The only way I can learn anything is by making mistakes," he said wearily, "but there are so many things to learn in this peculiar country. As soon as we can, we need to fence every foot of our range so this can't happen again. If we'd had it fenced, we'd have had our cattle at home. They could have taken shelter in our own school section canyon, or in the little gulch near our dugout instead of over on the flats near the Pattersons'. They would have been out of the wind and closer to feed."

Fencing was also on the mind of somebody else, they discovered. A week later Ray Patterson came riding up, his horse in a lather and dark anger in his face.

"Womble's riders are fencing our water hole," he said, "and they're also building a fence right through the middle of my wheat field. There's five of 'em and they've all got rifles as well as shovels and post-hole diggers. They say Womble was using all this land long before we got here."

Fritz laid aside the chain harness he was patching and stood, feeling a chilled sweat prickling the back of his neck. Womble was changing from free range to fenced free range. He didn't own it, but he was fencing it anyhow. Fritz tried to think calmly. He knew with dull certainty how the ranchman probably intended to dispose of them.

"This is his big move," said Fritz. "It's now or never with him. He'll probably send them over here tomorrow. He's got us beat in numbers and firepower. Since there's no law out here, he thinks we'll quit and sell out to him at his price."

He looked at Patterson and was struck by the change in his friend. Ray's mop of red hair seemed standing straight up and his teeth were clenched between his thick lips.

"Lend me your Colt," Ray pleaded, his crossed eyes flashing with fury. "The only language he understands is force. We've got to fight him. We can cut his fences during the night and take the wire off them to build fences of our own. We can steal his beef and eat it. We can set fire to his range."

Although Fritz felt angry and uneasy, Ray's blind rage acted as a deterrent upon him.

"They'll be looking for that, Ray," he said quietly. "They're probably already organized to meet it. We've got to think of some new way to cross him, something besides force, something he

191

hasn't thought of or doesn't think we'll do. Maybe we could reach him through the territorial courts.''

They decided to go to Woodward and try. In thirty minutes they were on their way, both families riding in the Romberg wagon with Fritz driving and Ray traveling alongside on horseback.

At the last moment Fritz took along a quart fruit jar of his wild grape wine for John Geist.

''How can you think of wine at a time like this?'' fretted Freda.

''He's German, too,'' said Fritz. ''I'll wager he likes wine.''

The Strip weather had done a complete turnabout. It was now warm and mild. The prairie was spicy and aromatic and had an emerald sheen, but in his nagging unrest, Fritz scarcely noticed.

They stopped briefly at the Coopers. Mrs. Cooper and Zella were hoeing in the garden. Orvus, his mouth full of chewing tobacco, was mending harness in the yard. Mattie had a horse saddled and was packing to attend a sick woman on Otter Creek.

Fritz explained the emergency and told them where they were going.

Mattie looked quickly at her father. ''Dad,'' she said, ''they kin water their cattle at our spring, cain't they?''

Orvus took a spit shot at a weed six feet away and sprayed it cleanly. He turned on her.

''Shet yer head,'' he snapped peevishly. ''I'm not takin' sides in their feud with Womble. That's between them and him.''

Ray Patterson glared at him. Jacob's lips began to puff out fiercely. Wanting to forestall trouble, Fritz got back in the wagon and took the lines.

''Thank you anyhow,'' he said. ''We don't want to discommode you.'' Actually he didn't blame Cooper too greatly. If he sided with the Rombergs, Womble might refuse to buy his creek bottom hay.

They hurried on, reaching Woodward just before dark, and established themselves at the wagonyard. With almost the last coins in their possession, Fritz paid for his half of the charge for subsisting the horses. In the camp house, Freda, Daisy, and Sarah began preparing supper from the scanty provisions they had brought.

Next morning Fritz and Ray went early to the Geist Mercantile store and bank. Fritz found the banker in the "Hole-in-the-Wall" and introduced him to Ray. He gave the quart of wine to Geist.

"This was made from wild grapes that grow just fifty yards from our dugout," said Fritz. "We thought you might like to try it."

John Geist's eyes glowed appreciatively. "Thank you," he said. "I just wrote you a letter yesterday and sent it down on the train to Shattuck," he added. "Your windmill got here. We left it crated in the depot so we can ship it to you by local freight today."

Fritz told him about Womble's latest transgression. "We want to move on him legally right now," said Fritz. "We think that's better than shooting and bloodshed. But we don't know how to start."

Geist's sharp eyes under the bushy black brows twinkled knowledgeably.

"I'd say you've got lots of law on your side," he said. "Fencing land that is not the property of the fence-builder is a direct violation of the Federal statutes. Also, I believe you told me last time you were here that his herd twice damaged your feed crop. I think you could file charges against him on both counts. You'll need a lawyer. Of course, all this will cost you money—I'd say about ten dollars to start. Have either of you got any money?"

Feeling helpless and embarrassed, Fritz shook his head.

"No, sir," he said.

"No, sir," echoed Ray Patterson.

Geist picked up the glass paperweight on his desk and moved it a foot to the right.

"I'll help you," he said. "I'd want every light in the room on if I was suing Sam Womble. I'll get Owen Tarketon for you. Owen will light all the wicks. He's a good lawyer, and well-known. Anybody he goes after will know they've been in a lawsuit. He'll work fast, too. We can go see him right now, if you're ready."

Standing, he reached for his coat. "Then we'll call on Jack Floyd, the United States marshal," he added. "He's been busy lately, but I think he'll see us. Two nights ago, while breaking up the robbery of another mercantile store here, he and one of his deputies got in a gun battle and shot and killed the outlaw, a cowboy who used to ride for Womble, big fellow by the name of Jim Yoakum."

Fritz's head came up. His mouth worked briefly, but he could not speak. He didn't want to believe it, but you had to believe death. He looked down at his broken shoes. Then something choked up within him and he wanted to go outside. Instead he got only as far as the end of the room.

Ashamed of his emotion, he turned his back on them. He sniffed once and swallowed. How was he going to tell Jacob and Sarah?

When he regained control of himself, he told John Geist about the many friendly things Jim Yoakum had done for the Rombergs.

"He was a good man, and a kind man," he said. "My family will miss him."

When Geist took them to see Owen Tarketon, the lawyer suggested that Fritz sue Womble for four hundred dollars' damages to the Romberg kafir crop. The court clerk issued a summons commanding Womble to answer in twenty days or be in default. Tarketon also levied a writ of attachment on Womble's cattle in case they couldn't serve the summons on him.

"Four hundred is probably more than you lost," the lawyer explained. "We couldn't get more but we could get less."

In behalf of Patterson, Tarketon filed an injunction forbidding Womble from building any fence until further order of the court. It was signed by George Wheelock, the same judge who had fined Fritz forty dollars for taking wood for fuel from the brakes of the Beaver River a year and a half earlier. When he saw John Geist and Owen Tarketon with Fritz, Wheelock became almost genial and bustled busily about.

Later Geist conducted them to the United States marshal's

office. He introduced them to Jack Floyd, the marshal, a big mild-mannered man who filled his swivel chair to overflowing. Floyd told them how Jim Yoakum had died.

"He got clean away with nine hundred dollars," the marshal said, "but he went back to the store for a pair of silk sleeve-holders that he had admired. I guess the holdup was going so easy that he didn't expect trouble. One of my deputies who had got there meanwhile shot him."

Again Fritz felt the pinching in his throat. "I'll bet the sleeve-holders were purple," he said when he found his voice.

Floyd said, "As a matter of fact, I believe they were. Wait a minute." Leaning over, he rustled in a pigeonhole of his desk and extracted them.

"Yep," he said, "they're purple all right. How did you know?" Fritz explained.

"We buried him this morning," the marshal went on. "He was a lonesome type and never told nobody who his relatives were or where they lived. When the undertaker laid him out, he found a bullet wound in his left shoulder. It had healed cleanly."

Fritz wasn't surprised. It would have to heal cleanly if Mattie Cooper dressed it. I must take her a bottle of turpentine for her medicine kit, he reminded himself. And get another for ourselves.

Geist switched the conversation to the necessity of Floyd's quickly serving the papers on Womble so that further damage could be avoided.

With a small pocket comb, the marshal groomed his black mustache. "It's a long drive, but I've made longer ones," he sighed. "I guess I'll go in my buggy."

"Sir," said Fritz, "if you want to come down tomorrow on the passenger train, I could meet you at Shattuck with an extra saddle horse and you could ride to Womble's. It would be only ten miles that way. And I'd take you back to Shattuck afterward so you could catch the night train back here. Or you could stay all night with us."

195

"I guess I'd better take the buggy," Floyd decided. "I got another set of papers to serve over on Wolf Creek."

Back on the claim, Fritz looked at his wheat and felt a sudden rush of excitement. They'd had no winter that year until spring, and very little spring until almost summer. But the snow and the rain together had provided constant moisture. The wheat stood as thick as the hair on a dog's back. And to Fritz it was almost time to prove the ranchmen wrong and to bring to fulfillment his father's dream.

He decided to erect the windmill on his school section so that prospective customers could see it function in a natural range habitat, amid grass and cows. He and Ray began digging the well, casing the hole with native rock as they descended. Jacob took his turn with the shovel.

At eighteen feet, they struck good water. They installed a pump cylinder in the bottom of the hole and a sucker rod and pipe. They covered the well with a cedar platform. Then they drove both wagons to Shattuck to fetch the mill.

In the depot freight room the dismantled windmill lay scattered all over the premises. But Fritz had been studying Mattie's Sears Roebuck catalogue. He knew where every piece belonged, as he fingered them lovingly, patiently explaining to Ray and Jacob and the depot agent the function of each. Fascinated, Jacob listened carefully. Soon he could describe the action of the machinery almost as well as Fritz. The transit of the monster over the hills from Shattuck to the school section was achieved without incident.

Setting up the steel tower, they assembled the mill and vane on top of that. Soon the mill was in operation. Fritz felt a thrill of satisfaction. The whining of its blades and the splash of its water spilling into the oblong steel tank that Geist had also sent would become the sound of the prairie, he knew.

On the second morning after they had moved their calves to the school section, and the animals were gathered around the tank, gentled by the slaking of their thirsts, Sam Womble rode up on his gray mare. Sitting deep in his Apple Horn saddle, he rolled himself a cigarette, sizing up the whole operation. He had ceased trying to fence their water hole, so they knew that Jack Floyd had served his summons.

"Good morning, Mr. Womble." Fritz's greeting was polite but inwardly he felt a cool, hard anger.

As usual, Womble looked riled and stiff-necked.

"Who owns that thing?" he asked.

"I do," said Fritz.

He swung down off his horse and, holding the reins, faced Womble. "I'm selling them for the Geist Brothers Mercantile in Woodward," he said. "They don't cost much. Only about thirty dollars."

The low cost seemed to surprise Womble. For a moment he sat his mare, smoking and scowling. He was watching the mill revolve in the wind and smelling the fresh water pouring from its spout. He seemed more subdued than usual.

"Drop the damage suit against me an' I might buy one," he barked suddenly in his gravelly voice, then lost his breath in a fit of coughing. As Fritz waited for it to subside, elation coursed through him. Womble was worried about the lawsuits.

"I don't want you to buy it for that reason," said Fritz. "I want you to buy it because you need it. You've got the biggest range in this part of the Strip. You need half a dozen or more windmills. You need them right now."

Fritz kept talking. If he could persuade his worst enemy to buy a windmill, Geist might be impressed enough to give him the full financial backing he needed.

"You've got a big range, Mr. Womble," he pressed, "but you're wasting half of it. The only part you can use is the grass close to your streams and it soon gets trampled out and eaten by your cows. You've got rich grass in the rest of it, in your back country. But you can't use it. There's no water there and your cows can't walk that far to graze, then walk back to the stream to drink. Even if they could they'd soon walk off their flesh."

197

Fritz sat down on the edge of the tank, hands on knees, and continued to lay out the logic of it. It was logic that applied to every ranchman in the Strip, he knew.

"If you put down windmills in your back country, you'd open up a whole new range. You could put in cross fences and have a whole system of pastures—summer pastures, winter pastures, horse pastures, bull pastures, pastures for Herefords or whatever blooded stock you start. You could double or triple the size of your herds. You could fence your cattle away from the fertile land along your streams and plant it to forage crops to supplement your range. You could grow your own hay."

He was talking so reasonably that Womble was listening and thinking.

"Barbed wire and fence posts cost money," he growled.

"I know they do," replied Fritz, "but if you buy windmills, you'd double or triple your herd. You could afford to build a fence from here to Woodward."

Fencing was very much on Womble's mind, Fritz knew. It was common knowledge that Bob Quinlan was fencing his whole domain. And northwest of Womble, the Steeple-H was illegally enclosing government land as well as what they owned. Talk of barbed wire was everywhere. The galvanized strands stapled solidly to green cedar posts would revolutionize the Strip cattle industry.

The cowman sucked deeply from his cigarette. Again his eye fell upon Fritz's calves switching their tails contentedly after drinking their fill and cropping the back country range. Suddenly he flipped his cigarette into the green buffalo grass.

"How about dropping the damage suit if I buy one?" he asked, squinting shrewdly.

Fritz stood, shortening his reins and flipping the ends to one side. It was time to move in on Womble. He spoke evenly, but he could feel the blood pounding in his temples.

"Let's shuck it right down to the cob," he said. "What you're saying is that you'll buy one thirty-dollar windmill off which I'd get a small commission if I forgot about your cows eating four hundred dollars' worth of our kafir corn. I'm not that thickheaded. You've seen this windmill work and you know what it will do. You need six or eight windmills and you need them fast. You'll probably buy them soon from somebody. Every ranchman is going to start buying them."

Curbing his irritation, Fritz steadied himself. "If you'll buy them from me, I'll meet you in Woodward Friday and we'll go see John Geist and sign a contract. Then we could go see Mr. Tarketon and I might reduce the amount of my suit and settle out of court. But you're still going to have to pay for destroying our crop. My family's too poor to take a loss like that."

Womble glared at him. His bloodshot eyes glittered. Then he straightened, gathering his bridle reins in his pudgy hands. His voice tightened.

"Today's Tuesday," he barked. "I'll meet you at Geist's office in Woodward Friday mornin' at nine o'clock and we'll talk about it. But I ain't gonna buy six of them things. I might buy two."

Fritz scowled right back at him. "The more you buy, the more reasonable I'll be about my kafir corn loss," he said.

Womble's face was a mottled and furious gray. His look was still flint-hard. Turning the gray mare, he drove in the spurs and galloped off toward his ranch at a pounding run.

Ray Patterson, who'd been lounging in the background, came forward, staring at Fritz with admiration.

"You can sure sell them windmills, Fritzy," he said, shaking his head incredulously. "Listening to you reason with him, I decided I needed ten or twelve for my own little spread."

Fritz drew a long breath and blew it out with relief. "You know that you can always use this one until we talk Geist into backing us both," he said. He looked into the distance at Womble's receding form. "The thing that sold Womble was finding out how much richer windmills will make him."

"Why did you put off the showdown with him until Friday?" Patterson asked.

"So I could show the windmill to Bob Quinlan Wednesday," explained Fritz. "He's promised to ride over and inspect it then."

Mounting, they rode toward their dugouts. And behind them on its pointed tower the mill spun smoothly and busily and musically as it lifted water from the up-country soil.

THE SUNDAY CALL

True to his promise, Bob Quinlan galloped up Wednesday morning. And with him, astride the mouse-colored grulla, came one Fritz was glad to see—Dobie.

She was dressed almost like one of the Quinlan cowboys—a big hat cocked over one eye, a green bandanna, long riding skirt, and boots. Her blonde braid, freshly plaited, tumbled down one shoulder and had an orange ribbon on it.

"Why the ribbon?" asked Fritz.

"To show people I'm feminine," said Dobie. "I'm going to a rodeo tomorrow. Dad may let me ride in it. Why can't I be a lady on or off a bull?" She's prettier than a spotted dog under a red wagon, Fritz thought.

Freda and Jacob came up from the garden. Sarah, almost hidden from view in one of Freda's aprons with the wide strings doubled back in front and tied there, emerged from the kitchen where she was washing the breakfast pots and pans. Greetings were said all around.

201

After Freda served coffee, Fritz showed them the wheat that was about ready to head and also the new sod home they would occupy as soon as they could afford glass and frames.

"Gonna have any kafir for sale?" asked Quinlan.

"Yes sir," said Fritz. "Jacob and I just planted it."

"I'll need some horse feed this winter," the ranchman revealed. "Maybe we can make a deal."

"Yes, sir," said Fritz.

Saddling Joe for Jacob, Fritz rode Jack bareback and the four of them set out for the school section to see the windmill. Once they arrived, Fritz explained to Quinlan how it worked and why every ranchman needed them, as he had previously told Womble. Then he left Jacob to expound on additional details.

"Sir, may I borrow your daughter for a few minutes?" Fritz asked the ranchman. "I want to show her our canyon." With one arm, he pointed to the long valley ahead, with its red walls, and the dark green void that filled it.

"You can't see it from here but it's full of cedar." He grinned. "Now that we have our own cedar we won't need to borrow any from the government."

Quinlan nodded and turned with interest to Jacob who, coached by Fritz, could now interpret windmills from pump to vane.

Fritz and Dobie rode off together. Their riding styles contrasted strangely. While Fritz, bareback on Jack, bounced all over his mount, Dobie sat Duke as smoothly as if she were riding in a canoe.

At the head of the canyon they stopped and looked down into a sweet-smelling vista of cedars, hackberry, and shade where the low cooing of the mourning doves told the world of its sequestered loveliness.

Without really intending to, Fritz began showing Dobie where someday he planned to build a spacious half-dugout for his own bachelor home. It would have walls of split cedar logs chinked with mud and gravel and a roof of cedar shingles split by hand off a block locked in a vise and put into finished condition by a drawknife.

"I'm going to build a fireplace so I can have the best smell in the world—green cedar burning—and its blue smoke going out my chimney." said Fritz. "I'm going to have an earthen floor, dark and cool, with braided rugs on it and Indian blankets on the walls." It was plain that he wanted the best in prairie elegance.

"How long will you live in it?" Dobie asked.

"For several years, I guess," replied Fritz. "Until I earn the money to build a wooden house."

"Are you going to live in it alone?"

"Sure," laughed Fritz, "until I get married."

Dobie looped her reins around the saddle horn and folded her arms across her breast. "You been doing any thinking about what girl you might want to live in it with you?"

"Yes," said Fritz, "some."

"Who?"

He tried to joke about it. After all, he'd only meant to show her the canyon. "I haven't decided yet," he said. "I've got the list culled down to seven or eight."

"Am I one of the seven or eight?" Dobie asked.

"Yes," said Fritz.

"Who are some of the others?" she persisted. "Who do I have to beat out?"

Enjoying the raillery, which at times approached reality, Fritz said, "You don't know them. They're from everywhere—Alva, Wichita, Kansas City, Amarillo, Dalhart, Beaver, Caldwell."

"You must be carrying the United States mail," said Dobie, dryly.

Fritz said, "You've got some beaus, too. Who was the one who called on you while I was setting fence posts at your place?"

"Oh, let's see," said Dobie, "Walter Foster came by, I think."

"Who's Walter Foster?" Fritz inquired. "Is he the one whose father lights his cigar with ten-dollar bills?"

"No," said Dobie. "His dad owns half the Steeple H ranch. You're thinking about Sam Morris whose dad owns the bank at Waynoka. He's already proposed twice."

Fritz blinked and tugged at his shirt collar. "*Ach*, Dobie," he said, "you've got them coming from way up on the Cimarron in Kansas. Who else would I have to beat out?"

"Oh, I don't know," said Dobie. "The Hardeman boys come by once in a while. And Jess Tandy whose dad owns the Bar-Z. He gets mad at daddy for not letting him take me to a dance unchaperoned."

Fritz shot a quick sideways glance at her, then began twisting Jack's bridle rein, thinking—thinking that while his conquests were invented, hers seemed real.

"Am I the only nester who gets to see you?" he asked.

"I guess so," said Dobie. "Nester boys call on nester girls, I think. Like that cute little Mattie you introduced me to at the Shattuck box supper. Do you like her?"

Fritz wet his lips with his tongue. "Yes," he said. Her questions were so direct.

"You seemed to enjoy her company at the box supper," said Dobie.

Fritz raised his eyebrows in protest. "I tried to buy your box," he reminded her.

Dobie's horse took a step forward, stretching out his lips for the new buffalo grass. Dobie put her right hand on his rump so she could lean around to look at Fritz.

"If I proved to be the dark-horse winner and moved over here, where could Duke, my horse, stay?"

Fritz said, "Knowing how well you like him, I suppose we'd have to keep him in the dugout with you. I could sleep outside in the wagon. I've been doing it so much, guarding my kafir from Sam Womble, that my pockets are full of seed."

Dobie's mouth twitched mischievously. She said, "Let's let Duke have the dugout and I'll sleep in the wagon with you."

Fritz's blush was like the glow of the aurora borealis lighting up the northern skies.

Both horses were grazing forward, a step at a time. "I may pick the girl who can cook and sew the best," he said.

Dobie stared into the grassy distance and got real quiet. "I know I don't do either very well," she said. "I've spent too much time in the corral."

Ahead of them in a buffalo wallow a flock of red-winged blackbirds were feeding in a manner suggesting a rolling wheel, the birds in the back lifting and alighting ahead of those in front as they sang their rich multitoned chorus.

"Don't you think we're too young to be talking about getting married?" asked Fritz.

"No," said Dobie.

Fritz flanked Jack forward two steps and peered around at her. "I'm so young that legally I'd almost have to get my mother's consent first," he said.

"You're not too young to think about it," Dobie insisted. "I think about it all the time."

"I think about it some," acknowledged Fritz, "when I'm not thinking about how I'm going to keep Womble's cows from eating our kafir, or how to get money enough to fence the school section, or how I'm going to keep Jacob and Sarah in school, or how we're going to keep from starving."

Reaching down with her left hand, Dobie loosened the tight riding skirt that was pinching her left knee. She said, "You wouldn't starve if you were on a ranch, I bet. You'd make a good ranchman."

"I'm always going to raise some stock," Fritz said, "but farming's what I like best. It's in my blood."

"In the years we don't get rain you may have to water your fields with your blood and I wouldn't want that to happen," said Dobie.

Fritz shifted his position on Jack. "It's not going to happen,

205

Dobie. When the dry years come I'll fall back on our cattle, and our kafir, and our truck garden, and my implement-selling business. I'm going to make it, one way or another.''

He guided Jack closer, so that he could lean over and take her hand. "You're an awfully sweet girl," he said, and meant it.

Now it was she whose face flared rosy red. "Is that all you're going to say?" she asked.

"Yes," he said, but he held her hand most of the way back to the windmill.

Later he wondered, does she really want to build a nest or was she just funning me like she always does? He decided that it was a little of both.

Back at the dugout, he gave Bob Quinlan a quart of the wild grape wine.

"Mr. Quinlan," he said, "this hasn't got anything to do with whether you buy the windmills. I appreciate all you've done for us and the advice you've given us."

At Woodward Friday morning, Womble and Geist were waiting. Womble purchased four windmills after Ray Patterson promised to sink them for him at a wage Geist suggested and Womble agreed upon after growling about it. Then they went to see Owen Tarketon.

At Tarketon's suggestion, Fritz reduced his damage suit to two hundred dollars cash if paid on the spot. After considerable grumbling, Womble wrote out the check.

Later Fritz and Geist sat down in the banker's office. Geist picked up the glass paperweight. He moved it two feet to the right, then returned it to its original location.

"I'll finance you fully," he said. "When you sold Sam Womble you also sold me. You check out fine with all your references."

He smiled. "Your wine checked out fine, too. It's *spritzig*, as my father used to say. It puts a tingle on the tongue. Now. How much will you need and how do you propose to spend it? Maybe I can advise you, save you some money."

Fritz said, "Mr. Geist, Ray Patterson and I each have a good wheat crop. It's about ripe and ready to cut. The big April snow and the spring rains really boosted it. The heads are large and maturing to full size. Ray has forty acres and we have fifty. That's too much to cut by hand with a scythe, and to flail with tree limbs. It would take us until Christmas."

Geist said, "There's a fellow living near Gage who owns a horse-powered hand-feed threshing machine worked by four or five teams circling round and round. He's only about twelve miles from you. I think I can get him for you. His charges are reasonable. Also, I'll credit you with one of our new Buckeye binders. That'll solve your cutting problem."

"Ray and I each have a wagon, but we'll need two more wagons and teams to help us haul the wheat to Shattuck," Fritz went on.

Geist nodded. "There's a fellow farming over on Wolf Creek who hauls freight on the Mobeetie and Fort Elliott trails. He got laid off. He needs work. He has two teams and two big wagons. I can get him for you." Marveling at Geist's acquaintanceship with the new country, Fritz began to see how helpful it was to have a banker for a business confidant.

Fritz faced him squarely. "Mr. Geist, will you back Ray Patterson, my neighbor, too? We do nearly everything together."

When Geist picked up the paperweight and set it down decisively with no horizontal shifting, Fritz knew that his answer would be favorable.

Geist nodded. "I will. Have him come and see me today before he leaves. What else?"

"Sir," said Fritz, "the most expensive thing we need is a young purebred Hereford bull so we can get started in blooded stock. Also enough barbed wire and posts to fully fence our land so we'll have exclusive use of the bull after we get him. And several young cows for breeding purposes—some of them jerseys so my mother can market dairy products."

"Can't you cut the posts from the cedar in your school-section canyon?" asked Geist.

"Sir, I could," replied Fritz, "but it would strip every tree from it. Besides, I want to use that cedar for another purpose."

With a pencil he had sharpened with a pocketknife, Geist scribbled notes on a pad. "I'm very interested in your Hereford project," he said. "Even with native cows, the first cross of a Hereford sire gets results. Later I can help you buy Hereford cows, if you like."

Fritz said, "We'll also need another windmill to put down near our new sod house so we can irrigate the orchard and our truck garden. I wish I could think of some way to irrigate our wheat with water out of the ground so we can have a bumper yield every year. I'm still trying to figure that out. We'll need plenty of pipe so we can run windmill water into a smokehouse I'll build, and into our kitchen and bathroom and onto our lawn." He was adopting Mattie Cooper's suggestion regarding this.

Geist kept nodding and making notes, accepting the formidable list without blinking. "I can help you get the best price possible for most of this," he said. "Also, I think you're going to be surprised how much you'll make from your wheat. The market looks very good."

He was right. For some of the wheat, Fritz and Ray Patterson were paid $1.25 per bushel. From the Rombergs' fifty acres nine hundred dollars was realized after all expenses were paid. Patterson did nearly as well. And they would still have the kafir crop, the new binder, the cattle, Womble's two hundred dollars minus legal fees, and Fritz's commissions for the sale of farm implements, windmills, and barbed wire.

And Fritz's thoughts went tenderly back to his father. He believed that Frederic would have been proud of him. He had proved his manhood. Frederic had made a wise decision when he brought his family from the tyranny of south Texas to the freedom of the Strip. Fritz was proud of himself for not having let his father, or himself, down.

On a later trip to Woodward to get their wheat checks, Fritz

208

bought dishes of homemade ice cream at the hotel for himself and Ray Patterson.

"Heavenly scissors!" ejaculated Ray. "We're rich. What are you going to do with all your extra money?"

Fritz licked the melting cream off the sides of his spoon, enjoying the vanilla taste.

"Bank it," he said, "and earn more to go with it so we can stand off the hard times that are sure to come later. There's plenty to spend it for up ahead. Someday soon I'll buy a nice tombstone for my father's grave at Shattuck. And a new chapel organ for my mother. And a riding horse and boy's saddle for Jacob. Some dresses for Sarah. New shoes and clothing for our whole family, including something nice to wear to church and school functions. We need chickens, pigs, new harness. Also windows and doors for our new soddy. And when we can afford it, a surrey so my mother and sister can ride comfortably to church and on the long trips to Shattuck and Woodward. It sounds like a lot, but it's no more than most of the ranchers have."

Fritz was proud of having been able to endure against the stiff challenge thrown out by the land and the elements. He had hung on tenaciously and won. The more he had sacrificed and the harder he had worked, the more he came to appreciate himself. The struggle had broadened his character and made him a man.

All through the wheat harvest, Fritz had thought about marriage and its responsibilities.

I know I'm only sixteen, he told himself as he drove Jack and Joe to the new binder, watching the blades shear the stalks and the machine tie them into bundles. But I'm a man in every other way. If I'm old enough to make a living for my family, why am I not also old enough to decide on what girl I'm going to start going with and which one I'm going to marry?

Deciding that was filled with difficulty, and before he thought it out, he and Jacob and Ray had sleeved the sweat from their foreheads a thousand times as they shocked all the wheat by hand, dug the beards out of their gloves, and waited for the arrival of the thresher.

The choice lay between Dobie Quinlan and Mattie Cooper. They were the only girls he really knew. Both of them were young, too, Dobie sixteen, Mattie fifteen. But on the frontier girls grew up faster and became dependable wives and mothers sooner than the girls in towns and villages.

Not until they fed the last of the bundles into the thresher's maw with pitchforks did he finally figure it out.

Dobie was cute and articulate, but he couldn't imagine her as a wife who could cope with drought, disaster, and terrifically hard work on the farm. She hadn't had the experience of living through poverty and need. Her parents were probably pointing her for a union with some young ranchman so that someday there would be a fusion of two cattle empires.

When he got down to thinking which of the two he couldn't bear to live without, the more certain he was that Mattie was the girl for the rest of his life. She's a treasure, he told himself, who should be cherished, treated tenderly, and appreciated. Frederic would have approved of her, he felt sure.

He could see her face light up happily, warming the atmosphere, when he had put his arm around her before taking her home from dressing Jim Yoakum's gunshot wound. Nobody else could make his pulses sing the way she had that night.

Mattie was better adapted to be a stock farmer's wife. She could cook, sew, doctor, work hard, and manage on next to nothing. She was a good thinker with a head full of sound ideas. She was interested in making a home. She had spirit, too. Although she was kind and compassionate, you couldn't run over her or treat her discourteously.

Of course, she'd be gone a lot, nursing sick people and doing it all for nothing, but soon the country would become so settled that every hamlet would have its own physician.

That Orvus, her father, was a Sooner didn't bother Fritz now, as it once had. Someday, people who got their land by soonering would be as respectable as anybody. It hadn't been Mattie's decision to enter the country before the proclamation date, anyhow. She had just followed her family.

And as she had told Ben Hornaday at the Shattuck box supper, the original Sooners were the ranchmen who had moved in with their herds a full decade ahead of the homesteaders, monopolizing several sections instead of settling on one lone quarter.

He thought, I think she likes me, but I'd better let her know I'm interested in her or she may marry somebody else. After all, she sees lots of people, carrying that old brown canvas medical kit around the country. Somebody's sure to pick her off.

On the Saturday night after they finished the wheat harvest Fritz sent Jacob on horseback to the Coopers to ask Mattie if he could call on her Sunday afternoon.

"What did she say?" he asked when Jacob returned.

"She said she'd be home," Jacob reported indifferently. "When are you going to buy me that saddle, Brother?"

That night Fritz drew a tub of gyp water from the well and with a bar of homemade soap bathed his sun-browned body. Next afternoon he donned the best he had, a shirt of faded cotton twill and a pair of much-washed blue overalls, and rode to the Coopers. He hadn't yet had time to purchase new clothing with his wheat money.

As he tethered Jack to the clothesline pole and walked to the Cooper shack, his footsteps slowed and he felt a nervous sensation in the pit of his stomach. It was odd how she had changed from a skinny, shaggy-haired moppet to the poised sweet person she was now. But maybe it was he who had done most of the changing. Her black head would fit snugly under his chin, he knew.

He knocked. Presently the door opened. There stood Zella, as big-eyed and startled as Mattie herself had formerly been. Without a word, she ducked back inside, leaving him standing alone on the wooden stoop. And then came Mattie.

211

"Fritz," she said, smiling and opening the door wider. And there was warmth in her voice and with it a trace of confusion that he did not understand.

It was obvious that she had been expecting him. She wore the same blue dress that she had worn at the box supper and the most infallible proof of all were the shoes on her feet. Her hair, brushed back smoothly and terminating at the base of her neck in that captivating bun, was further adorned by a brown velvet bow doubled back widely. She looked as fresh and clean as a young willow sprig after a rain.

"Come in, come in," she insisted, leading him past her mother, who was sewing, and into the parlor. And then something fell from its high place in his heart with a sickening thud.

Clifton Powell, the schoolmaster, sat on the worn red parlor divan in his shirt sleeves, one muscular arm draped familiarly along its tufted back. Neatly combed and shaved, he looked confident and at ease. His pants were creased and his hair tallowed. He wore a white shirt and tie. His attire far outshone that of Fritz. Bitterly, Fritz was struck at how attractive Mattie and Powell looked together.

When the schoolteacher got up to shake hands after Mattie introduced them, he loomed over Fritz like a railroad water tank over a locomotive tender. His grip was firm.

On a nearby stand-table the partly open box of candy he had brought was labeled "Molasses Mint Kisses." A cold chill clutched at Fritz's midsection. His knees were buckling. He wanted to sit down.

He was too late. He had lost. It was for Powell that she was dressed so nicely.

"I'm sorry," Fritz stammered, "I didn't know you had company." He wondered if Jacob had misunderstood her reply. He turned to leave.

Alarm and deep concern flooded the girl's face. She looked at him with startled eyes, a straight questing look with the wonder lingering.

She spun around, facing Clifton Powell.

"Mr. Powell," she said, "kin I get you to 'scuse me fer a minute? I'll kem right back in." Fritz thought, what's going on here? She's excited about something or she wouldn't have lapsed into her old way of speaking.

The schoolmaster nodded. "Certainly," he said. But as his dark eyes probed their faces he had lost some of his easy assurance.

Mattie led Fritz past her mother and Zella, out of the house and into the backyard near Jack. The horse was noisily cropping buffalo grass and seemed oblivious to the fact that he was partly screening them from view. Why do we always have all our meetings in her backyard, Fritz asked himself.

For a moment, the girl drew back from him, her lips parted breathlessly. She searched his face quickly and desperately. Obeying some spontaneous instinct, Fritz held out his arms.

To his astonishment, she came lightly, eagerly into them and her head fitted under his jaw as if it had belonged there always. For a moment Fritz held her, his blood pounding, wild fire in his veins. Then he put his finger beneath her chin and, lifting it, kissed her long and tenderly.

As he held her close, he could taste the clean loveliness of her hair and feel her pliant body trembling. And, he thought, here I am kissing her and liking it when I've spent the last three years trying to shake her off!

"I ben lookin' fer you all afternoon," she said tremulously, her face pressed against his old cotton twill shirt. "I got so tard of waitin'. Then he rode up. I couldn'ta driv him off when he'd rid fifteen mile to see me. He's been good to me. He's been learnin' me to speak correctly and fergit my Arkansaw vernacular, as he calls it. But I always fergit what he learned me when I see you."

Fritz said, "Don't worry about it. I like to hear you talk that way."

She put her hands on his chest and looked up at him imploringly.

"What am I gonna do 'bout him?" she asked.

Fritz chuckled resignedly. "Be nice to him," he said, "but not

213

too nice. I'll go on home. When he leaves, hang your sunbonnet on the clothesline and I'll come back.''

She held out one hand and his fingers curled around hers as he walked her back to the house. With one arm, he drew her closer and her nearness told him that they were on the threshold of something as lasting as this beautiful obstinate land that he was learning to conquer.